THE RELICANT CHRONICLES, BOOK 3
CROSSED BONES

I0562906

AARON ROSENBERG

CRAZY 8 PRESS

Kagiri woke to screams.

Rolling off the bed he came up on his feet, nihono in hand from where he had snatched it up but not yet drawn. Instead he merely held it at eye level, parallel to the ground, one hand on the grip, one on the scabbard. And, stilling himself, listened.

Then he burst from his tent, drawing the blade even as he shouldered the flap aside and stepped out into a night filled with chaos.

People were running every which way but he could see no direct reason for that, no fires licking up from other tents, no army trampling structure and inhabitant alike, no monster from nightmare gobbling up all in its path. Nothing but the same people he already knew, only panicked and shouting or sobbing or both.

Reaching out with the hand still holding the empty scabbard, he grabbed the nearest person and yanked them to a stop, his fingers firmly wrapped in the collar of their kitoro. It was Eisen, one of the newer members of their group, a stocky middle-aged man who claimed to be a legal clerk but whose hands bore the calluses and scars of many a brawl. Now he looked a mess, his bun sprouting hairs in all directions, his face sweaty and flushed, his eyes bleary.

"What has happened?" Kagiri demanded, giving the man a shake.

"We're under attack!' Eisen wailed, gripping his collar in turn and tugging it free. Then he was off and running again. Kagiri doubted the man had even registered who he was speaking to.

Several others charged past but they seemed just as dazed and he doubted he would learn anything more useful from them. But then he spotted a more disreputable-looking specimen and smiled.

Crazy 8 Press is an imprint of Clockworks

© 2025 by Aaron Rosenberg

Design by Aaron Rosenberg
Cover art by Lilly Repine
ISBN: 978-1-892544-29-2

To Jenifer, Adara, and Arthur, who are my true magic

Fyushu

KITINI

TABICHI

KORITO

IWIKARU

Yatamero

TATSUMA

SHITIMI

YUNIGIRI

OBANARI

CHIBIRI

SARUTO

HOCHIRO

BEZENKAI

MINIRI

Niginasi

NARIYARI

RIMBAKU

Scale _____ Miles

CAST OF CHARACTERS

Kagiri: a young man, older brother to Noniki. Also known as "Giri."

Noniki: the younger brother of Kagiri. Also known as "Niki."

Seikoku: a graverobber and thief from Ginzai

Hibikitsu: the young emperor of Rimbaku. Descended from the First Emperor, Taido Segei.

Misataki Shizumi: a gunso (sergeant) in the Honjofu, Rimbaku's elite warriors

Chimehara: a young woman living and working in Awaihinshi.

Maniko Kohori: Taikoro (Lord Commander) of the Honteno, Hibikitsu's household guard.

Kishin Narai: a wealthy merchant, leader of a cabal.

Shizu Yokori: Narai's second in the cabal.

Jiro Masute: Another member of the cabal.

Eien Kawatai: Another member of the cabal.

Fujiko Oritano: Final member of the cabal.

Joshi: Narai's man at arms, in charge of his guards.

Gento: the largest of Joshi's guards

Buntai: another guard

Hisa: another guard

Megu: another guard

Jitu Kanai: a potter from Ginzai

Kuma: a washer-woman from Shakomi

Isoro: a young herbalist

Sanedi: a basketweaver

Sukame and Minawa: an old married couple

Ratal: a fisherman

Amon: a netmender

Otokai: a horsetrader

Junko and Eiji: a couple who make clothes

Shisino sukudo: Hikibitsu's horse, "Speed of Thought." Nicknamed Shisi.

Diritan: a Honjofu

Nioko: another Honjofu

Ganema: Another Honjofu

Kenso: Another Honjofu

Akino: a Honjofu, one of Shizumi's most trusted men

Geniji: Another Honjofu, Shizumi's self-appointed bodyguard when in the field

Dairamu: Another Honjofu

Isano: Another Honjofu

Masai: Another Honjofu

Kori: Another Honjofu

Reiko: Another Honjofu

Fujibuki Haro: The Lord Commander (Taikoro) of the Honjofu. House crest: an otter wrapped around the sun.

Umibuki Nihiro: a former aiashe and recent Honteno

Hurito Yakai: a taisu in the aiashe

Itamon: a chuisu (lieutenant) in the Honteno

Reizei: another chuisu of the Honteno

Matsu: a servant in Aihiri

Amani Denbi: most senior of Hibikitsu's Imperial councilors, the Rojiri. House crest: silver star and crescent moon.

Sunao Tadazi: a Rojiri who is also Dogenriku, Lord General of the armies. House crest: a black bear.

Watane Yatahei: a Rojiri who is also Dogenkaishu, Lord Admiral of the navies. House crest: an emerald wave.

Orito Sadachi: another Rojiri

Yoshino Nanami: another Rojiri

Domo Haruta: another Rojiri

Itami Kane: a Honjofu

Suda: a young girl from the gutters of Suranmui

Kaemusei: the Silent Change, an inhuman being comprised of magic and hunger

Ibaru and Iraku: two brothers, Untouched, the hands of the Silent
    Change
Eisen: a "law clerk" and possible thug
Ryoji: an older gentleman
Futoba Kemi: a female boat captain, mistress of the Aio-akeo
    ("Autumn Love")
Master Eijiri: a wealthy merchant, minor noble, and the head of
    house Chohu, a merchant house specializing in gems
Madam Ponsoi: the senior housekeeper of House Chohu
Yuni: a cleaning lady in House Chohu
Ritaru: another cleaning lady in House Chohu
Master Ryoto and Mistress Etsuki: a married couple in House Chohu
Ruisoki: Ryota and Etsuko's son
Mistress Limini: another trader for House Chohu
Master Ganyeki: another trader for House Chohu
Ritsuro Okari: chuisu of the Honjofu
Baniko Anahi: the master of coin (a moneylender) of Jagimoto
Manari: a Honteno
Linai: another Honteno
Madam Ione: Chimehara's neighbor, a baker
Chiyu Akaii: a chuisu in the aiashe
Yoshitaro: an aiashe
Geido Shinen: one of the legendary Gensaiba matekan (wizards'
    warriors)
Shito Kibi: another of the legendary Gensaiba matekan
Onyoku Jeizen: another of the legendary Gensaiba matekan
Bushiki Kenin: another of the legendary Gensaiba matekan
Komu Setsui: another of the legendary Gensaiba matekan
Nikiyu Sinchu: another of the legendary Gensaiba matekan

CHAPTER ONE

"Listen," the voice said, soft as a whisper yet clear as a bell, and Kagiri knew it for his own, yet not. "Hear the way the air shifts, note the noise of the grass being trodden, detect the hint of breath being drawn. He is behind us, and approaching quickly, yet making an attempt at stealth."

"I hear him," Kagiri replied, detecting the hint of a pout in his response and hating that, yet finding it difficult to avoid when the voice left him feeling like a small child being lectured by a kindly yet impatient tutor.

"Hands at the ready," another voice broke in, just as quiet, just as close. "Settle your right upon the chahito, fingers gripping it loosely, almost stroking the metal there. If you decide to draw, you have only to slip your hand down the hilt. Your left you should rest against the scabbard, so that you might grip it and tug it downward as you free the blade."

To his irritation, Kagiri found himself doing exactly that, his hands obeying without conscious control.

Or at least, without *his* control.

"Stop that!" he hissed, and deliberately tugged both hands free of the weapon, hooking his thumbs in his sash instead. "I will decide when and if I should draw, not you!" Then, to forestall an argument, he pivoted on his heel, turning toward the man coming toward him.

It was Kishin Narai, as he had suspected it would be. The merchant was the most powerful of those following him, after all, and thus the most likely to approach him directly. Though even he had learned to be wary and to treat Kagiri with respect and no small amount of fear. After all, the man still bore a limp from the last time he and his fellows had thought they were in control of this group.

"We have found ships," Narai stated, bowing low enough that his broad face was momentarily concealed. "Three wide-decked ferries, simple crafts but enough to carry us across the river." They could have continued north, crossing farther up, but the closer they came the more closely watched the waters would be. Down here they had a better chance of approaching unnoticed, and that was an advantage they were loath to surrender.

Kagiri nodded. "Do we have enough food and water for the passage?" he asked, looking not at the merchant but at the wagons and carts and people spread out in a loose wave behind him. "I will not have any of those following me go hungry."

"Of course," Narai replied, dipping his broad shoulders again. "I will see to it." He backed away several paces before turning and heading for where the rest of the cabal waited near their tents. Kagiri knew that they would obey him. They were too afraid not to. But was that how he wished to control them, through terror? Would that not leave them resentful and eager for any chance to betray him?

"Fear is the only reliable method of control," a voice argued, different from the two before. "Loyalty, honor, friendship, even love, these can all wax and wane. They can shift with circumstances, changing as other relationships and responsibilities intrude. But fear, that is a constant. Once you make them afraid of you, they will remain so. As long as you do not lose your nerve."

"The only thing I am losing," Kagiri snarled in reply, "is patience with your prattling! Be still, the lot of you!" Angrily he turned away, looking back out over the water once more. They were at the edge of the Tonawa, second only to the more northerly Zinyang in size. From this vantage, nearly level with the river itself, he could not see its far shore, nor any land beyond. Only Awaihinshi itself was visible, and then only the topmost layers of the imperial city, rising from the water as if it were some sort of perfectly symmetrical shell piercing the river's surface. He knew that the city did not in fact float above the Tonowa, or even sit along its shore, but once they had made it across they would have only prairie and plains and then finally the Edishu left between them and their goal.

My goal, he corrected himself. *It is* my *goal, mine. Kagiri. No other.*

"You know that is not true," a fourth voice intruded. "To claim there is no other. It is in fact the farthest thing from the truth, for there are others. There is us. And without us, there is no you."

"You lie!" Kagiri snapped, biting down on each word before spitting it forth. "I am not you! You are not me! I am Kagiri! And you—you are nothing!"

"We are the Gensaiba," all four voices replied together, along with their two remaining brethren. "We saved you, Kagiri—never forget that. And now we are you, and you are us. You cannot be rid of us, not ever. We are here with you until the end."

"We shall see about that," Kagiri vowed, his hand tightening on his sword at last. He gazed out at the river, standing alone from his followers while in his mind he battled the six master warriors within. They had far more experience than him, far more knowledge, far more skill. But this was *his* body, *his* mind. He had not chosen to share it with them, he had not invited them into himself, and now he was determined to be rid of them somehow. No matter the cost.

But he knew that, however he accomplished that feat, it would have to be done before they reached Awaihinshi. For the Gensaiba were made for battle and conquest. If he allowed them to enter the fabled City of Polished Light, he was not sure he would ever be able to dislodge them from his mind, or his soul. That close to their prize, they would be all but unstoppable, and he might truly lose himself within their collective identity.

Even as he strode toward his men, his long legs eating up the intervening distance with smooth, powerful strides, he fought not to shudder at the thought of that, of being submerged forever within their constantly alternating array of personalities. Would he even survive as another voice, or would he simply be snuffed out, torn apart and scattered or consumed into the rest? They were ancient warriors, after all, legendary figures from the time before the great and terrible Schism that had torn this land apart and destroyed its magic. He was merely a boy from a small fishing village, seeking his fortune. If they were united against him, he doubted he could withstand their attack for long. And then the Gensaiba would be released upon the world, with no qualms against destroying anyone and anything that blocked them from obtaining their hearts' desire.

He could not allow that to happen.

CHAPTER TWO

"**W**ell," Noniki declared, sinking down onto a boulder as if the frown he bore on his broad, open face was an iron weight. "This is a problem."

"I warned you," Seikoku said, shifting beside him but remaining on her feet. The lithe former thief was not fond of sitting—she preferred always having the option to run. Though worry creased her brow as well, her lovely features were not nearly so grim as his, and the hand she rested on his shoulder was gentle, consoling, while her tone was mildly teasing. "I said not to assume this would all be easy."

"You were right," he admitted readily, and a part of him marveled at that. There had been a time, not all that long ago, when he could barely even conceive of being wrong. But much had happened since to convince him just how little he knew about the world and the way it worked, much less the way people thought and felt and behaved. Now he knew it was folly to try to be right all the time. His goal was simply to learn and grow and not make the same mistake twice. "I thought we'd be able to just, I don't know, beg passage," he concluded, waving his hand at the sight before them.

The hills dipped down just past where he sat, the slope gentle enough to walk down and lead beasts along but steep enough to make rapid progress as the land flowed toward the broad ribbon of gleaming silver and blue flowing past its edge. This was the Wagata, the first of the two rivers they would have to cross to reach Awaihinshi, and while a fraction of the Tonawa that coursed past to the east, it was still far too broad and quick and deep for them to attempt to wade or even swim. Boats were the only way to cross.

Twisting slightly, he studied the crowd that had paused behind him and Seikoku. Jitu Kanai was closest, the sturdy potter nearby as always, and he could also pick out Kuma and Isoro and Sanedi and Sukame and Minawa and many others. There were close to thirty people behind him now, for even as they had lost Madam Ushi and Chisigi and Isoko—though "lost" was hardly accurate, given that they had in fact been murdered by Yori, who had claimed to be a farmer but it seemed had in truth been a spy and an assassin—they had gained several new additions to their little mobile community. The newcomers, like the rest, had been curious about Noniki and his lack of aishone—his refusal to use them, in point of fact, and his refutation of the Relicant Touch and the society based upon its use—and had chosen to accompany him to the capital on his quest to speak with the emperor about the ills and flaws such a focus created. Noniki did not turn them away, for he was determined to welcome anyone who wished to join them, but it had created their current predicament.

For, with so many, they would require several boats. Perhaps as many as three or four.

And boats cost money to hire. Money they did not possess.

Kanai approached, along with the old woman Minawa, who had in some ways taken Madam Ushi's place as the sharp-eyed, sharp-tongued wrangler of their odd little flock. Along with Seikoku herself, though Noniki hesitated to point that out to her—for someone who prided herself so much on being a loner, the former graverobber had proven remarkably good at connecting with others, and extremely adept at swaying people to one side or another when there were disputes or questions as to which way to go. Now, with the three of them ringed about him, Noniki felt half like a taisho conferring with his issas and half like a schoolboy being lectured by his teachers.

"So?" Minawa asked, her words as blunt as her features and as lacking in deception. "How much did they want?"

"For all of us?" Noniki sighed, worrying the thick jade band he wore on his thumb, a gift from Seikoku as they had departed Ginzai what felt like a lifetime ago. "Fifteen gold."

That elicted a gasp from the old woman, and Kanai's mouth fell open. "So much?" the potter managed to mumble. "That's a fortune!"

"There are a great many of us," Seikoku pointed out, "and we are not traveling lightly." She did not bother to add that she and Noniki and even Kanai were, in fact, as the three of them each had brought only a small pack with clothes, bedroll, and a few small accessories. But some of the others in their little troupe had come more heavily laden, with carts and rickshaws and even wagons. Why, Isoro had the entire herbalist collection she had inherited from her mother, all the little jars and vials and boxes packed carefully away in teak drawers that lined the walls of her enclosed cart. That was not something that could be packed into a small bag, nor could it be left behind!

The problem was that, while many of the group did possess a quantity of personal items or tools and implements, none of them had a great deal of money. Certainly not enough for them to assemble fifteen gold coins! But without that money, Noniki had no idea how they would make their way across.

And this was just the Wagata! He could only assume that crossing the Edishu would cost just as much, if not more, since it ran practically to Awaihinshi's front gates! What would they do then?

"We will take up a collection," Minawa suggested. "Each of us has at least a few bronze stashed away, I'm sure. Sukame and I certainly do. That should make a start of it." She scowled, studying the river and the boats dotting its nearer shore. "Perhaps we can find a sympathetic soul who will ferry us over for less," she said, though her tone indicated she did not place much hope in this happening. "There may be one among these captains and sailors who agrees with you about the Relicant Touch and how it is stifling our people."

"Perhaps," Noniki agreed, "though that would mean speaking with each of them and broaching such a topic, which will take time. And might attract other unwanted attentions." He was referring to the emperor, of course, for they could only assume Yori had been working for Rimbaku's ruler, or at least someone in his inner circle, one of the advisors known as the Rogiri, perhaps. Who else would have such cause for concern about Noniki and his statements as to set a trained killer upon him?

"If only there were another way across," Kanai said softly. "A bridge, perhaps? Or a spot shallow enough we could wade across, as we did the Tonawa?"

"We were lucky with the Tonawa," Minawa told him. "That bend is one of the only places along its length where it's possible to cross on foot." They had also been lucky that Chisigi, who had been a fisherman, knew of those shallows from many years of fishing in that area. They could easily have walked right past that section of river without ever noticing. They had no such experts among them here.

But, he realized, they did have someone who was an expert at getting into places she shouldn't, often by finding new approaches or discovering paths that had not been blocked as carefully as they should. "How would you get across?" he asked Seikoku, turning his full attention toward her. "If it were just you and I, say, but we still lacked any coin. What would you do?"

She frowned, those lovely eyes of hers gazing out at the water and beyond, seeing not the real world but a land of possibilities. "I would steal a boat," she replied after a moment, a small smile playing over her lips. "Just a small one, and we could leave it on the far shore for its owner to reclaim." She laughed, a trifle bitterly. "I don't suppose even I could steal four large ferries, though." At first she had been reticent about her former activities, but weeks on the road together had broken down many walls among the people in their little circle, and there were few secrets left when you were walking and sleeping and bathing beside the same people day after day.

"Probably not the best way to impress upon people that we mean them no harm," Noniki agreed, though he was smiling as well. They had encountered several, during their trek up from Ginzai, who had felt that his approach to the Relicant Touch was a direct attack upon their way of life—which it was—and upon their own success—which it was not, or at least he had not intended it as such. But there would always be those, he had realized, who had accumulated wealth and property and prosperity and reputation and lived in constant fear of losing those things, and to them his suggestions could indeed be seen as a threat, albeit an oblique and general one that would most likely take generations to achieve. Still, those interactions had made him all the more determined to appear nonthreatening whenever possible, and he doubted largescale theft would fit in with such a goal.

Kanai sighed, rubbing at his chin with thick, blunt fingers. "If only I had a kiln," he stated slowly, for his words always emerged with no great haste, matching the thoughts that rose unhurriedly to his lips. "Then I could craft us a boat of our own." He grinned. "Though perhaps a ceramic hull would not be much use, eh?"

Noniki started to agree that, indeed, such a craft might prove less than seaworthy, but Minawa interrupted him. The old woman turned to Kanai and, much to his and everyone's surprise, grabbed his face in both hands and planted a solid smack of a kiss upon his lips.

"That is genius!" she declared, her eyes shining. "I knew you could not be half as dumb as you act!"

"I—" the poor potter clearly did not know how to respond to this, his hands going unbidden to his lips as if to ascertain the treatment they had just received. "Uh, no?"

Noniki glanced up at Seikoku, raising an eyebrow in unspoken question, and saw her face light up as if the sun had just broken through the clouds and shone down upon her and her alone. "Oh!" she said. "Oh, you're right! Of course! That is brilliant!" And she, too, stepped up to the befuddled Kanai and kissed him, causing the poor man to blush scarlet as if the same sun were now setting in his broad face.

"I am afraid I am lagging behind here," Noniki remarked dryly, "though I promise, Kanai, that when it is explained to me I will refrain from adding to your recent tokens of affection, since I cannot hope to match the beauty of its two donors." Minawa laughed at that, a deep, braying sound as honest as the rest of her, while Seikoku smiled and colored prettily before hurrying to speak, perhaps to prevent any further compliments.

"Kanai has exactly the right idea," she explained quickly. "Just the wrong composition." She smiled, gesturing toward the crowd waiting patiently behind them. "We have canvas and wood aplenty," she pointed out. "We can disassemble the wagons and carts and fashion rafts from them. Those will get us across the Wagata and the Edishu both—we can either rebuild our vehicles once we cross here or simply carry the rafts as-is." She beamed at Kanai, at Noniki, at the crowd, at the world in general. "I am sure that, among us, we will have those who are good with woodworking and can help with such a project. Anyone who isn't can still follow instructions, carry things to the water, and otherwise make themselves useful."

Noniki considered this. "I like it," he agreed after a moment. "And the fact that we will be making our way across under our own power, using our own materials and our own skills—well, that is exactly what we talk about, is it not? Not relying upon the gifts of others, not expecting anyone else to do things for us, but doing them ourselves? How better to arrive at Awaihinshi than by the fruits of our own labors?" Rising to his feet, he clapped a hand on Kanai's shoulder. "You are as wise as ever, my friend," he told the potter. "And I am, as always grateful to have you with us."

That compliment, at least, the other man was able to accept with only a mild stutter and a quick flush of pleasure, along with a dip of his head. He was grinning, however, when he turned toward the rest of their community and, along with Seikoku, Minawa, and Noniki himself, began telling them what they had in mind.

CHAPTER THREE

"Your Majesty!"

Hibikitsu, Echo of Victory, the Emperor of Rimbaku, whirled at the shout, his hand going reflexively to his nihono, Kosshiki. It was only when he registered the armor of the Honjofu that he relaxed, and even then only slightly, for he did not recognize the woman barreling toward him in such haste and it would hardly be impossible to imagine someone stealing the garb of his personal guard in order to get within striking distance of him. After all, the Fyushans had certainly behaved with far less honor, and though they had acknowledged defeat and taken their dejected soldiers back over the mountains he would not put it past them to try one last, desperate stratagem to remove him and gain control of his kingdom.

Clearly he was not alone in this thought, for Diritan and Nioko nudged their own horses forward, intercepting the newcomer well shy of where Hibikitsu waited on Shisi. Upon closing with the woman, they exchanged word and small gestures, and then parted to allow her through, bringing their steeds around to fall into place on either side of her.

"This is Ganema," Diritan stated, the three of them halting a few paces from Shisi. "She and I trained together."

"Your Majesty." Ganema saluted, hand over fist to chest. Though her armor and weapons appeared well-maintained, her face and her steed's were covered in sweat, causing the road dust to cling to them like a film. "I apologize for my unseemly appearance, but this message could not wait."

"What is it?" he asked, waving her to sit upright again.

"We have just received news from Awaihinshi, sire," the warrior replied, still out of breath. It seemed she had exerted herself nearly as much as her horse. "The capital is under attack!"

"What?" Now she had his full attention, and he nudged Shisi closer, shifting the black stallion sideways so that he could be face-to-face with the woman. "What do you mean? By whom? When did this begin?" His hands clenched the reins until his fingers ached, as if he could somehow spur Shisi into a gallop that would magically transport him the many leagues back home, but he forced himself to stillness as he waited for her to regain enough control to reply.

"We do not know exactly, Your Majesty," was her answer when it came, between gulps of air. "We received word only this morning, but it seems···confused. An earlier message got delayed and arrived at the same time as another, more recent one." She paused to organize her thoughts, then continued in a more measured tone, "Maniko Kohori sent word of an attack upon the Imperial Compound by···it appears by members of the Rojiri and their household guards."

"The Rojiri?" Hibikitsu ground his teeth together, all but spitting the title. "Those arrogant, presumptuous, entitled···they have gone too far this time!" At the same time, a part of him—that part that was calmer and wiser—voiced a separate thought:

This was his fault.

After all, he had chosen to leave the safety of the City of Polished Light, something no emperor had done in several generations. Indeed, most had rarely left Aihiri, the Imperial Compound at the city's peak, and then only to parade through the city's lower levels on festive occasions such as an imperial wedding or the birth of an heir. Certainly he had startled his imperial counselors when he had declared that he would take charge of the nation's defense himself, once they had received word of the Fyushan attack across their northern border. None of them had expected such initiative from him, or such a departure from tradition, and several had tried to argue against his going, yet he had made up his mind and had departed with his Honjofu.

And evidently those same counselors had seen this as too

good an opportunity to pass up, with the throne suddenly vacant for the first time in living memory. No doubt they had even hoped the Fyushans would do their work for them and ensure that he did not live to return and reclaim his rightful place.

"Which Rojiri?" he demanded now. "I would know who has betrayed me."

Ganema shook her head. "The message was unclear, Your Majesty," she stated, lowering her gaze in apology, though the fault was not hers. Still, Hibikitsu knew he had once been prone to fly into a rage at far less. Fortunately, his recent experiences had taught him some control as well as, he hoped, some wisdom. Though none of it had been without cost. "All we know for certain is that there have been attempts to take control of the compound, and the Honteno have been resisting."

"Of course they have," he muttered, unclenching his fists and straightening. Maniko Kohori was one of the most loyal individuals he had ever known, and utterly without personal ambition beyond serving her empire and protecting her emperor. That was why he had left her and her Honteno in charge of the throneroom and his personal quarters while he was gone, precisely to prevent any of the Rojiiri from getting ideas of exceeding their station and claiming imperial prerogatives for themselves. It seemed he had been right to be concerned. He hoped Kohori was well—though still a powerful warrior herself, she was no longer young, and though the household guard were hand-picked and each highly formidable, they were not a large cohort.

Glancing up from his reverie, he realized that Ganema was waiting, and not just for orders. "What else?" he asked, attempting to soften his tone to indicate that his displeasure was not with her but with these events she was merely relaying.

"The newer message," the warrior explained, looking almost pained by the words she was forced to speak. "It indicates sightings of massed groups approaching the city from without." There were guards posted at various points along the shore, at the mouth of each of the rivers bordering the imperial region of Saruto, and atop hills overlooking Awaihinshi, their only duty to issue an alert if they spied any threat approaching the capital. But Hibikitsu had never heard of them actually having to fulfill that function. That was why Saruto was in the middle of the empire, so that any would-be foe would have to either cover half Rimbaku or sail leagues around it to approach the city and thus could be spotted and headed off long before they came within sight of its walls.

"What sort of groups?" he asked. "And from where?" Belatedly he realized she had indeed said "groups," plural, and added, "And just how many are there?"

"Two, Your Majesty," she answered. "One approaching from the south and the other from the east. Neither is massive, perhaps less than a hundred, but both seem determined, and⋯" here she faltered again. "Your pardon, sire, but the reports suggest each is led by someone of great authority. The report seems garbled, but there is something about 'visible intensity' and 'commanding presence.' There is a note that says the leader of one, the group from the east, may be the Butcher of the Kindichi." She bowed again, indicating she had reached the end of her report, and then straightened, fist to her chest in salute, a warrior awaiting orders.

Hibikitsu frowned, digesting this. A hundred was not so many, certainly not enough to pierce the city's defenses, but what was this about "intensity" and "presence"? His sentries were trained to deliver details clearly and succinctly, so such a sloppy and vague report showed something was most definitely wrong, either with their perceptions or with the individuals they had observed. Either way, he did not like the timing of all this—not one but two strange groups approaching his city, from two different directions, and both while he was not in residence? It smacked of careful planning and deliberate strategy, perhaps some plan to close on the city from two sides and thus take possession before he could return.

And that last part—'The Butcher of the Kindichi'? What did that mean? He wracked his brain, and a memory slowly emerged. "The Kindichi," he said aloud, "those were the bandits down in Nariyari, yes?" His Honjofu shrugged—none of them had been present during any of those conversations, of course, and most likely their Taikoro had not bothered to inform them of the matter—but he was certain of it now. They had been wreaking havoc in the southern province and when a bantao had been dispatched to deal with them, these "bosses" had sent back the soldiers' heads. A full shotao had gone in next—with the same results. The commander of the aiashe, Sunao Tadazi, had formally requested aid from the Honjofu, and Hibikitsu had agreed and dispatched Fujibuki Haro himself to assemble a chotao and deal with the matter. He had heard nothing of the matter since, having left himself shortly after that. Had the Kindichi destroyed the Honjofu as easily as they had the aiashe? Was this "Butcher" of theirs responsible for Haro's death and countless others? That would make this individual a dangerous figure indeed!

At least that made his own course clear. "Alert your fellows," he told Duritan. "We ride for Tabichi with all speed. Send a messenger on ahead, all the way to the docks—tell them we will need their fastest boat, large enough to accommodate myself and my Honjofu, and that it should be ready to set out the moment we reach it." They had set out from Furukotai the day before but had been heading south, on the trail back down to the capital, and with all Korito and then Yunigiri to cover they had been setting a comfortable pace to not wear out their horses. Now, however, they would be turning their steeds to the west, and speed was of the essence. Taisho Daishin had brought his troops over on boats, as ordered, and would be returning the same way—he would simply have one boat less, since the Honjofu would reach the docks well ahead of the foot soldiers. It would be a hard ride, but there would be time enough for their mounts to rest once they were left behind or, like Shisi, loaded onto the boats that would be waiting. And from the harbors in Tabichi they could sail straight back to Awaihinshi. Depending upon the winds, they might be able to beat these two groups to the city. If not, they should still be able to show up hard at their heels and prevent either from consolidating any sort of hold they managed to claim on the capital.

"Thank you, Ganema," he told the Honjofu, and she dipped her head. "I appreciate your haste in bringing me this news. Ride back with us to the boats." She saluted again and fell into place behind as he wheeled his horse about and then, with the mountains behind him and the shore out of sight many miles ahead, kicked Shisi's flanks and urged the stallion into a gallop. Responding to his urgency his horse reared once, neighed, and then flung himself forward, eating up the uneven ground in a hard, punishing charge that caused the landscape to blur past. Hibikitsu gritted his teeth and held on, enduring the pain each jolt sent hammering up his spine, dimly aware of his warriors racing along beside him. His focus was on one thing now, and one thing only—returning home to Awaihinshi.

And the First Emperor pity anyone foolish enough to stand in his way.

CHAPTER FOUR

"**H**ai!" Misataki Shizumi shouted, arms taut where they held her nihono above her head, the blade curving back behind her. Around her, the rest of the Honjofu matched her cry and her pose, over a hundred swords gleaming in the morning light, their silvery blades a stark contrast to the black lacquered armor the elite warriors all wore.

"Hai!" she called out again, and as she forced the air from her lungs she yanked her arms down, sweeping her sword down in a vicious cut that whistled through the damp air. Her fellow soldiers mirrored her motion, and the practice yard was filled with the sharp keening of so many blades cutting through the dawn at once, underlaid with the creak of armor as it adjusted to that motion.

"Hold!" That call came from the man who stood ahead and facing the rest of them, an unprepossessing figure save for his well-oiled mustache and the gold trim to his armor, which marked him as not just a Honjofu but their Taikoro. Still, the very fact that he was here, much less leading this exercise, was a continuing source of mystery and wonder to her.

Now Fujibuki Haro straightened, shifting effortlessly from a fighting stance to a relaxed pose, sheathing his blade without looking down, using only his fingers to mark the entrance of his scabbard and sliding the sword home in a single smooth motion. That was another ongoing surprise for Shizumi. When she had last been here in Aihiri, her commanding officer had been utterly incompetent as a swordsman, at least when left to his own devices. True, once he downed aishone he became an expert warrior, but despite being a ranking noble and thus rich and powerful with access to many relic bones he rarely saw the need to make use of them. Certainly he would never have done so for something as trivial—to him—as a morning practice!

Yet when she had returned to the capital—only two days behind Haro, who had raced back to answer a plea for help from Maniko Kohori and her household guard—she had found a very different man than the leader she had last seen lounging and sipping tea down in Bezenkai. Her commander now carried himself like a soldier, a warrior, and participated in activities such as this. It was a wonder to her, though certainly she did not wish to question whatever had transformed him from his former preening, sneering self to this man she was almost beginning to respect.

He shifted to study her in turn and she stiffened, worried that some of her thoughts might have shown on her face, lowering her head in salute since she could not clasp hand to chest while bearing a naked blade. "I must return to my offices, to handle some urgent matters," their commander called out, even his voice clearer and more authoritative than it had been before. "In my absence, I leave your eminently capable gunso, Misataki Shizumi, to continue your training." And he dipped his head toward her, his fist rising to his chest.

"Hai, Takoro," she replied. "I will not fail you." Sheathing her blade long enough to return the salute, she stepped forward, taking his place as he moved aside, and pivoted to face the rest of the Honjofu, all of whom were watching her intently. She was pleased to see the respect evident in most of their faces, for she had worked hard to prove herself here, having two major strikes against her as both a woman and a commoner, and while one or two still bore sneers they were careful to wipe those expressions away when she glanced in their direction. They might deride her in private but they would obey her in public, and that was what mattered most.

The members of her usual bantao, of course, were arrayed across the front, around the position she had just vacated, and in them she saw not only respect but personal admiration. Geniji grinned openly at her, the big woman as incapable of restraining her emotions as ever, and Akino winked when his eye caught hers.

Shizumi schooled herself not to react, silently cursing him for his constant attempts to goad her, though she knew that, too, was a mark of respect from the quick-witted and equally sharp-tongued warrior. Still, now was not the time.

Instead she steeled herself, mentally checking her stance, her hands falling automatically to her sword and drawing it in one quick move, the blade a shining arc that swept out before her and left a rainbow shimmer in its wake. Sweeping it back to a vertical line beginning at her belly and lancing out from there, her other hand rising from the scabbard and falling into place beneath the first on the silk-corded handle, she drew in a deep breath before bellowing out, "First position, hai!"

"Hai!" The collective shout echoed the yard, and she allowed herself a faint smile, studying the row upon row of warriors mirroring her every move. Except for the thrill of battle itself, there was no place she would rather be than right here, right now.

How odd that she had Fujibaki Haro to thank for that.

An hour or so later, showered and attired in clean hosode and hakami beneath her armor—for the Taikoro had declared that the Honjofu should wear their armor whenever possible, even at times like now when she was not officially on duty, another departure from past practice—Shizumi nodded at the two warriors standing guard and then rapped sharply upon the door to her commander's study.

"Enter," came the call from within, and she slid the paneled door aside, stepping through and shutting it again behind her.

The room was a handsome one, and she had always grudgingly admitted that, whatever else could be said about her superior, he had excellent taste. Scrolls hung upon the wall, one displaying a painted version of the otter wrapped around the sun that was the symbol of House Fujibaki and the other showing a pair of dragons twined together mid-air in what could be battle or lovemaking or perhaps both. A lovely folding screen stood against the back wall, its panels not made of the traditional framework with rice-paper squares but instead solid wood panes covered in beaten gold upon which had been layered a scene of flowering branches emerging from the morning fog, each petal distinct and made of inlaid ivory so that they shone brightly against the softer background, the branches themselves painted upon the gold with careful strokes. Before that was the Taikoro's desk, a traditional affair of low, polished wood surprisingly devoid of trinkets and sculptures and holding only brushes, ink dish, parchment, and a small stone carving of a prancing otter used to hold the parchment in place while writing. This was not how the surface had looked the last time she had been in these rooms, and again she wondered at the change.

She mentioned nothing of this, however, as she saluted, saying only, "You wished to see me, Taikoro?"

"Hai," her commander agreed, leaning back in his seat to regard her. "I wished to ask your opinion, gunso," he explained slowly, stroking his mustache—his pride in that facial ornament had not changed, at least! "What do you think of our recent morning practices?"

Surprised by the question, Shizumi took a moment to consider and to formulate her reply. At least she did not have to lie when she finally said, "I think they are going very well, sir. The Honjofu always benefit from regular exercise and practice, and having you lead them has been a significant benefit to morale and to a sense of cohesion."

"Yes," the Taikoro said slowly. "And practicing in full armor? I know that is not your usual style." Indeed, Shizumi was forced to repress a shudder, for her superior had spent many mornings watching her practice in only hosode and ponmei, alternating between condescension at her need to better herself, snide remarks at her waste of aishone on such meaningless exercise, and leering at her body with the sweat-soaked undershirt and thin pants clinging to her like a second skin. Now, however, she did not see any hint of lust or ridicule in his gaze, nor hear any in his voice. Consequently, she took his question as a serious one and answered it in kind.

"It is not," she agreed carefully, "but I feel it is indeed useful for us all. It is one thing to wield a blade while wearing only light clothing and another to handle it while encumbered with armor." The Honjofu wore superior armor, of course, carefully crafted to fit them and designed for maximum protection while still allowing as much freedom of movement as possible. Still, no armor could allow full motion without being so flimsy or spread apart as to be little better than cloth itself. She had seen many unseasoned soldiers die because they had not accounted for the difference, and indeed had taken advantage of that unpreparedness many times when facing enemies, using their sudden limitations against them.

Haro nodded. "Thank you, gunso," he told her. "I value your input. You are one of our finest, and I have nothing but respect and admiration for you." The way he said that had Shizumi studying him, trying to spot the insult hidden within that apparent compliment, but if it was there it was concealed too cleverly for her to pick up on.

"You honor me, Taikoro," she replied instead, bowing low and saluting. "I live to serve the Empire."

"So do we all," he stated, saluting in return. "That is all for now. You may go about your regular duties. And thank you."

As she turned to go, however, he called after her, "Oh, one more thing." When she glanced back, he was drumming his fingers idly upon the edge of his desk. "Has there been anything further about that body you and Taikoro Maniko discovered on the palace grounds?"

"No, Taikoro," she answered, shifting to face him once more as she gave her report. "The Honteno are handling the investigation, and I have heard nothing further." She could not help but shiver a little, remembering the horrific scene they had found that morning, the body shriveled and blackened as if by an intense flame, the face frozen in abject terror, the empty eyes staring out at them in silent recrimination.

"Hm, yes, of course," Haro said. "That is as it should be, for of course the grounds fall under the Honteno's care. Still, please offer your assistance to Taikoro Maniko, on my behalf. Assure her that the Honjofu stand ready to assist her in any way necessary."

"Hai, I will, Taikoro," Shizumi replied, saluting again. There did not seem to be anything further, and she departed the office more confused than ever. That interview had been brief, direct, businesslike, and respectful.

In short, nothing like any encounter she had ever had with Fujibaki Haro in the past.

What had happened to her commanding officer, she wondered yet again as she made her way back toward her own bunk. And was it too much to hope that it might be permanent?

CHAPTER FIVE

U mibuki Nihiro could hardly believe his luck. He had served as an aiashe for the past four years, rising from a mere foot soldier to gocho and finally gunso. He hoped to eventually move up to at least shosu, though he knew that was long odds because it was the first rung of the officer ranks and his family, though noble, was only a minor offshoot of a greater house and not particularly wealthy or prestigious enough on their own to win him such a promotion. Still, stranger things had happened.

Such as his current situation. Nihiro had just returned from a patrol when he'd been summoned to his taisu's office. There his superior, a tough but not unreasonable woman named Hurito Yakai, introduced him to her visitor, whose name was Itamon. But it was not the guest's face or features that stunned Nihiro almost into silence, so that he stammered over his own name like a small child on their first day at lessons. It was Itamon's armor, which was not the plain, functional gear of the standard army. This man's armor featured a proper deo and karute instead of the aiashe's simple maikaro and jingaso. Moreover, it was lacquered in solid crimson, denoting him as a member of the Honteno, the Imperial Household Guard who protected the Imperial Compound and the Emperor himself. Further, Itamon's breastplate bore the gold bars of a chuisu at his shoulders and above the browpiece of his helm.

"Umibuki," Taisu Hurito stated, her voice as flat and grating as usual but her sharp eyes surprisingly kind. "Chuisu Itamon here has come to see if I have any soldiers I think would fit in well with the Honteno. I've recommended you for the job. If you're interested, that is."

He almost thought he caught a quirk at the corner of her lips as she said that, but of course that was impossible, for everyone knew that Hurito Yakai lacked even the slightest hint of a sense of humor. Still, she had to know what she was saying. Would he be interested? In joining the Honteno, one of the finest forces in the nation? In serving exclusively in Aihiri, answering directly to Tai-koro Maniko herself and protecting the Emperor's own person?

What kind of fool would he be if he were not?

"I would be honored to serve," he replied when he'd found his voice, and the chuisu grinned at him, the smile lighting up his broad face. He clapped Nihiro on the shoulder as if they were old friends.

"Excellent!" The Honteno said. "In that case, go gather your things and come meet me back here. I'll square things with your taisu and then we'll head up the hill together, get you situated, geared up, all that."

Nihiro glanced at Yakai, for she was still his superior until declared otherwise, and she nodded. "You are a good soldier and I'm sorry to lose you," she told him, "but I think you will fare well in the Honteno, and it seems they've a need for good soldiers right now." She saluted him, and he returned the gesture before backing out and running to the barracks like demons themselves were at his back.

It took him less than five minutes to throw everything into his bakiro and race back. He arrived, red-faced and out of breath, to find Itamon leaning against the taisu's doorframe, arms crossed, looking amused.

"You can leave your armor and weapons here," the Honteno pointed out, gesturing toward the bench beside him. "We'll get you outfitted properly once we're up top."

Nihiro nodded and hastily removed all the markings that made him aiashe, until finally he was standing in only hosode and ponmei. He pulled a shatage from his bag so that he did not feel quite so naked. At least his nihono was still at his side, secured by a simple silk sash! That was the ancestral blade of his house, and thus his to bear no matter where he went.

Once the Honteno nodded his approval they set off, wending

their way up through the tiers of the city, for the aiashe were stationed in Mazihini, at the very bottom, to be able to deploy along the outer walls quickly. Itamon proved to be a pleasant companion, friendly and chatty without being overly familiar, and more quickly than he'd expected Nihiro found himself stepping through the pure white marble walls that separated the very highest level from the rest.

Not pausing to let him drink in the sight—"you'll get used to it"—Itamon led him straight to the Honteno's barracks, and to his new commanding officer, Maniko Kohori. Nihiro had seen her before, though only at a distance, and was surprised at the warmth that radiated from the stern-looking woman, despite her evident fatigue and what he thought might also be grief.

"Welcome, Umibuki Nihiro," she said once Itamon had introduced him and handed over his service record, clearly obtained from Hurito Yakai. "I appreciate your joining us. We have recently suffered some losses, which I'm sure you'll hear more about later, and so we are actively trying to refill our ranks." She glanced quickly at the scroll, studying a few of the details scribed upon it, then nodded. "Judging by this, I'd say you will be an excellent addition."

He saluted, then, and bowed deeply. "It is my honor to serve," he told her. "I promise you I will do my best."

That won a smile from her. "That is all anyone can ask." She nodded to the man still beside him. "Itamon will show you your quarters, get you outfitted, and explain your basic duties. We'll speak again later." The dismissal was clear, and Nihiro was not at all taken aback by it, for it was evident that his new superior had a great deal on her mind.

Getting him settled took the better part of the day, and his head was still awhirl when he was told he had an hour or so before dinner and was free to wander the grounds and familiarize himself with the place. Nihiro felt as if he were in a waking dream as he stepped from the barracks and stopped to admire the beautiful, lush lawn spread out before him, and the neat rows of ornamental trees and bushes carefully spaced to form straight avenues and narrower, winding paths. It was beautiful, far moreso than any of the home gardens he had seen in the lower levels, and now this was to be his home and his place of work, all in one.

Several men and women walked past, two in the red of the Honteno—the same crimson hue he now wore—and one in the black of the Honjofu. Of course, the Bone Warriors were also quartered here. Itamon had said that the two groups normally kept a respectful distance from each other, but that right now they were working more closely together because of the recent reduction in the Honteno's numbers. He had promised to explain more about that over dinner.

Another man strolled by, also in black enameled armor but with gold trim, and as he passed beneath a nearby lantern his mustache gleamed in the light, looking enameled itself. Nihiro started, for he knew that mustache and that face!

"Haro!" he shouted, hopping down from the low porch and rushing over. "Haro, it's me!"

Fujibuki Haro started at the sudden intrusion into his personal space but recovered quickly and bowed. "Yes, hello," he replied, but it was clear from his tone that he had not yet made the connection.

"Haro, it's me, Umibuki Nihiro," he continued, leaning in so the other man could see his features more clearly. "You know, your cousin?" For the Umibuki were an offshoot of the more powerful Fujibuki. Further, he and Haro were of the same generation and had grown up together in the manner of boys some six or seven years apart, seeing each other regularly at full clan events and whenever their parents had visited each other.

Now Haro's face lit up. "Ah, Hiro!" he said, laughing and embracing him quickly. "Of course! I didn't recognize you at first! How good to see you, cousin!" He stepped back, still holding Nihiro by the shoulders. "And a Honteno? How did I not know that before?"

"Oh, this is new," Nihiro replied, grinning. "They just recruited me from the aiashe today. Not bad, eh? And hey, that means we'll be seeing each other regularly, right? Though of course you're a mighty Taikoro and I'm just a lowly Honteno, not even a gocho anymore. At least, not yet." He nudged his cousin in the ribs, and Haro chuckled obligingly.

"Yes, we will run into each other, I'm sure," he agreed, stroking his mustache thoughtfully. "Though I am busy, of course. And it would not do for anyone to think I am favoring you, especially over my own men."

"No, of course not," Nihiro agreed quickly. Haro had always placed great stock in appearances and particularly in following proper codes of behavior. He would never wish to show favoritism because it could be seen as ignoble, and that was the one fate his cousin feared most of all.

Still, seeing him here, now, Nihiro could not help but rib him a little. "So, I see you are still oiling your mustache?" he said, leaning in and lowering his voice in case anyone else walked past. "Tell me, are you still scenting your Subayaki oil with lilacs and lavender, or have you changed to a more masculine scent at last?" The oil, derived from seeds of the common camellia, was often used for hair care, but Haro had always complained that it smelled musty to him, so he had his servants scent his. Which would have been fine if he had not gone with such a delicate, traditionally feminine choice!

"Ha, no, still the same scents," Haro had agreed, his smile slightly strained. "Actually, cousin, now that I think on it, there is something I should really discuss with you, a family matter, as it were. I'm sure I can trust you to be discreet, as we are related?" Nihiro had barely begun to promise his silence before Haro was guiding him off the path and into the gardens, down one of the smaller paths and well away from the lights.

He's grown stronger over the years, Nihiro thought, feeling the iron grip his cousin had upon his arm, the way he tugged him along so quickly he was almost out of breath. He could barely see their surroundings now, as dusk began to settle, for the rest of the lanterns had not yet been lit. But his guide clearly knew where he was going and did not falter once as he took them deep into the maze of plants, finally releasing Nihiro's arm just as he rounded a final bush and disappeared momentarily into the shadows gathered there.

"All right, you've brought me all the way out here," Nihiro groused, rubbing at his arm. "What is it you needed to tell me?"

"It is only this," Haro replied, his silhouette barely visible in the dark there, his voice strangely husky. "Luck was not with you when you chose to join the Honteno today."

And with that the man that had been Nihiro's cousin lunged from the shadows, his body elongating oddly, his limbs themselves an inky black and trailing wisps as if made from smoke, his fingers long and taloned. But it was his features, his hideously stretched and distorted features, that were the worst of all, and Nihiro felt his own blood curdling, his bowels loosening, as he raised his hands before his face and opened his mouth to scream.

Something sharp and jagged tore through his throat before any sound could emerge. And then there was only the darkness, leaping forward hungrily to claim him.

CHAPTER SIX

"**S**eikoku! Seikoku!"

She glanced up at the sound of her name, and after only a second of casting about located the source—Isoro, who was barreling toward her, long hair come loose from its usual braids and fluttering like a silken pennant, robes in disarray, face flushed. Instantly Seikoku was on her feet and met the young herbalist halfway, catching her firmly but gently to halt her headlong flight.

"What's wrong?" she asked, checking behind the other woman in case of some threat. Had Yori returned? Was the spy-turned-assassin done with slow poisons and now resorting to more overt methods?

"It's my cart," Isoro wailed, clutching at her shoulders, her eyes wide. "They're tearing it apart!"

"What?" Seikoku was already moving, clasping Isoro's hand in hers to drag the woman along as they retraced her steps. She didn't run but she did step quickly, and within minutes she had reached the site of contention, right along the shore as their entire community worked to convert their wagons and carts into rafts to take them all across. There was Isoro's cart, easily identifiable because of its high sides and the lack of any openings save for the tightly fitted door at the rear. And there, true as true, were two men struggling to detach one of the rear wheels from its axle while another was up on the cart itself and busy prying at the hinges on its door.

"STOP!" She shouted, charging forward. She leaped up onto the cart without pause and slapped the one man's hands away from the door. With his stocky build, unkempt bun, and hairy, sunburnt arms, she recognized him even before he turned an astonished face her way. "Ratal, what in all the bones do you think you're doing?"

The fisherman scratched his nose, which was peeling—it seemed that, unlike many who spent their lives working in the sun, he had never developed any sort of tolerance to its rays and spent his life perpetually reddened and chapped. "We need to build rafts," he answered after a second's thought. "That's what you said."

She ground her teeth to keep from yelling further, knowing that wouldn't help. "Yes, we do need to build rafts," she agreed slowly, struggling to keep her tone calm and level. "But do you remember what else we said?" He shook his head, and she glanced over at his two companions. "Amon? Otokai? Do you remember?"

The two of them exchanged worried looks, and finally Amon answered, "Was it when you said we needed to respect people's property?" He had been a netmender in a small village not far from here, and his fingers were so heavily callused he could pluck coals from the cookfire without burning himself.

"That's exactly right," she assured him. "We have to respect people's property. We can't just go yanking apart things that aren't ours, can we?" All three men shook their head. "Now, this cart belongs to Isoro, here." She waved the herbalist over. "Ratal, you know that—she gave you that ointment for your skin. Which means you know how important her herbs are, not just to her but to everyone. And what do you think would happen to all those herbs she has if they were to get wet during the crossing?"

"They'd be ruined?" Otokai offered hesitantly. He was a horse-trader and had a keen eye for animal flesh, and a quick tongue, but right now he was cowering like a dog that had disobeyed and knew it, awaiting its punishment.

"Utterly," Isoro confirmed. "I'd have nothing left, nothing to help heal people's burns and cuts and stomach aches. Nothing to sell to help provide food for the community, either." Now that the men had stopped she had regained some of her composure, and her voice was low and soothing, which only made the men look even more ashamed.

"Sorry," Ratal mumbled. "It seemed like such good, solid wood, we just thought···" He trailed off, ducking his head. "Sorry." His hands rose and patted the door as if to prove it was still secure.

Seikoku blew out a breath. "Look," she said, "it's good that you're helping. We need that. But next time, don't just take it upon yourself to decide what needs to be done, yeah? Ask me or Kanai or Minawa." She glanced about, studying some of the others from their troupe who were nearby. "Here," she said after a second, pointing at a couple a short ways distant who were struggling to disassemble their wagon. "Junko and Eiji look like they could use some extra hands. They're taking their wagon apart—why don't you go see if you can help? Just remember," she called as the trio hurried off to do as she'd suggested, "that it's their property, so let them tell you what can be taken apart and what needs to be saved!" The pair in question were tailors but she knew that most of their silk and cotton and other cloth was kept wrapped in oil-skin, so as long as those were tied securely they should be able to make the journey safely. Besides, Junko was tough—she would keep them in line.

"Thank you," Isoro told her as she hopped down to the shore, her feet sinking slightly in the damp earth there. The air here was invigorating, she noted as she took a deep breath and held it, savoring the moisture and the scent of it. Ginzai had a river running through it as well, the Yoto, but comparing that to the Wagata was like comparing an earthworm to a mamusha, the two being roughly similar in shape but far different in size, texture, and disposition. And like that venomous snake, Seikoku thought the river before them was intimidating in its bulk, though at least it did not hiss and spit and lunge at them—it merely flowed along, oblivious to their desire to cross it, uncaring that their destinies lay beyond its farther shore.

"I don't know what I'd have done if they'd wrecked it," the herbalist was saying, and Seikoku forced her attention back to the conversation. "Mother and I···we spent so much time gathering everything."

Seikoku laid her hand on the other woman's arm, reminding

herself yet again that Isoro was roughly her own age and possibly a little older. She seemed much younger, but then she'd always had her mother to take care of her, to look after her, to teach her and guide her and even to a degree shelter her. Up until Yori had killed the senior herbalist, that is. "Of course," she said now. "I'm glad I could help. Just let me know if they give you any more trouble, okay?" She thought for a moment before continuing, "You're going to need some help with your cart. If you keep an eye on Ratal and the others, they should be fine, now that they know not to just do whatever they think is best."

Isoro nodded. "I'll ask them to help, then," she agreed. "Noniki suggested I just put my entire cart on a raft and take it across in one piece, to keep anything inside from getting ruined." Her long, solemn face brightened. "Oh! I could store some of the others' things inside it! That way they wouldn't get wet either!"

"That's an excellent idea," Seikoku agreed, tapping her fingers against her chin. "Yes, you're right—your cart is probably the closest one we have to being watertight, so we should use that to store anything that absolutely can't get wet and bring them all across together." She smiled. "I'll talk to Kanai and Minawa and we'll put together a list, see what we can fit without damaging any of your things." She waved and set off, searching for the potter and the old farmer. Noniki she spotted walking the shore, stopping to talk with each person along the way, but she decided not to bother him. He already had his hands full keeping everyone cheerful and focused and together. That was fine, she only needed Kanai and Minawa for this. Between the three of them, they'd see it done.

That brought her up short. At one point, she wondered, had that happened? When Noniki had reappeared in Ginzai, she'd been impressed by the changes in him. He was as handsome as ever, of course—and as seemingly unaware of that—but the careless, brash boy she'd met in the cemeteries had become a quiet, thoughtful young man. His heart had been just as big and just as open, but now he had deep thoughts to go along with that, so when he'd announced he was leaving again she had decided to accompany him. As had Kanai. It had just been the three of them, three friends traveling together, and if she and Kanai had begun to see Noniki as a teacher his gentle ways and unassuming manner—and willingness to laugh at himself—had kept them from placing him on a pedestal. When Madam Ushi and Kuma had arrived and joined them, he'd welcomed them, of course, and she and Kanai had done the same, for how could they not? What claim did they have on their friend's time and attention when he was so happy to share it and there was in fact so much to go around? So their trio had become a quintet and had continued to grow from there. But it had always stayed a loose-knit, friendly little community, with everyone pitching in where they could.

So when had she and Kanai and Minawa become the ones everyone else turned to for advice and support and help? When had it fallen to them to make decisions for the group as a whole?

Because it had, she saw now. The three of them dealt with most of the everyday matters. If something felt too big or important for them, they took it to Noniki, but often he just asked their advice and deferred to their judgement.

How had she turned into some sort of community leader? She'd always cared for others, of course—back home she'd spent most of the money she'd stolen on her neighbors, making sure people like Mother Pidiri and her grandson Noru had enough to eat—but she'd done that on the sly, like most everything else, not caring about taking credit for such deeds and preferring to do them in her own time and her own way. Now people came to her with their problems. Isoro had run looking for her, not anyone else.

And she had handled it, she realized. She had fixed the situation. Ratal and his friends had listened to her, done what she'd told them, and everything was fine.

It was a strange feeling, this. Being respected. Being looked up to. Being expected to have the answers. And, perhaps more than anything else, being open in who she was, what her role was, what she did and what she could do.

In fact, something else leapt into her mind and was so stunning she nearly toppled over, right there on the shore—

Isoro had shouted "Seikoku!" when she'd run to her.

That was how everyone else here knew her as well.

Which wouldn't have been odd—it was her name, after all—if not for the fact that, back in Ginzai, she had used different names around different people. Hintaro, her grocer friend, had known her as Mistress Keiko. To Mother Pidiri and the others in her building she'd been Koko. Different names for different roles, different faces.

But here everyone knew her by her true name. She wasn't hiding at all, or pretending, or lying. She was, for perhaps the first time since she had been forced to fend for herself all those long years ago, being completely honest and upfront with everyone around her.

She was surprised to discover just how much she liked it.

CHAPTER SEVEN

Maniko Kohori felt like she had just drifted off to sleep when the shouting started. She was out of bed, on her feet and grabbing her robe before she even registered that they were calling her name. By the time they had reached her door she was sliding the panel open, nihono tucked into her sash and yanoi in hand. To his credit, Itamon gaped for only a second upon finding his superior already dressed and alert. Then he saluted.

"Another body, Taikoro," he gasped out, chest heaving in evidence of the speed with which he had raced to deliver this dire news. "In the gardens. Again."

"Ash!" She swept past him and out the door, taking the lead along the hall to the stairs and down them to the general level of the Honteno barracks. Her rank would have provided her with separate quarters if she'd wanted them, but they would have been in a different part of the compound and she preferred to be here with her warriors. This way, when there was trouble—as now—there was no need to send runners in two different directions. "I gave orders to bottle that place up!" she snapped as she marched through, waving half-asleep soldiers aside when they glanced up and reached groggily for their gear. A crowd was not going to help here.

"You did," Itamon agreed, the chuisu having regained his breath and keeping up with her easily, his shorter stride balanced by significantly fewer years. "And we've done our best. But there's a lot of ground to cover, and not a lot of us to manage it." There was no remonstrance in his tone, though she wouldn't have faulted him if there had been—it had been an impossible order, expecting a score of warriors to completely lock down a space that size, and she knew it.

She was also sure her warriors had done their best.

"The Honjofu?" she asked, reaching the outer door, which already stood open, allowing the crisp night air to glide in. Two men stood at attention there, one to either side, and saluted as she stepped through the open barrier, onto the low porch beyond, and then hopped down to the ground without pause. Now, however, she did slow and turn, since she did not know where in the grounds she was headed.

"We've not told them yet," her lieutenant answered, joining her and taking the front now, moving quickly and quietly across the yard toward the far side. "I thought it best to wait and see if you wished to include them."

Kohori nodded. She had been making heavy use of the elite warriors the past few days, ever since they'd returned and helped her crush the Rojiris' attempted coup. She'd had little choice—with half her Honteno dead or sidelined from wounds, she'd needed the Honjofu to supplement her own forces if she were to have any hope of maintaining proper security in the compound. No matter what price Haro had set, she'd have paid it.

And thus far, she had been lucky. Her fellow Taikoro had not demanded anything of her. In fact, he had been surprisingly generous about that. True, when he'd returned his first act had been to execute Etsuya Kenshin, the most belligerent of the imperial councilors and one of the only two to have still been openly committing treason at the time. By doing so, Haro had taken credit for stopping the coup, relegating Kohori herself to the secondary role of holding the rebellious forces at bay until he could arrive and deal with them properly. But she could hardly fault him for that, and in fact his killing Etsuya had saved her a great deal of trouble. He could have demanded all manner of reparation for deigning to come to her aid, and she suspected he would as soon as the Emperor returned, but normally she would have expected Haro to at least needle her about that, to hint at all the things he would require of her in that sly, oily, arrogant manner of his.

Instead, when they had encountered one another he had been distant but polite, even considerate. Strange behavior for a man she had grown to detest but she could hardly question such a gift, especially at a time like this.

Still, better to keep them out of this if at all possible.

As if her thoughts had demanded an immediate response, the sound of footsteps fast approaching drifted through the night air, outpacing a single figure striding rapidly toward her and Itamon. As they drew nearer, lantern light shone on the lacquered black of the newcomer's armor, the polished chahito of a sword—and the single gold bar at the stranger's shoulders. A gunso of the Honjofu, then, and given the height and build it could only be one of the two. Which was why Kohori paused long enough to swivel about as the person reached them.

"Gunso Misataki," she stated, hands to her chest in the traditional salute. "You are out late this night."

"Taikoro Maniko," Misataki Shizumi replied, returning the salute along with a bow, since hers was the inferior rank. "I could say the same of you." She lowered her hand, exasperation on her face. "Ash, I'm no good at diplomacy, never was! I heard there was another murder. I came to help."

How did you hear, and so quickly? Kohori wanted to ask. But, unlike the younger woman, she was skilled at politics, or at least enough so that she kept the question from her face and tone, saying only, "Thank you for your kind offer but this is a security matter and therefore falls under the Honteno's jurisdiction. I will be sure to notify your Taikoro should I need assistance."

They were close enough now that she could see the younger woman's scowl. "He sent me," she answered, fisting her hands upon her hips. "I have been instructed to offer my assistance on his behalf, and to assure you that 'the Honjofu stand ready to assist you in any way necessary.'"

"Ah." Kohori spared herself only an instant to glare reproachfully up at the night sky, as if that velvety, star-studded expanse were to blame. *Well, I did bring this upon myself,* she admitted. *I'd wondered at Haro's unusual kindness in not calling in any of those markers yet. And now here is one of them, glaring at me as if this were my doing. Which, in a way, it is.* "Then I thank you for your aid, Gunso Misataki," she declared. "We were on our way there now." She gestured for Itamon to continue leading the way as the Honjofu fell in beside them.

"Please, call me Shizumi. Do we know who it is yet?" the Honjofu sergeant asked, matching their pace with little effort. She had taken the time to don her full armor, Kohori noticed—or else she had not yet been to bed, despite the late hour.

"No," Itamon answered over his shoulder, shrugging an apology at Kohori for speaking without checking with her first. As if that would have been possible while in motion! "I only just received the report that a body had been found and came straightaway to inform you." Those last words were meant for Kohori alone, she knew, and the message was clear enough. Her subordinate was asking, in a very subtle way, whether he should keep their unintended companion out of the loop as far as any further incidents.

But that would never do. Haro had made his intentions plain by sending her the way he had, and by the message she carried. To slight Misataki Shizumi now was to slight her Taikoro, to whom Kohori owed a great debt. Thus she swallowed any accompanying bitterness and replied, "You did right, Itamon, but in future please send to Gunso Misataki—your pardon, Shizumi—as well." He acknowledged the order—and its broader meaning—with a mere wave of his hand, never breaking stride, and for the next few moments the three of them traveled in silence, broken only by the rustle of their boots upon the grass and the louder crunch when they crossed paths of crushed stone and shell.

Aihiri was large enough that it took several minutes before they finally slowed. They were nearly to the far corner of the compound, Kohori knew. It was an area dominated by garden mazes and she had a brief flash of young Hibikitsu, when he was still just a boy and only the heir-apparent, racing through the twisting hedges, laughing with delight as she and several other servants and guards ran after, attempting to keep up. He had always been possessed of quick emotions but back then they had turned as much to sudden, spontaneous joy as to the dark bursts of anger he had displayed thus far as Emperor.

Several guards stood at attention as they approached one of the maze entrances and parted to let the three of them past. Another waited farther in beside one of the hanging lanterns, now lit to indicate their destination. It was Reizei, her other chuisu, and Kohori frowned to see the woman there.

"Why are you out of bed?" she demanded as they closed the distance. "You should not be on that leg at all, let alone traipsing all the way over here in the middle of the night!" Reizei had taken a blow to the leg during the fighting over the throne room, and though the blade had not passed all the way through her haidoto it had punctured the thigh guard and driven those jagged edges and splinters into her thigh. She would recover full use of her leg in time, but only if she did not overexert herself while it healed.

Her lieutenant dipped her head in apology. "I was careful," she promised, and stamped the yanoi she was putting her weight upon. "Someone had to stand guard while Itamon went to tell you. That doesn't require a lot of mobility." Her gaze flicked to Shizumi, standing silently to the side, but she did not ask. She knew her commander would tell her if she needed to know. "It's around the corner, just here."

"Fine," Kohori grumbled now, annoyed that her own soldiers were not heeding her advice. "You can go back now. Slowly. We will handle this from here." She returned Reizei's parting salute and took the lantern off its hook, stepping around the bush that blocked her view.

She could not tell if the gasp that arose came from her, from Shizumi, or from Itamon. Certainly all three of them froze, staring down at the twisted, blackened body curled up on the ground before them. It was very similar to the one she and Shizumi had discovered the previous night, also out here in the gardens—the appearance of having been burned, the way the mouth was open in a scream that had doubtless never emerged given the throat and the vicious, powerful cut bisecting it and much of the neck, the cracked and blackened teeth. There were two noticeable differences here, however.

"He's one of yours," Shizumi whispered, crouching just out of the figure's reach. In the lantern's light it was easy enough to make out the crimson of the armor encasing the corpse, making it look as if he had bled out even after being burned.

And it *was* a he. Kohori could tell that from the build, the shape of the hands and jaw and hips and eyes.

Which was the other change from before. Then, the body had stared up at them with empty eye sockets. This man's eyes were intact—or at least they were still present, for they had burst from the heat, leaving only a blackened, gooey mess behind.

Why the change, however, she wondered, stooping to examine the body more closely. What had caused this murder to differ from the last? Was it a change in the intended goal, or some other factor?

Itamon joined her and stifled a quick curse. "What?" she demanded.

"It's Umibuki," he answered, his words grim and sharp. "Umibuki Nihiro."

Shizumi twisted to study them. "What's so special about that?" she asked. Clearly she had caught the strangeness in Itamon's tone.

"He was a recent transfer," Kohori answered heavily, studying the body anew and trying to match it to the man she had met mere hours before. Yes, the build matched, as did what she could see of the features, and the armor was new, without a single scratch. Which was interesting in and of itself—whatever had burned the man had not damaged his armor in the slightest. She reached out and rested one finger against the chestplate. It was not even warm. "Today was his first day."

"Ah." Beside her, the Honjofu dipped her head. "I'm sorry." The grimace that crossed her face indicated that she recognized the ridiculousness of that remark, for why would she be any sorrier they had lost a new recruit than if they'd lost someone who had served for years. But Kohori understood what she had meant and nodded her thanks.

After a few seconds more, she rose to her feet, ignoring the creaking of her knees. Ash, she was getting too old for this! "Look around," she ordered, raising the lantern high so that its light fell across the entire scene, encasing them and the body in a warm golden bubble. "See if you can find any clue as to what happened here. Who did this? When did it happen? How did they burn him but not his armor? Anything new would help. But do so carefully. Do not disturb anything. The idea is to observe, not to taint and destroy anything that could help us."

She had a sinking feeling, however, that they would not find anything useful. Oh, the grass might indicate that someone else had been here, but that could be assumed anyway, as it was unlikely Umibuki Nihiro had done this to himself. But there had been nothing useful at the last murder, nothing to help her figure out who had done this or even why, and she suspected this scene would prove much the same.

One thing was clear, however. One dead body, however strange, could be chalked up to some sort of isolated incident. Two meant there was a pattern. It also suggested that the individuals themselves were not the purpose. Whoever was doing this had a plan in mind, an end goal and a strategy for getting there.

Which told her that, whoever—or whatever—this was, it was only getting started.

CHAPTER EIGHT

The young girl stabbed again and again, putting the full weight of her small body behind each blow, her face twisted in what looked like anguish, eyes wide, lips back to bare gnashed teeth, nostrils flared. She did not stop, did not pause, did not so much as falter until a voice cried out, shattering the previous low-level rhythm of her blows.

"No!" The single syllable rang across the small space, freezing her hand mid-swing, her whole body vibrating from the need to continue its forward motion. "That's enough!" the speaker continued, striding forward into the light of the single lantern, which revealed a beautiful young woman in a comfortable blue silk kisoni patterned with emerald butterfly wings. Though she wore no makeup, her face was stunning, her eyes large and dark, her nose delicate, her lips full—and currently pursed in disapproval.

"You're doing it all wrong, Suda," Chimehara explained with a sigh, stepping up to the girl and gently grasping her wrist to guide her hand lower. It took considerable strength to force the limb free from its current taut position, and she tapped Suda on the shoulder with the fan in her other hand, not hard but with enough force to be noticed. "Relax, please," she instructed. "Take a deep breath, let it out, and all the tension with it."

The girl did as she was told, her body becoming more pliable as she released some of her stress, and Chimehara was able to adjust the girl's hand at last, guiding it down by her thigh. She plucked the knife free and reversed it before sliding the handle back into the girl's grip, so that now it was held low and angled up instead of over Suda's head and pointing down.

"Overhead blows are powerful, it's true," she told her young charge, stepping back again, her lovely features fading once more into the shadows that shrouded the rest of the room. "But they're sloppy, hard to control—and harder to conceal. Stab upward—you may not get as much force but your strike will be more subtle, more precise. And it is far easier to pierce the vitals from that angle. Try it."

Suda needed no further urging. She returned her attention to the figure before her—a man-shaped form made up of rushes wrapped around a bamboo frame and then padded with cotton. With a wordless cry she lunged into it, her knife's blade disappearing within the "body," only to reappear an instant later and then vanish again.

"Do you see the difference?" Chimehara asked, and the girl paused to consider that question, her own large, dark eyes scrunched in concentration. Finally she nodded. "Good. Now, I want you to aim for the heart." She had thoughtfully painted an outline of each organ on the unbleached cotton "skin," and written its name beside it.

The girl studied her victim, noting the heart's location. Then, quick as a snake, she stabbed her blade through that rough circle—and cried out when the knife rebounded, nearly slicing open her palm as it flew from her grip.

"What was that?" she demanded, rounding angrily on her mentor, who was struggling not to laugh. "You trapped it!" Her voice was as rough as ever.

"If by 'trapped it' you mean 'inserted bamboo where the major bones lie,' then yes, I most certainly did," Chimehara replied sharply. "There's a reason I told you to angle your blade up, not jab it forward like a spear. You hit the breastbone—it'd take a much larger, much stronger person than either of us, with a much heavier blade, to pierce the heart *that* way!" Retracing her steps and pausing to stoop and retrieve the ricocheted knife along the way, she nudged Suda aside with her hip and took the girl's place, gripping the weapon against her upper leg. Then she jabbed upward, through the ribs. "See?" She held the blade there so her pupil could examine what she'd done. "Between the ribs and up into the heart. Simple as threading a needle."

"I don't know nothing about thread and needle," the girl retorted, though her eyes were fastened on the weapon, drinking in every detail about its position.

"No, I realize that, Suda," Chimehara responded, biting back a sigh. "It's just an expression." Tugging the knife free, she flipped it over and offered it hilt-first to the girl. "Try it again."

The girl snatched the blade away so quickly she was tempted to count her fingers and elbowed her out of the way. This time the strike was perfect, as was the second one. And the third. And the fourth.

"Good." Chimehara patted the girl's head, ignoring the way she flinched from the unexpected contact. "Now try for the kidneys." She circled around, calling out different organs and watching as Suda located each one and then attempted to stab it. Sometimes there were no obstacles and she hit the mark on the first try. Other times her blade was blocked again, but Chimehara did not offer any further explanation. She let the girl figure things out for herself. It was, after all, the best way to remember what she learned.

It had only been two weeks since she had taken Suda in, but already the change was remarkable. The girl had nearly doubled her weight, for one thing. She had been skin and bones before, as were most children who survived by scrounging and begging and stealing in Suranmui. Now, though still slender, she at least did not look like some sort of akatai, skeletal and unwashed and out to steal people's souls.

The fact that, immediately upon bringing her home that first day, Chimehara had submerged the girl in the bath for a good hour, washing away years of caked-on dirt and grime, had something to do with the transformation as well. It had taken several more long immersions to remove all of it—until then Suda had looked a little like the reverse image of a tree pretending to be a girl, with each bend and fold darker than its surroundings like the seams in old bark—and nearly half Chimehara's oils and lotions to restore the girl's hair to something resembling passable, but at least now she could take Suda out in public without being utterly embarrassed. Or, more importantly, without drawing attention to themselves.

Which was why, after watching the girl impale her victim's spleen for the third time, she called out, "Right, tidy up, it's time to go on a little excursion." She smiled, careful not to let the expression crease the skin around her eyes. "Don't forget to bring the knife."

"Very well," she said a short while later. They had descended two levels, to Bejinuri, tier of artisans and craftsmen. The walls here were the color of red wisteria, a pale violet that all but shone in the afternoon light, and the streets were filled with people going about their daily business. Most wore simple clothes, unbleached or dyed a single color, patterns reserved for small flourishes like a sash or a headcloth, but here and there were wealthier folk, most likely patrons come to inquire after various projects or to hire for such work.

Chimehara had dressed much as she had the day she and Suda had met, in a simple wrap and scarf, though this time the wrap while still unbleached was at least of silk and the scarf, also silk, was a better green and threaded with flashes of blue and purple. Her sandals were better quality than before as well, all in all marking her as someone who could be either from here or from Sakiriti just above. Suda wore ponmei and hantien, being young enough to get away with such garb, and though simple and unadorned except for brighter thread at hem and cuff and collar, the fabric of each was of sufficient quality to offset its plain design.

"What are we doing?" the girl asked, twisting around to stare up at her from where they stood against the wall of a shop, watching the passersby. "Do you want me to kill someone?" The girl said it with no trace of repugnance or hesitation, but then she had grown up on the streets. She had no doubt killed before. Chimehara had not asked—her own childhood had been similar enough that she did not need to, and she had felt it was better for Suda to put all that behind her now. At least until it was needed.

For the moment, however, she shook her head. "Nothing quite so lethal today, I think," she answered, eyeing a couple strolling by. "No, I believe for today we will limit ourselves to simple theft. Show me how much you can collect in the next hour. I will meet you back here." And with that she strolled off toward a little bakery she knew had the most delightful nut-and-fig pastries. If the girl called after her or made any sort of noise, she did not hear it, nor did she stop to listen. Either Suda would pass this test or she would not, but she would do so on her own.

After what she judged to have been sufficient time, Chimehara returned to the same shop. There, sitting and waiting, was Suda.

"Still alive, then?" she said as she approached the girl. "Good."

Her pupil frowned at that. "Did you think I might be dead?" she asked.

"If you'd tried to steal from the wrong person, perhaps," Chimehara replied. "But no, I thought it more likely you'd run if that happened. In which case I would expect you to be smart enough to know that waiting for me here would no longer be viable." She leaned against the wall beside her young charge. "And how did you fare?"

In response, the girl reached into her jacket and extracted a small pouch, which she passed over. Tugging it open, Chimehara saw a collection of coins, most of them bronze but a few silver, plus several rings, a bracelet of amber and onyx beads, and a pair of earrings. "Now, how did you manage to snatch these?" she wondered aloud, admiring the last item. They were beautiful, carved from milky-pale jade into the shape of leaves but with gold edges and traceries and stems jointed together at the top and connected there to a carved jade acorn. Poking them inside the pouch they jingled slightly, and she was sure that when worn they would produce a lovely little chime every time the owner shifted her head.

Suda grinned, and as always the expression made her look her age and properly carefree, rather than like a tiny, grim woman.

"I found a jewelry stall and waited 'til a man walked away, then snatched his purse. Those were in it."

"Clever," Chimehara agreed. Far better to do that than try to steal them from a woman's ears. Which could be done, but not easily and not without a spot of blood or noise or both. "And the purse?"

"I tossed it in there, along with the rest." She nodded a short ways ahead and across the street, where a narrow gutter interrupted the curb. "But one at a time so they wouldn't clump up and get stuck."

"Very good." That had been exactly the right move—purses and pouches and iniro were often personalized, and thus easy to identify. Unless the container itself was inherently valuable, better to dispose of it and just keep the contents, which would be far harder to trace. "Some other time I will take you to a woman I know. She buys such things from time to time. We will see what we can get for these—and whatever it is, that is yours."

The girl's eyes, already large, widened until they almost seemed fit to swallow her head. "Mine?"

"Of course. You took them, therefore they're yours." Chimehara stroked the girl's hair—which, though still somewhat rough, was far better than it had been, and with repeated washings would soon be silky smooth—and smiled. "I'm teaching you how to take care of yourself—that would not work very well if I didn't let you keep at least some of what you'd earned, would it?" Besides, staking out a jewelry stall had been an inspired move, and she wanted to encourage such original thinking.

Suda thought about that moment, but when she finally glanced up her question was about something slightly different. "I will get to kill someone soon, though, won't I?" There was a pleading look in her eyes. "I don't want what you taught me this morning to go to waste."

"Oh, don't worry about that," Chimehara assured her as she led the way back through the tier toward the gates, and from there back home. "I promise you'll get to use that soon enough."

All in all, she felt the girl's training was coming along very well indeed.

CHAPTER NINE

A solitary cloud hovered in the sky over the little fishing village of Otimo, the ground directly beneath its blurred form darkened by its shade. But more than mere shadow covered that expanse; the grass seemed gray and lifeless, the soil beneath it equally blanched, even the pebbles and other rocks were stripped of any hue, and the few earthworms and beetles and flies within that small region lay mixed in among the rest, no more than lifeless husks. The only color and activity left there was within the cloud itself, for strange colors shimmered and swirled through it, flashes of light and shadow swimming and spiraling and churning so that anyone looking upon it might grow dizzy from the mere spectacle.

Not that anyone was watching the cloud. The people of Otimo had other concerns at the moment. Namely, savagely tearing into one another with tooth and nail, kicking and punching and scratching and attacking with any tools at their disposal. Harsh cries split the air, wordless bellows and inarticulate screams, for the villagers had become so incensed they could no longer speak coherently, their guttural noises the only sounds they had left beyond the thud of flesh against flesh and the faint hiss of flesh being torn asunder.

In the midst of this chaos stood two young men, barely more than boys, both slender to the point of emaciation, appearing only half a step removed from skeletons with their chalk-white skin and ash-gray hair. In their eyes, however, darkness danced, filling their sockets with a strange tumult whose madness was matched only by their bloodthirsty grins. Perhaps it was those feral expressions that kept the villagers at bay, for the violence encircled the pair but never touched them directly, howling men and women throwing themselves to the side to avoid coming into contact with the ghostly figures in their midst.

Or perhaps it was the bodies at their feet, shrunken and shriveled and dried like mummies left out in the sun. Bodies that had been fellow residents before they had stood up to the pair, sensing the danger within the seemingly fragile duo. Residents who had dared to raise a hand to one or both, to touch that washed-out flesh, and had collapsed in on themselves as a result, as if a thousand years had crashed down on them all at once.

And so Ibaru and Iraku stood and drank in the carnage they had caused, the mindless rage they had unleashed, the chaos they had summoned. The brothers stood and watched with their strange, dark eyes, smiles just barely touching their pale lips, and had breathed in the anger and hatred and bloodshed as if it were meat and wine.

While on the village's outskirts, the strange cloud called Kaemusei hovered, waiting.

At last, however, it seemed to grow impatient. It drifted forward, past the village edge, toward the water that lay beyond. As it floated along, wherever its shadow fell grew bleached and bare, devoid of life, devoid of vibrancy.

When it reached the water's edge, however, it stopped.

Back in the center of Otomi, the brothers glanced up. They felt their master's call deep within, a gnawing pain that grew swiftly stronger and sharper until it felt that their stomachs must burst from their bodies, their spines rip free from their torsos, their eyes explode from their head. Never before had they felt such impatience from the Silent, never before had it demanded their attendance and their obedience so swiftly and so unequivocally. For it was all too clear that it would not stop, would not let up, would not lessen its pull or the pain it caused them. Not until they obeyed.

Thus the brothers abandoned their play and their feast and, turning from the tumult, walked through the rest of Otomi, the buildings to either side crumbling as their fingers brushed wood and paper and thatch, to rejoin their master.

For a moment the three stood silently, staring out over the water. The river here was wide enough that they could barely make out the other side, and fast enough that a twig caught in the current went whipping past almost too quickly to follow. The brothers considered this watery obstacle for a moment. Kaemusei had made it abundantly clear that it wished to cross this river, and indeed the next one beyond, in order to reach the tiered city they had spied from the hilltop now behind them. But while it could simply drift lazily across, it had evidently grown accustomed to having someone to do its bidding, to act as its mouthpiece—and to enact its vengeance. It enjoyed having the brothers to serve as its eyes, its mouth, and its hands. It was not about to give that up so easily.

The question then became, how did they get across?

Ibaru glanced up at the Silent itself, his fathomless dark eyes considering. "Will you not simply carry us across?" he asked at last, his voice as flat and empty as a scraped-clean plate. "That would seem the quickest way."

In response their master dipped lower, its shadow engulfing them both. But as the boys reflexively raised their hands to protect their heads from this aerial assault, they felt a tug in their fingers. This was not the same as the pull they felt toward their master, however. That was akin to a fishhook tugging at a fish, the line growing taut as the hook distended the flesh it was planted within, towing it toward the fisherman. This was more like the pull of a river to a bowl of rice dropped beneath its surface. The water caught the rice up in its currents, tugging it this way and that, and the rice quickly came apart, drifting into its individual grains, each one floating in a different direction, and even those disintegrating until there was nothing left. That was how Ibaru felt now, and his brother as well. It was only in the hands at the moment, but it felt as if someone were unraveling their flesh, unbinding the skin layer by layer, diffusing the bones like tea in hot water, letting the joints and tendons come apart and start drifting away. The particles rose and were sucked into Kaemusei, which grew slightly brighter in response as it absorbed some of its servants' essence.

Then it withdrew, and the brothers collapsed on the shore, relieved to feel the boundaries of their own flesh reassert itself once more. It was as if someone had begun unspooling them, starting with their hands, but had suddenly decided that the whole process was a waste of time and had tossed it aside unfinished.

That did answer the question, at least. Their master was not unwilling to bear them, merely incapable—at least, without destroying everything they were now and thus defeating the purpose of bringing them along at all. Which only meant the brothers would have to figure a way across on their own.

"We can take a boat," Iraku suggested, and they glanced around themselves, as if just noticing that they were on the border of a fishing village. After all, there had been no time to learn of the town's history, not when their very presence incited violence. Now, however, they stood for a second, admiring the many boats tied to sturdy docks up and down this stretch of the river.

A boat did indeed make sense, and although neither of them knew anything about sailing, they only needed to make it to the river's farther shore. Surely that was within their abilities, especially with the Silent itself hovering overhead to protect them.

Though they were unacquainted with water travel, the brothers eyed each of the various craft around them carefully, walking up and down the strip of sandy dirt that ran the length of the docks. Finally Ibaru paused beside one. It was a small boat, lacking any manner of sail, but it seemed sturdy, solidly made without any cracks or holes to be spied, and there were two oars laid across the supports within it. Paddling seemed far easier than sailing, and the brothers had been granted great strength and endurance when Kaemusei had chosen them as its servants and followers. They had little doubt they could row themselves across.

When Ibaru crossed the dock and reached out to rest his hand upon the boat's side, however, in order to leap into its shallow curve, the wood there, weather-beaten and solid but a second before, crumbled away. He climbed in nonetheless and set his foot down on the bottom—only to have it crash through to the water lurking beneath, instantly soaking him up to the knee. The

water was a shock in another sense as well, for it seemed Ibaru's
destructive touch had no effect on the liquid. Presumably that was
because the water had no component parts to dissolve into and
aging it did not alter it appreciably—centuries-old water was still
just as cold and just as wet. He yanked his leg free, rearing back
up in the process, and stumbled backward from the sudden shift
in balance. The wood beneath his other foot was already beginning to give way, having crumbled to the point that water was
seeping through it like a sponge. Iraku caught him before he could
fall on his rear and bodily hauled his brother back onto the dock
and from there onto the sand beyond. After helping Ibaru right
himself, the brothers stared at the dock before them, bowing from
their passage, and at the prow of the small boat even now sinking
under the water, the rope that still connected it to the dock being
pulled taut as the ruined vessel vanished from sight.

Clearly this was going to require additional thought.

There were other small boats here, and the brothers chose a
second one of similar size and complexity. This time, they linked
arms and simultaneously leaped down into the boat, Ibaru then
laying his hand on the rope and causing it to shrivel and fall away,
freeing the small craft from its tether, while Iraku kicked them
away from the dock and reached for the nearest oar. The wooden
implement disintegrated at his touch and the boat's bottom gave
way an instant later, plunging both brothers up to their waists in
the cold river water. Only the fact that their torsos became wedged
into the damaged boat kept them from going under completely,
and with every second of contact those holes grew wider. They
flailed about as the boat came apart all around them, swallowing
water and then choking and coughing on it as they grabbed for
the dock, which collapsed in their hands. Finally they managed
to haul themselves up onto the rocks and dirt piled up beneath
the start of the wooden dock and lay there, gasping for air, their
breath whistling in and out as they struggled to calm themselves.

That was not going to work. Not without some additional
precautions.

Once they had recovered, the brothers rose to their feet,

shivering slightly for they were still drenched, and climbed back up onto the dock. Taking care not to stop and stand still but to keep moving in order to alleviate some of the damage their touch caused, they quickly approached the third small boat. Only this time, they did not close on the tiny vessel emptyhanded. Instead each brother held a large, flat chunk of wood. These were pieces that had been torn from other, larger boats, and although they were flaking away at the edges the centers were still solid.

Together the brothers tossed their precious cargo into the bottom of the third boat. Then they climbed in, carefully, grasping onto the dock instead of the boat—and each placed themselves directly atop one of those wooden slabs. This time when Ibaru removed the rope and Iraku shoved them clear of the docks, the boat itself remained intact, the slabs slowly falling apart beneath their feet but protecting the boat from harm.

The only question was, could they get all the way across the river before the wood crumbled away like everything else, leaving nothing between them and the boat that was, in turn, the only thing between them and countless tubs and buckets and basins of water? Or would the wood not get them far enough across for the boat to survive long enough to finish the trek? Would they instead wind up being dumped into the water once more, but this time halfway across the river, which even their strength might not be enough to ford safely?

Though not keen to test their luck in this way, the brothers knew they were about to find out. For the Silent wished them to cross this river, and so cross this river they would, or least make every attempt within their power.

Still, it was with a spurt of something thought long-gone which they belatedly realized must be fear that the brothers picked up their oars and began rowing, shoving the little boat forward across the waves like an arrow shot from a bow. Their only hope was that their speed would prove greater than the boat's rate of decay.

They were, in a very real sense, betting their life on that slim possibility, particularly since their master had already demonstrated that it would be unable to aid them if they failed, its touch being far more deadly than any immersion. The idea of taking such a risk, and of being in such danger, was both terrifying and oddly exhilarating, and for the first time since their transformation the brothers felt themselves to be alive due to something other than the violence and rage they engendered in others. That only made them row all the harder, and river water sprayed about them as they hurled their small craft through the water and toward the far shore. Kaemusei floating along above them, its feathery bulk shading their efforts, only the frenetic motion within it providing any indication of its own sense of urgency.

CHAPTER TEN

Kagiri woke to screams.

Rolling off the bed he came up on his feet, nihono in hand from where he had snatched it up but not yet drawn. Instead he merely held it at eye level, parallel to the ground, one hand on the grip, one on the scabbard. And, stilling himself, listened.

Then he burst from his tent, drawing the blade even as he shouldered the flap aside and stepped out into a night filled with chaos.

People were running every which way but he could see no direct reason for that, no fires licking up from other tents, no army trampling structure and inhabitant alike, no monster from nightmare gobbling up all in its path. Nothing but the same people he already knew, only panicked and shouting or sobbing or both.

Reaching out with the hand still holding the empty scabbard, he grabbed the nearest person and yanked them to a stop, his fingers firmly wrapped in the collar of their kitoro. It was Eisen, one of the newer members of their group, a stocky middle-aged man who claimed to be a legal clerk but whose hands bore the calluses and scars of many a brawl. Now he looked a mess, his bun sprouting hairs in all directions, his face sweaty and flushed, his eyes bleary.

"What has happened?" Kagiri demanded, giving the man a shake.

"We're under attack!' Eisen wailed, gripping his collar in turn and tugging it free. Then he was off and running again. Kagiri doubted the man had even registered who he was speaking to.

Several others charged past but they seemed just as dazed and he doubted he would learn anything more useful from them. But then he spotted a more disreputable-looking specimen and smiled.

"Joshi!" he shouted, striding toward the man. "What has happened?"

Joshi turned at the sound of his name, and naked relief broke across his face like a sunrise. "My lord!" he hurried to close the distance and bowed. "Some kind of wild beasts! They downed two of our horses, and then one of them shredded old Ryoji's tent!" He saluted, though sloppily. "I was coming to tell you!"

"You just did," Kagiri pointed out. Resheathing his blade, he clapped his companion on the shoulder. "Let's go."

As they trotted toward Ryoji's tent, Kagiri considered the man beside him. When they'd first met, Joshi had been Narai's man at arms and the leader of his personal guard. Though crude in both appearance and manner, Joshi had proven himself to be capable and passably intelligent. He had quickly figured out who was truly in charge of this expedition—more quickly than his erstwhile employer, in fact—and had taken to looking to Kagiri for instructions, particularly when there was trouble.

Shortly before they'd reached the Tonawa, Kagiri had come to a decision. He had taken Joshi and Gento and the other guards and begun to train them. Every morning at dawn he led them through daily exercises, then taught them both swordsmanship and unarmed combat.

"You are a fool," Nikiyu Sinchu had been quick to point out, as eager to find fault as ever. "These men do not answer to you, they serve their masters—the same men who thought to be *your* masters, if you recall. And who are not only because they are afraid of you. If you train their guards to be able to best you, what control do you have over them then?"

The other Gensaiba had agreed, but Kagiri had stood firm. "I am not training their men," he'd answered carefully. "I am training mine. You will see."

Now, despite the general panic all around him, he smiled slightly. Joshi had not gone to Narai and the other merchants. The guard had come to find him. That was why Kagiri was training him and the others. Yes, they would be more competent, more capable—more dangerous. But he had no fear of them turning that training upon him. His working with the guards was only binding them to him more tightly. They received their coin from the merchants, but they took their lead from him. Exactly as they should.

Gento and Buntai were waiting by the tent—what was left of it. The silken panels had been shredded on one side, long jagged tears running down them, and either whatever had done that or Ryoji himself in his panic to escape had then pushed or shoved hard enough to splinter several of the bamboo rods supporting the structure, causing the whole thing to collapse into a muddled heap. At least the old man himself was off to one side, sitting on a stump cradling a large cup of steaming tea.

"Did anyone see anything?" Kagiri asked as he and Joshi joined the other two, distractedly returning their salute. "I'm guessing Ryoji didn't, but anyone else nearby? I'd like to know what kind of animal we're dealing with."

"We aren't," Buntai answered. He squatted down and pushed aside one corner of the ruined tent, then tapped the ground there. "Not unless those animals have suddenly sprouted human feet." Because, sure enough, there was a footprint in the mud just past him. And, even though it was evidently barefoot, there was no way to mistake it for any other creature's.

"You're saying a person did this?" Kagiri nudged one of the damaged tent panels. This close, it was abundantly clear that it had been torn apart. "What about the horses?"

None of the others had been to check on those yet, so they all went together. It wasn't far—Ryoji had lived on the outskirts of their makeshift community, preferring to be alone with his thoughts. In a matter of minutes they had reached the enclosure where they kept the horses. Before they had even come in sight of another living thing, Kagiri flinched back, his nostrils flaring as he tasted a familiar scent on the cool air.

It was blood.

And it was very fresh, sharp and rich and almost cloying.

He spotted the source at once, a large, unmoving bulk near the outer line they had created for their makeshift pasture. Approaching it carefully, he saw that it was one of the many horses they possessed, either to draw carts and wagons or for riding. This one had a warm chestnut coat and a lighter, almost ivory mane.

It also, he noted by the light of the torch Gento held up, had had its throat torn out. Hence the amount of blood that had been sprayed around this area. But the wound itself—"bring that closer," Kagiri instructed, squatting down, and the gigantic guard obediently stooped, shoving the torch almost up against the dead horse. Yes, now he could see it clearly, and judging by the rough, jagged tears that had been made? And the marks along the flank, where large chunks had been torn loose?

Buntai was correct.

This was no animal.

"A man did this," he told his men, rising to his feet. "I doubt it's anyone here, however. Most likely a savage living among the trees." Saruto had small copses of woods dotting the landscape, which was pleasant to look at and offered occasional cover from rain but also meant there were places bandits and others could hide. The nearest to their camp was perhaps fifteen minutes' hard walk directly from where he stood now.

"Should we go after him?" Joshi asked. "He could come after more horses—or more people—if we don't."

Kagiri considered that, silently consulting the Gensaiba for their thoughts, but then realized he had already made up his mind. "You are completely correct," he told the leader of his guard. "We can't leave an unknown threat nearby. Gather a few of the others and we'll see what we can find."

"Give me a little light and I can track him," Komu Setsui offered in his head as he watched the guards run to find their cohorts. Kagiri was not surprised to hear this. Setsui was the group's master archer, after all, and very little escaped her sharp eyes. He was also pleased to note the hint of approval in her tone, signaling that she, at least, agreed with his decision. Not that it mattered even if they did not. He had already spoken.

After a few moments Joshi returned, now with not only Gento

and Buntai but Hisa and Megu following him. All of them had paused to fetch their chokoto and seeing the guards with those cheap weapons reminded Kagiri that he really should acquire nihono for them all. The curved blades were far better made, more agile, with sharper edges and better balance. Before, he would not have wasted such a sword on the guards, but now they were nearly ready to handle nihono with the care and skill such weapons deserved. He could hear not only Sinchu but Geido Shinen scoffing but ignored them both.

Still, six seemed extreme for a hunting party, particularly when the quarry was one barbaric man. "Joshi, Gento, Megu, you three stay here," Kagiri instructed. "Keep an eye on the horses and the perimeter, in case he circles back for another meal. Joshi, you're in charge." The guard leader had looked about to argue at being left behind but puffed up slightly at that and saluted instead. "Buntai, Hisa, you come with me." Taking the lantern Megu offered him, he stalked off, the two guards trotting after him.

As soon as they stepped beyond the horse line the world seemed to plunge into darkness. Kagiri had not even realized just how much light their encampment produced until it was behind him—looking back over his shoulder, the collection of torches and lanterns and cookfires was nearly blinding. He had to blink several times and squeeze his eyes shut before he could see again in the near-darkness ahead.

"I've got him," Setsui announced, and Kagiri saw the place where the grass had been bent and crushed by a heavy foot. Another spot appeared up ahead, and another past that, and now he had the trail. Which led into the nearest copse, as he'd suspected, but then continued through and past that, to a farther clearing surrounded by smaller bushes rather than trees.

"Carefully," he warned as they approached. He shuttered the lantern so its light would not give them away and shifted it to his left hand so that his right was free to draw his sword if necessary. Then, with the two guards close by his side, he stepped boldly into the clearing—

—and found himself facing not a lone man but a small

collection of people, men and women and even some children, all sitting in a rough circle sharing food.

Food that looked suspiciously like raw chunks of bloody horse meat.

Everyone started as Kagiri stepped into sight, and leaped to their feet but did not stand up fully, staying crouched instead. They all had their hands out and loose at their sides, even the children, and all of them had fingernails so long and sharp they resembled talons.

Or claws.

The man who stepped forward to confront Kagiri was shorter than him, wiry but also half-starved, and his face and hands were both wet with blood.

"You killed one of our horses," Kagiri pointed out, stopping a few feet away from the stranger. "I don't suppose you have money to pay for that?"

The man stared. Then he hissed, half raising his hands as if to fight—or to defend himself.

"We don't want to hurt anyone," Kagiri tried again. "But you have to stay away from our animals.'"

Beside him, Buntai slapped his knee. "Merciful Bones, that's who they are," the guard exclaimed. "They're Dobuichi!"

Kagiri frowned, not turning around, his eyes still locked on the stranger. "Animal Touched? I am not familiar with the term."

It was Hisa who answered, her voice as sharp as her expression was bored, which was to say vastly. "They use their aitachi to draw from animal bones," she explained. "There're pockets of 'em all over Rimbaku but they tend to stick to the wilds, so most people never even see one."

Now that he knew what to look for, Hisa's explanation made sense. The man carried himself with a certain compact grace, like a wolf, relaxed but still ready to fight or flee in an instant. His clothes were tattered and torn, little more than rags, and his feet were of course bare. His face, beneath blood and sweat, showed no signs of humanity, save for the way his eyes took notice of everyone and everything, sizing up the men and woman arrayed before him. That was the look of a predator, yes, but not of an animal. Unfortunately, animals could not be reasoned with. Even if men sometimes could.

"Let's go," he told Buntai and Hisa, and retreated, backing away from the bushes and the copse and marching back toward camp.

"We're just going to leave them?" Buntai asked, jogging to keep up. "What if they attack us again?"

Kagiri shook his head. "We leave in the morning. We'll simply post a more robust guard until then. Once we've put a day or so's distance between them and us, I think they will fall upon prey a bit closer to home."

"And if they don't?" Hisa asked softly.

"Then we will make sure they cannot bother us anymore," he answered, his tone not sharp but certainly decisive.

Inside, he was still turning over this new information he had found. The Dobuichi. He could feel as much as hear the various Gensaiba scoffing at his decision, mocking the strange group they had just seen and berating Kagiri for being so soft as to let them go unharmed. But he had not spared that man and the others because he was squeamish.

He had spared them because they were barely human any longer. If they acted like animals, lived like animals, they should be treated as such. And one did not pause an entire caravan to go after the one wolf that had been bold enough to sneak down and steal a chicken. Nor did you hunt down the wolf, and its family, and butcher them all. You defended yourself against them, killed them if necessary, but you did not seek them out, nor did you harbor a grudge. They were merely animals, after all, and doing what they must to survive.

Though he would never admit it even to the Gensaiba sharing his brain, Kagiri found himself admiring the Dobuichi. No convoluted politics and confusing papers for them! They worried only about survival—and about keeping their pack together. Simple goals, but that made them attainable.

As they returned, filled the others in on what they'd found, and instructed them to prepare the community to move on in the morning, Kagiri noticed something else odd—

Except for those one or two interjection and offers to help, the Gensaiba had kept almost entirely silent. That was highly unusual for them—

But it was nice to make his own decisions without having a half dozen people constantly correcting him or arguing with him or both.

Kagiri knew he should appreciate that behavior now, as a buffer against the next time they resumed their constant bickering with him and with each other.

Which was why, once he was sure Joshi and the others had everything well in hand, Kagiri returned to his tent and all but flung himself down on the bed.

When he fell asleep shortly thereafter, he dreamt of light and color and the elements—and knew the dreams for his own and no one else's.

It was glorious.

CHAPTER ELEVEN

The day they were finally ready to cross the Wagata dawned cold and wet, the sky like gray silk, shimmering and flickering with bits of light but mostly a soft, muted color, the air thick and heavy with moisture that often coalesced into drops but soaked skin and cloth regardless. It was miserable, and the river responded in kind, its waters threshing about, rising and falling with more than its usual vigor even as it continued to race past.

"We're going to row across that?" Ratal asked, glancing toward the river as they all sat together huddled around a single large cooking fire—they had built it well back from the water's edge to avoid any chance of a stray spark leaping to one of the boats they'd assembled, and had a rough shelter over it to keep the rain from dowsing it prematurely.

Though "boats" was being generous, Noniki admitted, idly twisting the thick jade ring around his thumb as he surveyed the scene. These were barely more than rafts, pieces of wood and bamboo lashed together to form mostly stable, mostly watertight platforms upon which they could stand and balance their meager belongings. Only a few, like the one for Isoro, had any sort of a lip to keep the river from sloshing across it. For the rest, well, everyone had accepted that they would be wet and uncomfortable—the plan was to launch, row as quickly as possible, and then immediately upon landing build a nice big fire to warm up and dry off.

That might prove difficult if this rain continued, however. He knew he was not alone in hoping it would end soon.

For now, however, he just said, "If it is still like that when we leave, then yes. We cannot sit and wait and hope for better weather." They had been using up their food at a prodigious rate since they'd reached the shore, where it was harder to forage and the river's rapid pace made fishing iffy at best. Noniki was praying that the space between the Wagata and Edishu would prove more fertile, giving them a chance to restock before that had to cross that second river. That crossing, at least, would deposit them more or less at Awaihinshi's doorstep.

At that point, finding food would be the least of their worries.

There were grunts and moans around the fire, but no one objected, not even Ratal. They all knew that they could not wait much longer. It had already taken them several days more than expected to get everything ready enough to even make the attempt. If they delayed, their determination might falter, and other factors could intrude to slow them down further.

They had to go now and hope for the best.

The First Emperor seemed to smile upon their endeavor, for as they broke up and returned to their crafts to lash down the last items, the rain ceased. The sky was still monochrome, but the shimmering behind it brightened, the sun now fully up and sending its rays through the veil, and the temperature rose from being chilly to pleasantly brisk. The Wagata calmed in turn—though still fast-paced, its waters were smoother now, not nearly as frenzied.

"We will be carried at an angle," Noniki pointed out to everyone as they disassembled the shelter and tossed water on the fire, then gathered the still-smoking wood to take along. They could not afford to waste anything they might still be able to use. "Just row as hard as you can and do your best to keep yourself facing across. If you get completely turned sideways it will be twice as hard to muscle yourself out of that current and to the farther shore."

"If that does happen," Ratal added, "Row backwards." A few of the others scoffed, and Noniki held up a hand. They quieted at once, but the fisherman was not offended—he chuckled and shook his head as he continued. "I know, it sounds daft, but trust me—if the current catches you, your best bet is to hold in place until we can pull you across." They had found as many lengths of stout rope as they could spare from creating the rafts themselves, and in some places were using knotted lengths of silk instead. These were passed from boat to boat, each boat clinging to the patchwork lifeline. The plan was for Noniki, Seikoku, and Kanai to take the lead and Ratal, Amon, and Isoro to bring up the rear, with stronger members of their group spaced out evenly so that each raft had at least one person who could row hard and at least one to grip the rope and haul their vessel along. Isoro's converted wagon was the heaviest of their crafts so it would serve as the anchor, while Noniki and his two original companions had the least in the way of belongings so their raft was lightest and quickest. They would tug the rope as taut as possible as soon as they had beached—it was too much to hope that they might find something to tie the rope's end around, and the three of them would not have enough weight to keep the boats from slipping, but each new craft that made it across would add extra hands to help, and extra weight to anchor the end. Eventually they should be as much pulling the boats to them as expecting them to row themselves across.

It was a good plan, the best they could come up with given their current resources, and Noniki took no credit for it, for the idea had come from Seikoku and Ratal, the thief and the fisherman putting their heads together to devise the best chance they had to all make it across successfully.

That hadn't stopped some of the others from praising him for the idea, even when he'd corrected them. Fortunately, Seikoku had not been offended.

"You're the leader here," she'd reminded him gently, even teasingly, her eyes alight. "I'm just the brains behind the throne." Then she'd laughed and skipped back when he'd swatted at her. Noniki was, as always, glad she had decided to accompany him. He wasn't sure how he'd have managed all this long way without her sharp mind and, just as importantly, her quick wit and warm smile. She brightened his day and lifted his spirits in a way nothing else ever had.

He only wished he knew how to tell her that.

Setting those ruminations aside for the moment, he helped collect the firewood and carry it to a woven basket Sanedi had created for that purpose. This was then lashed to the front of his own raft—he and Seikoku and Kanai would set the fire as soon as they crossed, so that it would be blazing its warm welcome to the others. It would also double as a beacon, giving them something to target as they made their way over the water.

He hoped and prayed everything went that smoothly.

"It really is astonishingly good luck that the rain stopped," Seikoku remarked as she and Noniki pushed their raft out into the water and hopped onboard. Kanai was already standing on it, the potter being a little older and less agile than they were.

Noniki laughed at her as he took the other oar—rough-shaped but functional, carved from a former wagon axle—from Kanai and settled into position on the left, shoving the broader end into the water and pushing them out into the river proper. "Are you going to tell me, like the others have, that the First Emperor is blessing our endeavor?" he teased, grunting from the effort to propel their raft across the swift currents. At least the water had calmed somewhat!

"No," she answered slowly. "I don't think it's the First Emperor at all." She regarded him with a surprisingly serious expression for once. "I have a completely different theory, but I'm not sure you'll want to hear it."

"What? Why not?" He could only speak between rows, and could not turn to face her fully, as the bulk of his attention had to remain with the water trying to force them to the side and into the river's central channel, which would sweep them east in a heartbeat if he let it. "Go ahead and tell me, I'm curious to know."

Surprisingly, it was Kanai who answered from the raft's other side. "Have you ever noticed," the potter remarked, seemingly randomly, "how mild and pleasant the weather has been throughout our journey?"

"What?" Noniki laughed, nodding his chin toward the gray-hued sky above. "You call this mild and pleasant?"

"It isn't pouring," Seikoku replied, checking the rope tied to their rear to be sure the knot was still secure. "It's not even raining now. And it's not freezing cold, either—or boiling hot, with the sun beating down on us." Her head tilted to one side as she considered. "In fact, I'd say it's the perfect weather for what we're doing."

"Exactly," Kanai agreed. "Perfect weather. As it has been, the whole way. Every day, perfect." Many assumed the potter was not terribly bright because he was slow to speech and sometimes missed the obvious. But Noniki had known the man long enough, starting back when he and Kagiri had been stuck as hired help toiling away at the Happoa Kappua, to know that he simply considered deeply and took his time before shaping those thoughts into words. Some of those notions, when they emerged, were surprisingly deep, and often wise.

Still—perfect weather, the whole way here? That was impossible, and he said so.

"It should be, yes," was his friend's response, coupled with a slow, secretive smile. "But I believe there is a reason for it—and I suspect it is the same one Seikoku has twigged to." He nodded at the young thief, who had settled into a cross-legged position at the back, one hand on the rope. "Please, continue."

She sighed and scrubbed at her face with her free hand. "I'm not sure I should," she admitted after a second. "It's···a bit unbelievable, even though everything fits. And I'm not sure if saying it would help any. It might mess everything up."

"The truth should always be heard," Kanai declared. "Tell him." The order had surprising weight, and Seikoku frowned but complied.

"It's you," she told Noniki without a trace of jest. "You're the reason for the weather."

"What?" he asked again, feeling like one of those birds that could only learn a single word and repeated it endlessly, but unable to come up with anything better. "You think I'm, what, controlling the weather?"

"Yes," she told him bluntly, and Kanai nodded. "You have been from the start." She bit her lip. "You just don't know it."

"That's···insane!" he burst out, unable to contain himself. He wanted to turn and face them both, but the river sent a small wave, rippling their raft up and down, and he had to keep his attention on the water and their treacherously slow progress across it. "How would I be doing something like that?"

"Magic," his two friends answered simultaneously.

"Magic? That's crazy!" he told them, struggling with his oar. "What, you think I'm a matekai now? I grew up on those tales too, you know—Mother Utu used to tell us stories of them. The Matekai who ruled the land before the Schism, their faithful Gensaiba at their side." He laughed. "I loved those stories! But that's all they are, stories. I'm no wizard."

"No?" Seikoku's eyes flashed at him. "Then how do you explain it? And not just the weather! Remember when you confronted Yori? Remember what happened?"

"He ran," Noniki replied shortly.

"Before that," she insisted. "He attacked you—but the wind blew him back. Then he tried again—and the fire flared up, burning him. You think those were happy accidents?"

"So you're saying I did that?" he asked. He did remember those events, though it was hazy, all caught up in a blur—he'd been furious to learn that one of their own had betrayed them, had been murdering their friends, and had confronted the man in a hot rage, his old temper flaring again in a way it hadn't since the monks of the Hakara Ikibanichi had saved his life and helped him center himself again. "How?"

"I···don't know," his friend admitted after a long pause. "I don't think you do, either. But you are doing it. Nothing else makes sense."

That provoked a snort from him. "*That* makes sense to you? That I'm a wizard like in the old stories? That I can control fire and water and weather with my mind? So what were the options that *didn't* make sense?"

Kanai had kept quiet during this back-and-forth, but now he interrupted again. "Did you know," the potter said conversationally, "I can't swim. Never learned how."

Seikoku shrugged impatiently. "Me either. So?" The Yoto was barely more than a stream where it passed through Ginzai, so that made sense.

Now the potter smiled as he set his oar down on the raft. "Noniki?" he said softly, his jaw set, as determined as they had ever seen him. "Help."

And he stepped off the raft, plummeting into the river like an iron cauldron, the water instantly closing over his head.

"NO!" Noniki tossed his oar and dove into the water himself before he even had a chance to think about what he was doing. He had grown up on the water, and was as comfortable there as on land, but the Wagata was a torrential downpour compared to the steady rainfall back home, and he was momentarily blinded by its speed and force as he struggled to see through its depths. His vision was too blurred to make anything out, however, and after a second he was forced to surface, lungs bursting, head bobbing above the water as he clutched the side of the raft and stared out over the river's expanse. "No!"

Seikoku leaned in close, her face inches from his own, tears streaking down her cheeks but her own gaze resolute. "You have to save him," she told him fiercely. "You're the only one who can."

Noniki shook his head—but deep inside, something rebelled against his own denial. Rebelled and broke free. Energy washed through him and over him, invigorating him, making each hair stand on end and every muscle and joint and inch of skin tingle with life. Whatever it was, it made him feel powerful, and the sounds of the water all around receded, leaving a quiet space in his mind where only his own thoughts and emotions dwelled— and that new something, which he could tell at once was not alien at all but truly a part of him.

NO, that something declared, but not to him—to the river that had just taken his friend. GIVE HIM BACK.

And, overwhelmed by the sheer force of that inner voice, the water obeyed.

At first it was a dimple on the surface just behind him, the water dipping down instead of flowing forward with the rest. Soon more and more began to dive into that rapidly expanding depression, the current being sucked down and around into a whirlpool.

Then, with an explosive sound and a shower of droplets

everywhere, the current reversed itself. The whirlpool became a waterspout, the swirling going from downward to sky-high in a heartbeat, the water towering overhead in a tottering cone—

—and at its very peak, shocked into gasping for air, body still encased in water but arms and limbs exposed, was Kanai.

SET HIM DOWN, Noniki commanded in his mind, and again the water hastened to comply. The spout teetered, tipped, elongated—and came arcing down, down, down before depositing the potter almost gently, the water splashing on the ground as it dissipated around him.

On the far bank of the Wagata.

TAKE US THERE, was Noniki's next order, and the river current, only just restored to the surface from where it had distended upward, bent to the side, shooting the raft with him clinging to its side and Seikoku flattened atop it racing across the broad channel and up onto the shore. They came to a bumpy stop mere feet from where their friend lay on his back, still gasping, eyes wide, a big, bemused, triumphant smile stretched across his face.

"You idiot!" Noniki staggered to his feet long enough to stumble over to the potter and collapse to his knees beside the man, pounding him on the chest and shoulder. "You almost died!"

"But I didn't," Kanai replied, coughing up water but sounding insanely pleased with himself for someone who had nearly drowned. "You saved me."

"You did," a calm, gentle voice agreed as a hand came to rest on his shoulder. It was Seikoku, still pale from the suddenness of their passage, who knelt beside the two of them. "You did that, Noniki. No one else. Do you see that now?"

He couldn't very well deny it, not without making himself a liar to these two who he cared about and trusted completely, just as he knew they trusted him. Not now, when that inner voice had awakened and he somehow knew it would never sleep again. "Yes," he admitted finally, shaking his head. "I supposed I did."

"You know what that means, don't you?" she continued, her hand still a spot of welcome warmth against him.

"What, that I'm a matekai?" he asked, glancing up at her.

"Well, yes, that as well," she agreed with a smirk. "But first it means you can rescue our friends before the river sweeps them all the way back to Ginzai."

"Ha!" Laughing, lightened as he always was by her, Noniki struggled to his feet and turned to face the river once more.

Then, with a smile, he ordered the river to calm itself and allow the rest of their community to make it safely across to join them, while behind him Seikoku helped Kania to stand and the two of them set about starting a fire.

CHAPTER TWELVE

Hibikitsu had never been on a boat before. Which was no great surprise, considering that, before this trek, he had never even left Awaihinshi.

What was a surprise, at least to him, was how much he liked it.

Standing at the prow of the *Aio-akeo* as it sliced through the water, his feet braced against the hull, his shins pressing against the low lip, one hand wrapped firmly around the sailline stretching out behind him to where the boat's single large sail billowed as it caught the wind, smelling the sharp, cool, salt tang of the water racing past beneath him, land in easy view on both sides but nothing ahead but sea and sky, he found that he did not have to think, did not have to plan, did not have to posture or pose. He could simply breathe and be. Out here he was not the Echo of Victory, not the ruler of all Rimbaku, not the king of a failing empire. Here he was just a man on a boat, letting the wind ruffle his hair and the sun beat down upon his face.

A part of him wished he could stay here, just like this, forever.

The muted cough behind him made him sigh. Of course that could never be the case. It was simply not his fate. "Yes?" he said without bothering to turn, trying to preserve the illusion at least a few moments longer.

"Pardon, Your Majesty." It was Ganema. "The captain reports that, if the winds remain favorable, we should reach Awaihinshi in a matter of days."

"Very good." He frowned. "Where are Diritan and Nioko?" Those two had become his personal guards, and it seemed strange for it not to be one of the two of them reporting to him now.

"Ah···" Was that embarrassment he heard in the warrior

woman's voice? "They are···indisposed, Your Majesty."

Hibikitsu did glance at her, then, and caught the unmistakable glint of amusement in her eye, though she kept her expression neutral. "Indisposed?" he asked. "What do you mean?" A notion occurred to him—were his two guards romantically involved, and currently engaged in amorous activities? They had never displayed such a connection in all the time he had traveled with them, but being Honjofu they would of course keep such distractions safely walled away while on duty. Now, on this boat where there were no threats, they might have decided that it would be safe to indulge their carnal passions once more.

That seemed unlikely, however, given their usual devotion, and Ganema confirmed this when she explained, "They are both ill, Your Majesty. Not everyone takes to traveling by boat as well as you."

"Really?" He considered that. It had taken him perhaps an hour to get used to the rocking motion of the deck beneath his feet, that was true, but beyond that he had experienced no discomfort. "Do you suffer from such an ailment, Ganema?"

Now she allowed her amusement to surface a bit more. "No, Your Majesty. But I often travel by boat, as it is the fastest way to deliver news and orders along the waterways. Diritan and Nioko are both unused to such things, and it has hit them hard." She gestured behind her, down the length of the ship. Looking that way, Hibikitsu caught sight of several figures, Honjofu by their armor, bent over the railing in the rear. "They will recover," Ganema assured him. "For many, once they are sick a while and then fall asleep they are fine."

"Strange." He shook his head, then used the ropeline to swivel back around. "Well, give Daiso Futoba my thanks, and assure her again that she will be well compensated for her aid." The *Aioakeo*'s captain, a short, grizzled woman named Futoba Kemi who could have been anywhere from thirty to ninety, had not been entirely pleased to be pressed into service. Her boat, a typical single-mast takaneburi, was primarily meant for river work with its flat bottom. Traveling the channel between Tabichi and Iwikaru was fine, since the sea was not so deep there, but taking the boat all the way down past Tatsuma, past Yunigiri, to Saruto—that was well beyond its normal scope. Especially when it was packed with a dozen or so Honjofu—and one horse, for Hibikitsu had adamantly refused to leave Shisi behind.

Still Futoba could not ignore an Imperial command. And she would be paid handsomely for her time, more than she would make in a month of her usual short runs.

Besides which, Shisi was being perfectly well behaved. The horse had been placed in the widest of the boat's sections, between crossbars separating the front and the middle, and had neighed once when the boat had gotten underway, then had promptly fallen asleep. Evidently the stallion was faring better than some of Hibikitsu's elite soldiers!

"Was there anything else?" he asked Ganema now.

"No, sire," she answered. "Will you wish for food at some point?"

"Let me know when the rest of you eat, and I will join you," he replied. He did not miss the almost inaudible gasp she uttered at that, and smiled. "Do not worry over it," he assured her, for she had not traveled with him for long. "As you no doubt noticed on our ride here, I do not stand on ceremony while we are on the road and I have no intention of doing so onboard this boat, either." She had nearly fainted with shock that first night when Hibikitsu had swung down from his saddle, squatted by the fire, and accepted a plate of fish and rice from one of the others, eating by scooping food into his mouth with his fingers just like the rest of them, then washing it down with swigs from the wineskin they handed around. He wasn't sure why she had thought he might behave differently here on the *Aio-akeo*. Perhaps because there was someone else around? But Daiso Futoba was a commoner herself and would surely be eating with them, so why shouldn't he? Wasn't it said that every captain was like a king on their own ship, and ruled with absolute power? Then he was not in command here at all and could hardly be blamed for grouping himself with his warriors instead of keeping aloof and separate.

None of which negated the fact that he would be forced to distance himself again once they returned home, of course. It was one thing to sit and eat and even sleep near the others while they were riding or sailing, but back in Awaihinshi he would be expected to maintain a certain decorum and a certain separateness. There, he was once again Emperor of Rimbaku, and as such he would dine alone, except when he invited other nobles to a formal dinner.

It was not something he was looking forward to.

Again that small part of him asked, *then why go back at all? Why not remain here? Purchase a boat like this one—perhaps even the Aio-akeo itself—and take up life as a boat captain, ferrying freight and passengers to and fro? Let someone else worry about the fate of the empire for a change?*

But he knew he would not do that. He had been bred to this duty, but more than that, he felt a responsibility to see it through. Not for his parents or their parents and all their other ancestors before them, but for people like Daiso Futoba or the little girl Kome, who they had settled with a kindly but childless couple back in Furukotai, or the countless others he had met along his travels. Those people were depending upon him to protect them, to make their lives better, and unless he met someone who he felt was better equipped to shoulder that weight he would not be able to cast it aside. Such was his fate, and he accepted that.

Still, he intended to enjoy this moment while it lasted. And to have others like it in future. Where was it written that the Emperor must spend his whole life cooped up in Aihiri like a bird in a jeweled cage? And even if it was written, he would change it! He was the emperor, after all.

Motion ahead caught his eye, and he set such ruminations aside to study it more closely. There, some distance before them, the water seemed almost to dip, swirling in and down like it was draining from a tub, though the general level around them seemed to remain more or less constant. What was that? He glanced about, but Futoba was at the back, her hand on the tiller, and if she noticed anything amiss it did not cause her to shift either her stance or her stolid expression. Ganema had retreated, but another of the Honjofu, a man named Kenso who told the worst jokes but was so amused himself that it became funny anyway, had just ducked under the sail and was now in the same section as Shisi. "Kenso!" he called

The man immediately straightened, hurried over, and saluted. "Yes, sire?" His voice always struck Hibikitsu as surprisingly high, given his broad shoulders and gruff features.

"What is that?" he asked, gesturing toward the dip in the water, which still seemed roughly the same distance ahead of them, and no more pronounced than before. "There, in the water?"

Kenso peered ahead, shielding his eyes from the sun's glare, but after a moment he shook his head. "I don't see anything, sire. Where, exactly?"

Hibikitsu started to point it out but then thought better of it. "Ah, never mind, I think it was just the sun reflecting. Do not worry yourself about it." He almost apologized for bothering the other man but stopped himself just in time. Emperors did not apologize to soldiers.

The Honjofu shrugged good-naturedly and wandered back away, leaving Hibikitsu to ponder this. He could see the dip clearly, but evidently Kenso could not. Why was that? Did it mean something ill? Or was he merely imagining it? Was that a problem, if the ruler of the land started seeing things?

He returned his attention to the dip—and had to swallow the gasp that threatened to erupt. For the dip had vanished! In its place the water now spun upward, creating a strange funnel shape that spun in place, bending and twisting—and then dropped back down, collapsing back into the river as a whole. Just like that it was gone, and the water was smooth once more, or as smooth as it could be as it slid by, glittering in the sun.

Hibikitsu looked around. Clearly no one else had seen that, for there had been no outcry, no shouts, and no one was pointing and staring. The vision had been his and his alone.

But what did it mean? Was he going mad? Was it a message from the First Emperor—or from some demon or spirit trying to confuse him?

And if it was a message—what did it mean?

He returned his gaze to the waters, trying to once again find mindless solace there, but it was no use. His mind was racing, and the water offered only a reminder of this strange mystery that had now enfolded him in its wings.

CHAPTER THIRTEEN

Suda had already worried one kanashi free from her hair and tangled the second with the ribbon, leaving a knotted mass where she'd had a smooth tie just moments before. Chimehara sighed and stopped, halting the girl with a hand on her shoulder, which caused her to stiffen at once.

"It feels weird," the girl complained, directing a sideways glare her way. "Like someone's trying to tug me back by my hair."

A very real concern, and possibly a situation she'd had to deal with in the past, Chimehara knew. Certainly she had been restrained in such a way many times in her own youth. Now, however, she tried to keep from sighing again as she took the first kanashi from the girl—who had been clutching it like a dagger, low and at her side, the point ready to stab anyone who got too close—managed to extract the other, untied the ribbon, and, using the comb that had been stuck just before the bun, quickly restored her charge's hair to something resembling order.

"This is pointless, anyway," Suda complained. "Why do I need to get all fancied up like this?" She slid a finger under the collar of her kitoro, trying to pull it away from her neck. "I feel like someone's choking me!"

Chimehara resisted the urge to slap the girl's hand away. "No one is choking you," she said instead, allowing some sharpness into her words, and was pleased to see her pupil's hand immediately release the garment and return to her side. Cajoling, she had learned in short order, did not work with Suda, but strong discipline did—not beatings or anything like that, those would only make the girl more recalcitrant, but clear words and a sharp tone worked wonders. She was, after all, eager to please her mentor, and just as eager to stay in her good graces and continue to enjoy the benefits of such attention, meaning a warm place to sleep, her own bed, good food, and more.

That did mean, however, that she had to learn to put up with a few things she felt were unnecessary, annoying, and idiotic. This was one of them.

"It is not pointless at all," Chimehara explained. "This is the first time you are meeting any of my co-workers, and so it is important to make a good first impression. A clean, tidy appearance goes a long way toward that, as does keeping your mouth shut, minding your manners, and not attacking anyone." The girl stuck out her tongue at that, but giggled immediately after, and Chimehara could not help but smile as well.

Then, her task accomplished and her charge presentable once more, Chimehara took the girl by the hand and led her to the front gates of House Chohu.

Suda gazed up in awe at the massive gates, with their heavily inlaid wood and the beautiful carvings all across their panels, then craned her neck to gape at the panel above, with its jeweled house crest. "How much is all that worth?" she whispered, and Chimehara shushed her, for the righthand gate was gliding open, silent as ever on its oiled-daily hinges.

The woman standing in the widening gap was roughly Chimehara's height, perhaps twice her age, and nowhere near as pretty, though she was stately and carried a certain air of authority that had Suda immediately narrowing her eyes but also clapping her mouth shut. The woman's gaze twitched to the girl, then to Chimehara—and then her face broke into a wide, open smile even as she stepped back, making space for them both to enter.

The minute they had passed through she was closing the gate once more, then turning to engulf Chimehara in a hug.

"Oh, it is good to see you!" Madam Ponsoi declared, pulling back after a second to hold her at arm's length. "And I do believe you grow lovelier with each passing day. This must be your cousin."

"Yes, this is Suda," Chimehara confirmed. She had considered changing the girl's name to something a little more elegant but had decided against it. She was used to that name, after all. They could always change it when she grew older.

"Oh, lovely!" The senior housekeeper exclaimed, clapping her hands together. She bent at the waist, putting her face level with Suda's, and offered the girl a warm smile. "Welcome to House Chohu, Suda."

"Thank you," Suda replied, dropping into the curtsey Chimehara had spent hours teaching her. Honestly, the child could memorize the location of every vital organ in minutes, and the best angle and location to strike at each one—why did she still look half-drunk and half-paralyzed when she curtseyed? Not that Madam Ponsoi seemed to mind—she was beaming like the girl had just performed the most intricate dance imaginable, while reciting poetry flawlessly and playing a flute. "It is very kind of you to let me visit."

"But you're not a visitor," Madam Ponsoi replied, laughing and wrapping Suda in a quick hug. "You're family!" The girl only stiffened a little. After what Chimehara assumed had already been a great deal of abuse in her young life, it was understandable that she would not be comfortable with physical contact, especially if it was initiated without asking. Still, it was something she would have to adjust to if she wished to be out among other people on a regular basis. That was part of the reason for this visit. The other being that, after thinking long and hard about it and weighing the benefits and drawbacks to both options, Chimehara had decided it made more sense to include Suda in her House Chohu life than to try and hide her from them. It could have been done, of course, but that would cut Suda off from this potential source of contact, socialization, and information. It would also mean that, if anything were to happen to Chimehara, Suda would have nowhere to turn for support and aid. This way, she would already know everyone here and would be part of this world—it meant more exposure but also a good deal more security, and in the end she had deemed that to be worth it.

They just had to survive this first visit without Suda losing her composure and killing anyone. A prospect made significantly more difficult by the pair now descending upon them.

"Oh, she's adorable!" Yuni shrieked, charging in and wrapping Suda in a hug that threatened to swallow her whole. "I could just eat her up!"

"So lovely!" Ritaru agreed, yanking the girl free from her co-worker in order to administer her own engulfing embrace. "Aren't you the sweetest thing ever!" All Chimehara could see of Suda was her nearer hand, which was starting to twitch and stiffen into a claw. Uh oh.

Fortunately, Madam Ponsoi intervened. "Don't smother the poor girl!" she snapped, pulling the cleaning lady off Suda, who took a grateful step back and a deep breath. Chimehara found she was holding her own, watching this child she had adopted but still did not know fully. What would Suda do now? She was armed, of course—she never went anywhere without the knife Chimehara had given her, a slender, razor-sharp thing tucked into a snake-skin sheath along her right shin which she could draw in a heart-beat. Would she go for the blade? Attack one or more of these cloying but well-meaning women?

Instead, after glaring for just a second, the girl straightened—and bowed. "You must be Yuni and Ritaru," she said to the pair. "My cousin has told me so much about you, I feel as if I know you already." And she smiled at them, a friendly smile if a little calcu-lating. Not that these women would notice the distinction.

Chimehara allowed herself to breathe again, and when Suda caught her eye she nodded her approval, which made the girl brighten even more. The cleaning ladies, of course, were delighted, and quickly surrounded their visitor again, but this time they found a way to appeal to her far more, producing sweets from their pockets. As with any child, and especially one who had grown up hungry, the easiest way to Suda's heart was through her stomach.

While that was going on—now confident she could trust the girl to behave herself—Chimehara allowed Madam Ponsoi to steer her off to the side for a private conversation. "How are you, my dear?" the older woman asked. "Losing your aunt and uncle so suddenly—that must have been such a shock. And taking young

Suda in all by yourself—that's so good of you!" She clasped both of Chimehara's hands in her own, which were still strong and smooth despite all her years of hard work. "If there is ever anything you need, you know you have only to ask."

"Thank you," she replied, and realized that she meant it. Befriending the housekeeper, the cleaning ladies, and the rest of the staff had been a means to an end, of course—they were the ones who truly knew what was going on, and the ones with access to anything and everything. But they had taken her in without reservation and she could see now, with some surprise, that she had grown to feel genuine affection for them as well. How strange.

"Now, Master Eijiri wished for you to come see him as soon as you arrived," Madam Ponsoi was saying. "Before breakfast, even, if possible. So off you go! The girl too—he wants to meet her, I'm sure." The woman's smile assured her that this was not a bad thing, and so Chimehara let herself and Suda be gathered and shepherded along the halls toward the master of the house's private receiving room, which was on the other side of the central gardens, away from the communal spaces and general workrooms. Suda stared as they walked, openly admiring the beautiful tilework and lovely lattices and gorgeous flowers, which was fine as it both kept her quiet and made their guide feel a well-earned pride in the place she maintained so carefully.

As they walked, they passed a few other members of the house, all of whom either nodded and smiled or paused to say a quick hello. Every eye turned to Suda with interest but no real surprise, by which Chimehara knew that word of her "recent family tragedy" had already spread. That was exactly as she'd expected, however. She had been back several times since adopting Suda, but had manufactured that story to explain the girl's sudden appearance in her life and why she had missed a few days of work while getting Suda settled in and both of them adjusting to living together. She had made a point of telling Madam Ponsoi first, knowing it would spread quickly from there.

They passed one pair who did not acknowledge them at all, but then they seemed wrapped up in some misery of their own. Both looked wan and weak, their skin waxy and beaded with sweat, their eyes slightly glazed, and though leaning into each other they wobbled slightly as they trudged along the path. Madam Ponsoi tugged Chimehara and Suda to the side to let the couple past.

"Poor things," the housekeeper clucked after they had gone. "Do you know Master Ryoto and Mistress Etsuki?"

"A little," Chimehara confirmed. Etsuki worked in the counting room, where she had started when she'd first been admitted to House Chosu. Ryoto was a trader who specialized in carvings and inlays, installations rather than jewelry and accessories. They had been married for more than a decade and—"They have a son, do they not?"

"Yes, Ruisoki," Madam Ponsoi replied, pointing—and, indeed, a third figure was stalking along behind the stricken pair, so quietly she had not even noticed him at first. He looked to be about Suda's age, perhaps ten or twelve, and unlovely, with a blocky face and wide features, but he was neatly attired, everything precisely in place. As he passed he glanced up at Chimehara—and she started at the cold calculation she saw in that otherwise placid gaze.

"A quiet boy," the housekeeper continued after he had slipped by, oblivious to the recent exchange, "but so polite! He is struggling right now, the dear, what with both his parents being so sick. It's strange, too—no one else has fallen ill, just the two of them. Such a sad thing, and both of them so gentle and kind to everyone!"

"Indeed," Chimehara agreed. "I hope they recover soon." But, as they resumed their walk, she found herself thinking about the couple, their strange appearance, their son's odd glance, and what that might mean. The more she considered it, the more a certain suspicion formed in her head—and, along with it, an audacious, ambitious plan.

If she was correct, a terrible thing had occurred and was still happening right now.

What's more, it was something she could directly profit from. If she was careful.

Thrilled with this new idea, she draped an arm around Suda's shoulder, ignoring the almost imperceptible shudder in response, and tugged the girl close.

Yes, this could work out very nicely indeed, if she handled it right.

But then, handling things well was something she was exceedingly good at.

CHAPTER FOURTEEN

Things came to a head when they stopped for supplies, but it had started shortly before that.

They had been walking for two full days, after taking the rest of that first day to recover from the river crossing and then another full day to dismantle their makeshift rafts and rebuild the wagons and carts as best they could. Not all of them could be reconstructed exactly, of course, but an interesting thing had happened—in the process of taking the wheeled contrivances apart in the first place and putting different people together to man the various rafts they'd built, many of the old divisions had broken down. People who had always kept their belongings separate were now sharing them freely, mixing them together with their neighbors, pooling everything into one communal lot. So the fact that they were a cart or two short from what they'd had before didn't seem to matter—people just placed their things on another cart or wagon, sharing the effort of hauling it or driving it, and that was that. Isoro still kept hers mostly separate but that was simply because her herbs needed to be kept clean and dry. She did allow any of the others to store their valuables in her wagon, however, and, curiously, Amon had started helping her drive the wagon. They chatted as they rode, and it seemed to Seikoku that the young herbalist was teaching the netmender about herbs and poultices and healing methods.

In short, the effort of crossing the river had turned them from a community into a family.

Of course, there was a downside to that transformation, as well. Communities respected their leaders, their elders, and honored those people's decisions. Families tended to be more informal, which meant they questioned more—and quarreled more.

Which was why, on their second night in Saruto—which was, thus far, more lush and green than Bezenkai had been, its hills gentler, its streams prettier, almost like it was some idyllic land rather than reality—Kuma raised her head as they all sat around the fire finishing the evening meal and asked, "What are we doing, exactly?"

Everyone else went quiet, all the little conversations around the fire ceasing as all heads turned toward her. "What do you mean?" Noniki asked, setting his bowl aside and wiping his hands on the grass before him. "We are on our way to Awaihinshi, to speak to the emperor."

"Yes, but what will that actually accomplish?" the washer-woman asked.

"Why are you questioning now?" Minawa demanded, rounding on the other woman, her wrinkled face set in a glare. "When we have come so far? When *you* have?"

Kuma waved her off. "I chose to follow Noniki because I was tired of my life as it was," she answered, speaking loudly and clearly so all could hear. "He spoke of changing things, of making things better, and I wanted that. I needed that. Nothing was going to change if I stayed in Shakomi. So I left." She looked around at all of them, and her stony expression softened. "And it did get better. I found all of you. I found this community. This family. That never would have happened." She nodded at Noniki. "And I still believe in what you say, that we need change. I'm just asking, how do we do that? What will speaking with the emperor actually do to make that happen?"

"If we even get to speak to him." That was Ratal. "He's the emperor, right? Who're we? Fishermen and netmenders and washer-women and horse traders and farmers—we're all peasants. Do we really think anyone's going to let us even get close to him?"

That caused a murmur around the circle and Seikoku rose to her feet. She turned to face the rest of them, taking in their faces, their expressions. "Don't you have any faith?" she demanded. "Look how far we've come already! We didn't think we'd make it across the Wagata, did we? But we did! Noniki got us here—do you truly think he's going to stop now? Are you?"

The tenor of the murmuring shifted, becoming less doubtful, less dejected, and more cheerful, more energized. Then Noniki levered himself up.

"You want to know how we're going to change things?" he asked. He waited for the nods and cries of assent to die down before replying, "I don't know." Then he held up a hand for silence. "I don't. I don't have a grand argument mapped out in my head that I can present to the emperor and which will make him suddenly fall to his knees and cry, 'oh, how could I have been so blind?'" That brought a few chuckles. "I don't have a perfect map that shows 'start here and follow this route to reach a more enlightened and equal society.'" He looked around and smiled. "What I do have is friends. Friends from all along the route, from here all the way back to Ginzai, to Shakomi. Friends from many different occupations. Friends who believe, as I do, that we need to stop relying upon aitachi and aishone, that we need to stop looking to the past for answers, that the real answers, the right answers, are here in the present." His smile widened, becoming a grin, and showing him again for the eager, passionate boy he had been not so long ago. "I think, when faced with this many people with such a clear message, even an emperor will have to listen."

That seemed to satisfy everyone, and the meal ended, people breaking off to wash their plates and bowls, store the remainder of the evening's food, bank the fire, check on the horses, and a host of other small tasks. But Seikoku noticed that Noniki hadn't entirely answered the question. Because even if they did manage to reach the emperor, and he did listen, what were they going to say besides "the system is broken"? You couldn't just say that things didn't work—you had to offer a solution. If not a perfect map or a perfect argument, at least the start of one.

The fact that Noniki didn't seem to have even that much worried her.

"You should tell them," she said the next morning as they started out, her and Noniki taking the lead as was often the case.

"Tell them what?" he asked her. If the discussion last night had bothered him any, he gave no sign of it now—his forehead was unfurrowed, a gentle half-smile upon his face, and from time to time he paused in his relaxed pace to tilt his head up, eyes closed, and drink in the sunlight that washed across him.

"That you're a matekai."

He glanced over at her, just a shift of his eyes, and frowned. "I'm still not sure I even believe that myself," he stated, and laughed when she opened her mouth to argue. "Yes, I know, I saved Kanai, and pulled our boats across the river," he told her quickly. "I admit that. But···I haven't been able to do it again."

"What, toss us across a river?" She pretended to be shocked. "I hope not! We only just managed to get to this side in the first place!"

He laughed, as she'd intended, but didn't let her distract him. Not this time. "I've been trying to summon···something," he told her seriously. "Wind, rain, whatever. Nothing's happened." He shrugged. "Not much of a wizard if I can't do anything deliberately, am I?"

"I guess not." She snagged a long blade of grass, leaning down to snap it off just above the ground, and swished it back and forth as they walked. "What did it feel like, when you did it before?"

"Like something inside of me had woken up and taken control," he answered. "I've been trying to wake it back up since, but so far—nothing. Maybe it only works when I really need it." He laughed. "In which case, I hope it never works again!"

She thought about that, and had to admit it was not a bad answer. Besides, Noniki seemed happy and she did not want to spoil that. So she let it go. For now.

Two days later, they reached the town. It was the only one they'd seen the entire time they'd been in Saruto, and they desperately needed rice, flour, and several other necessities. "I will go into town," Minawa offered. "I can take Kanai, Ratal, maybe Junko. We will bring what coin we can gather and see what we can purchase with that."

Noniki nodded. It was Seikoku who said, "I should go with you."

But Minawa shook her head. "No, dear girl," the old woman told her. "Trust me, it is far better for you to remain here until we know what we are dealing with."

"Why?" Seikoku demanded, hands on her hips. "I can handle myself!"

"Of course you can," the old farmer agreed. "But that pretty face of yours, it can draw the wrong sort of attention, and we won't get much of a deal on anything if you're busy beating off men at the same time." She patted Seikoku's arm. "I will be fine." She winked, a gleam in her eye. "I have done this sort of thing before, you know."

Seikoku was still fuming when the old woman departed a few minutes later, taking the three she'd named with her, while everyone else waited just beyond the edge of town, far enough away that they could see anyone coming long before they got close. It was Minawa who looked ready to explode, however, when she returned a short while later—empty-handed.

"The unbelievable nerve!" the old woman declared, pounding one gnarled fist against a wagon wheel when she was finally amongst the community once more. "I've seen some gall in my day, some brazen arrogance, but this—this beats all!"

"What happened?" someone asked, voicing the question vibrating through the group as a whole.

Minawa glared and snarled and gnashed her teeth but seemed too worked up to answer. It was Kanai who replied instead.

"Their prices were a bit inflated," the potter told them all, earning him a snort and a murderous look from Minawa. "Perhaps more than a bit," he amended. "They were outrageous."

"How bad?" Seikoku asked.

"A gold for a sack of rice," he answered. The collective gasp could have shaken the door clean off a house. "Same for a sack of flour."

"That's insane!" Otokai cut in. "I've sold horses for a fraction of that! Good ones!"

Seikoku just shook her head. "I've seen this before," she said aloud. "Not to this degree, but the same principle. Supply and demand. They're the only village anywhere in sight, so they know anyone passing through has to be desperate. That means they can set the price to anything they want and people have to pay it—or starve."

"We can't pay that kind of money!" Sanedi cried. "We'd be able to get, what, a bag of rice and a bag of flour and nothing more? That's not enough for all of us to live on!" They had only been able to gather a little over two gold, and that was with everyone contributing all they had.

"I hate greedy people," Seikoku muttered, glaring at the town as if she could somehow force those responsible to think better of their actions by the sheer force of her displeasure. "They rob people blind and get away with it because they do it openly, in the name of commerce." Slowly, her frown faded, to be replaced by a smug little smirk. "Maybe it's time someone showed them what it feels like."

"What are you going to do?" Noniki asked. He looked worried. His gaze fell to his hands, and the ring there. "Perhaps this might be worth something?" he offered slowly, and she was touched to see how loath he was to part with her gift. But even if it was worth a fortune—and it might be, considering who she had stolen it from and the care they had taken to safeguard it—she had no way of exchanging the jade band for coin without drawing more attention than they could possibly want.

Besides, she had a far better idea.

"Don't worry about it," she told him. "I'll take care of this." Then she patted his arm. "The less you know about it, the better."

That night, well after dark, Seikoku set out for town on her own. She did not bring any coin with her, but she did carry her old tools, her rope and her picks and her small, sharp knives, all of which she had thought to pack and bring when she'd left Ginzai. She had not been sure she'd ever need them again, but she was glad now that she'd decided to lug them along, just in case.

She returned a few hours later and slipped back into her tent with no one the wiser. When the dawn broke the following morning, the sky lightening though it remained smothered in clouds, she was up, only the circles under her eyes indicating how little sleep she'd received, and off to find Minawa. By the time the rest had gathered for the morning meal, the old woman was gone, taking the same three companions with her.

A few hours later, Kuma raised a shout: "Wagon approaching!" Sure enough, there was a wagon riding toward them from the town. As it drew closer, they could see two figures driving it and two more walking alongside. Then it came closer still, and they saw that the driver was Minawa, with Ratal beside her. Kanai and Junko were the two on foot. When they finally pulled to a stop near Isoro's wagon, everyone saw that this new one was filled to the brim with supplies of all sorts.

"How did you manage to get all this?" Noniki asked, and the quartet just grinned.

"Did you talk them down to a reasonable price?" Kuma asked.

Minawa nodded, looking pleased as a well-fed cat. "I did get them to come down from the highway robbery they were asking before, yes." She grinned. "Apparently there's some fight left in this old toad after all."

But Otokai was looking over the wagon with a seasoned eye. "There is no way you bought all of this for only two gold," he stated flatly. "Even at normal prices, that would be almost impossible, and I can't imagine they were willing to discount it that much. What actually happened?"

Seikoku saved the old woman the trouble of lying further. "I gave her the money," she declared. "I didn't want her to say in case anyone got upset, but it was entirely me."

"What was?" Isoro asked. "Did you have all that money hidden away somewhere and didn't tell us?" The young herbalist's tone made it clear she did not believe that for a second.

"No." Seikoku sighed, then steeled herself, raising her chin and meeting her friends' gaze without flinching. "I stole it." That earned her varying degrees of shock, surprise, discomfort, and even awe as she continued, "I stole it from the town itself. More specifically, I took it from their moneylender. The same one who gets rich off driving the prices so high no one can afford to pay them directly."

"So," Sanedi said slowly, "you're saying we bought all these supplies from them, at the crazy prices they demanded, with their own money?"

"Exactly." She dared any of them to contradict her as she said, "they're stealing from everyone who passes through here! I decided to give them a little of their own back." She grinned. "They got their money back, anyway. Most of it."

Someone laughed. Then someone else did. Then everyone was laughing, some so hard they nearly fell over. Kanai and Ratal both had tears streaming down their faces and Amon and Junko both had to sit down, they were shaking so much. Seikoku laughed too, then, but more out of relief. She'd been afraid of how her friends—no, her family—would react to what she'd done.

Then a quiet voice cut through all the hilarity. "That's it."

Their amusement fell away as everyone turned to look at Noniki. Seikoku did flinch a little then, inside, for fear that she had upset him, that he was angry with her, that she had damaged their friendship.

But his eyes were shining as he continued, "That's it." Then he found Kuma. "You asked how we were going to change things," he told her. "This is how." He glanced back at Seikoku. "How did you steal the money?"

She frowned. "I snuck in through the window, found his coffers, picked the lock on them, and took what I felt we needed." She wasn't sure where he was going with this.

"And what aishone did you use for that?" Noniki asked next.

"Aishone?" That dragged a short chuckle from her. "None! I didn't need any. It was easy." And it had been. She'd worried that she would have forgotten how, after all this time on the road, but the minute she'd reached town everything had come back to her. And they didn't even have half the usual safeguards she'd learned to expect. Evidently being the only ones out here had made them careless.

"Easy?" Now he shook his head, but not angrily or even in disbelief. "Do you hear yourself?" he asked her, his gaze still bright but not nearly as warm as his smile. "You snuck in through the window—first floor or second?"

"Second."

"You got up into and through a second-story window," he repeated, "crept through the house without a sound, picked the lock on his coffers, took coin, and snuck back out, all without getting caught—and without a single aishone." Now he cocked his head to the side. "Where did those skills come from, then?"

"They—I—" Seikoku realized that everyone else had gone completely, utterly silent, hanging on her every word. She herself discovered she was listening just as intently, in just as much wonder, as she heard herself say, "They're mine. I taught myself how to do that."

"Exactly!" He grabbed her by the hands and spun her around, laughing like this was the best thing in the world, and she found she was laughing with him. She was still giggling and giddy and more than a little dizzy when he slowed to a stop. "You taught yourself, Seikoku! You earned those skills all on your own! No aishone necessary!" He fixed another of their group with his gaze. "Ratal! You helped build all those rafts. Did you use aishone for that?" The fisherman shook his head. "Amon, Isoro says she's teaching you about herbs and healing. Are you using aishone?" Another negative. "Kuma, you made last night's stew. Did that come from a relic bone?"

"If so, you should send it back!" someone called, to general laughter. But even though he laughed along, Noniki would not be turned from his point.

"This is how we change the world," he told them all. "Just like this. Learning new things. Mastering new skills. Not through our ancestors—just us, doing it ourselves. We are the living proof that the Relicant Touch is not only not necessary, it's holding us back. We can show the emperor—and everyone else—that this is the way of the future, the only way we can move forward as a people." He smiled, and the sun burst from the clouds to shine down upon him, bathing him in golden light. "We will show them all that we can do anything we set our mind to."

And when he winked at Seikoku, she knew he had found that inner voice once more.

CHAPTER FIFTEEN

No one was more surprised than Ritsuro Okari to learn that he was not in fact a killer.

Oh, he had done his share of killing, that was certain. One did not remain among the Honjofu long without being able to fulfill one's duty by protecting the Empire against all manner of threat—and "protecting it" typically meant finding whoever was posing that threat and eliminating them, once and for true. An elite warrior would hardly do the Emperor much good if he pardoned the realm's enemies and let them escape alive to plot another day.

Okari had not only managed to handle such responsibilities, he had excelled, demonstrating both loyalty and strength of arms with enough dedication and fervor to eventually earn a promotion to gunso. A few years later, he advanced to chuisu, which was exhilarating but also sobering, for the Honjofu were too small to require more than one lieutenant and had no other ranks above that save for the Taikoro himself. Which meant that the only way Okari could ever rise higher would be to someday become the elite unit's lord commander himself and that seemed improbable, what with his house being a minor one of no particular note. More likely when Fujibuki Haro retired the Emperor would appoint someone from one of the other powerful noble houses, who would posture and issue orders but would leave the real work to his or her officers.

That was acceptable, however. Okari had no illusions about his own merits. If he never rose above chuisu, well, at least he had attained that rank, and in one of the most illustrious and exclusive units in all Rimbaku.

He had handled his duties well, giving both his commander and his soldiers no reason to complain. Tough but fair, flexible but firm, always willing to shoulder his share of the work but cognizant of the best uses of his time, happy to bond with the men but also careful to keep just enough apart to remind them who was in charge, he liked to think he had been a model lieutenant.

Then fate chose to cast him a bad hand, in the form of the flux. The bloody, bloody flux.

He had been laid up for over a week, too feeble to stir from his bed, often unable to keep down even thin soup and tea. When that had finally passed and he had been able to sit up, then stumble to the washroom, he had lost nearly half his body weight and all his muscle. He moved like an old man, every limb shaking with each step, head wobbling side to side, back bent. But he had been moving.

It had taken him another week to truly be back on his feet and he was nowhere near fighting fit. He might never be again, if he were being honest—his muscles had all melted away, leaving him weak as a newborn and nearly as coordinated. The very notion of morning exercises and combat training were enough to make him groan in despair. He couldn't even draw his sword, not without the tip wavering and then dipping toward the ground.

But the strange part was, he'd discovered that he did not genuinely miss it.

Oh, he looked forward to being outdoors again, to strolling the grounds, sitting beneath the trees, perching on the sturdier shrubs, listening to the birds and feeling the wind fluttering on his cheeks. And the idea of exercising again, of building his strength back up, of being able to walk the length of the grounds without collapsing, wheezing and struggling for air, that did have a certain appeal.

But wielding a blade? Battling someone? Struggling to kill before he could be killed instead?

That was for younger, stronger men, Okari decided. He did not need that. Whatever burning desire he'd had to prove himself had long since died down. He still wished to serve his Emperor and do his duty and aid his fellow Honjofu, but perhaps never again on the field of battle.

Especially since he had found a very different field upon which to test his strength and brag about his victories.

Such as right now. As Okari sat back on his haunches, he regarded the scroll laid out before him with an air of pleasant surprise. It had taken him much of the past week but finally—finally!—he had solved their budgetary problem.

"It is all about the rice," he muttered to himself, flicking one finger at the spot where his scrawled calculations had come home to roost. "All about the rice."

And his discovery that they had been overbuying rice—and overpaying for what they bought—for the past several years? He would inform Taikoro Fujibuki, of course, as was his duty. But something of this magnitude—for it had long been a question as to why the Honjofu went through its allotted funds so quickly and still suffered a lack of several vital supplies throughout the year. Well, the Emperor would want to know that they had found an answer to that, absolutely. And although the Taikoro would ultimately take credit, as he did—as was his right—surely he would still mention Okari as the man who had taken that project upon himself, and solved it for him? The Emperor would hear his name, he had no doubt. And thus he would be pleased. He might even reward Okari for showing such loyalty, such singlemindedness, and such attention to detail.

Others among the Honjofu might wield a swifter sword or a more powerful bow, but none could handle the brush and the ledger half so well as he did now, so even though his arms ached and his back screamed and his eyes burned, still Okari kept his chin up and his smile broad but gentle. He might no longer pose a threat to other men and women, but no clerical error would be safe from his sight! Besides which, he had been surprised and pleased to discover that there was a great deal of pleasure to be found in the tidy lines of sales figures and stock items, and a certain sense of accomplishment as well in wrestling those same rows and columns into submission.

Which might have explained why, upon hearing a strange sound somewhere nearby, Okari reached for his brush rather than his sword, though the nihono did lie beside him upon the floor mat of the tiny room that served as both his bedchamber and, these days with the addition of a small writing desk squeezed up against one side, his study. "Hello?" he called out, belatedly restoring the brush to its place in his writing box and instead snaring the kogotano that resided beside it. He adjusted his grip upon the little knife so that its small, triangular blade extruded from the bottom of his curled fist, angled back up toward his forearm, ready to be whipped around and stabbed into anyone or no one at all, for no one answered. "Is anyone there?" he tried again, raising his voice. "Show yourself!"

No one moved, nothing emerged from the shadows that had just begun to settle around the little room as the sun began its nightly disappearance, and after a moment Okari lowered his makeshift weapon, finally setting it back in the box and lifting his hand to flex life and nimbleness back into his fingers.

And it was precisely then that a shadow fell directly across his desk.

"Hai!" Okari shouted, throwing himself from the desk and its newly distended shadow and only succeeding in slamming the back of his head against his bed and then knocking himself flat on his back. He scrambled back up to a sitting position, rubbing the sore spot he'd created, his eyes darting about as he scanned his surroundings, but still he saw nothing out of the ordinary. The shadow was evidently either a prank, a trick of the light, or both, and nothing more.

Carefully he struggled to his feet, still wobbly upon them, and then leaned over to roll up the scroll and retrieve that and the suzeri kabo, which he closed and clasped shut. The beautifully inlaid lacquered box had belonged to his family for generations but he had only begun using it in the past few weeks, when his illness had rendered him incapable of fulfilling his other duties. Now it had become his prized possession, and one he intended to use far more often.

He was still bent forward collecting the box when something dark lunged from the shadows and swept a long, slim flicker of night across his throat.

Okari gasped, the box and scroll tumbling to his feet as he clutched at his neck, feeling a burning line there and a cold numbness that seeped from it, spreading rapidly. His gaze went to the nihono at his feet but he discovered he could no longer hunch forward and his hands remained locked around his throat, unable or unwilling to reach for the distant sword instead. He stumbled back a step, barely keeping his balance, and the shadow moved with him, detaching itself enough from its surrounding gloom that he could now make out a definite figure there, and even two lighter patches that must serve as eyes. It glided closer to him, a slim arm lashing out to hook around his waist and catch him as he tripped and fell, easing him onto the bed behind him as gently as a drifting leaf. Yet Okari found he could not thank the strange creature, not when his throat was closing up and his chest was seizing, every banished breath a painful shudder that spiked the fear now racing through him.

He did not want to die, he realized. Not now, when he had finally found his calling. How odd to think that, after so many years wielding a sword, Okari had at least realized that his place was at the suzeri kabo instead! Only now, when he had learned that, was his time with brush and stone cut brutally short, ended before it had a chance to properly begin.

The numbness was spreading, all through his head and chest, deadening his senses and also dulling the pain from both the wound itself and the inability to breathe. The darkness was closing in, filling Okari's sight, but that shadow stayed at the forefront distinct from the general black that sought to claim him. It hovered there, watching and waiting, its hunger evident even through its inky black features, and Okari longed to spit at it in defiance but his mouth would no longer work, nor his lungs.

His last thought was that he hoped the scroll survived intact, because the Emperor would surely wish to see those projections about the rice. Then the darkness swooped in, filling his vision and stealing the last of his breath, and all calculations and tallies and totals faded away, along with everything else.

CHAPTER SIXTEEN

Shizumi was no longer in Awaihinshi.

Instead she was back in Botetsu, the little village in Yunigiri where she had grown up. Only this time she was no child, and it felt strange to stalk through the place as an adult, clad in her armor, her nihono by her side. She paced along the single road, which was nothing more than a wide dirt path that looped through the settlement. She studied the rough huts clustered on either side, with their steep, thatched roofs and their shingled walls, seeing them both as she had experienced them then and as she might view them now, a strange sensory overlay of the comfortable and the crude, the expansive and the cramped, the impressive and the ordinary. There were no people about, which she found strange, but not enough to keep her from continuing her tour along the winding path, passing by the small trading post and the tiny shrine and cemetery before finally reaching a tall, narrow cottage at the village's farthest edge, its walls neat, its roof rushes well-trimmed, its garden lush and lovingly maintained.

Her childhood home.

"Hello?" she called as she slid open the front door, peering into the room beyond. It was both sitting room and dining room, and kitchen as well, with a partial loft overhead serving as sleeping quarters. No one answered, but there was something cooking on the bed of lit coals at the center, something that sizzled and popped over the flames and filled the room with a delicious smell, a rich, deep scent.

The smell of roasting meat.

Stepping inside, she crossed the rough mats of the floor, resisting the urge to shed her boots, and approached the raised bamboo platform comprising the house's center, with the cookfire it had been built around. Had the food truly been left unattended? Her parents would never have been so careless. She stepped up onto the platform, the bundled stalks creaking beneath her weight, and crossed it carefully, with far more trepidation than she had as a child. She stopped beside the shallow rectangular firepit, glanced down—

—and tensed as she finally saw what was being cooked.

It was a human hand.

With a start, she sat up in bed, hands already reaching for her blade. It was sitting upon its rack, however, with her armor draped on the frame beside it. Neither of those objects would have been in her parents' home, and a quick glanced around confirmed that she was instead back in the barracks in Aihiri.

She had been dreaming.

"Ah!" Shizumi shouted, rubbing at her eyes. Talk about vivid! And so odd that she would see Botetsu, which she had not thought about in ages. What sort of omen was that?

And how, if she was already awake, was she still smelling that cooking meat?

In an instant she was out of bed, grabbing up her sword as she slid the panel open and stepped out into the hall. Shizumi was not big on abusing the privileges of her rank, but one she had happily accepted was the tiny private room afforded to her as a gunso. She slept a great deal better when she did not have to worry about someone trying to attack her—or worse—in her sleep. Of course, she slept best out on the road, bedding down on a hill or in a valley, her bantao spread out around her in their own bedrolls, the stars shining down from high above.

But if she couldn't have that, she would gladly take the room of her own, thank you.

Creeping silently down the hall—she had not bothered to grab her boots, though at least she slept in ponmei and hosode—she let her nose guide her. It did not lead her back toward the mess, however, or down the stairs to the main barracks. Instead it took her farther down the small upper hall her own room was upon, past the chamber belonging to her fellow gunso, Norio Shinjuru, to the third room in the row, which she knew was much like her own, only slightly larger.

Ritsuro Okari's room.

"Chuisu?" Shizimi called, rapping on the door's frame with one hand. "Are you all right in there?" When he didn't respond she tried again. "Chuisu Okari? It's Misataki Shizumi. May I enter?" Still no reply, and no sign of movement, but the smell was so strong here it brought tears to her eyes. That, and the bad feeling in her gut, overrode any sense of propriety—not that she'd ever had much of that.

Carefully she slid the door open—and stood, staring into the tiny room at the body curled up there on its bed, its entire form so badly burned its skin had developed a thin, flaky black crust like some sort of protective shell, its head tilted back, its mouth open in a soundless scream.

She nearly crossed the threshold, but stopped herself. This was the scene of a crime, and as such she needed to remember what Kohori had said before, out in the gardens: "Look around. See if you can find any clue as to what happened here. But do so carefully. Do not disturb anything. The idea is to observe, not to taint and destroy anything that could help us." So she stood there in the doorway instead, studying the little room, trying to remember everything she saw. Then she closed that door again and took the stairs down to the main barracks, where she found Akino, Geniji, Dairamu, and Kori all awake, sitting cross-legged on the floor between the beds and tossing dice together.

"Kori," she called out, selecting him both because he was closest to the door and because of the four he was the soldier she knew and trusted the least. "Apologies for interrupting the game, but I need you to deliver a message for me. It is beyond urgent."

"Beyond urgent, hey? Must be important." He winked at his teammates. "What is it? Are you out of face paint?" He laughed but his three companions did not join in, and his grin quickly soured. "Fine, what do you need?"

"Find Taikoro Maniko," Shizumi instructed. She struggled

with what to say, how much to tell him, because anything she said now would soon be all over the compound, possibly before the Honteno commander even received the message. But she couldn't not tell her, not if she wanted the older woman to trust and include her in turn. "Tell her to meet me here right away. And that it has happened again."

Taking a cue from her voice, Kori rose to his feet, saluted, and in two long steps was over by the door that led out onto the porch. Slipping through that door he quickly vanished from sight, leaving Shizumi with three of the people she relied upon most in the world. All of whom were watching her closely.

"What's this all about, hm?" Genji asked, folding massive arms across her equally large chest. "I'm guessing it has to do with whatever Haro told you that sent you chasing after Taikoro Maniko before. Am I right?"

Shizumi paused only a second before nodding. "There have been several deaths recently," she explained. "Strange ones, here in Aihiri. Our Taikoro told me to shadow his Honteno counterpart, to offer her whatever aid I could in solving this." She barely suppressed a shudder. "And now there is another."

It was Akino who narrowed his eyes. "You came from upstairs," he said, his voice as quiet as ever but his tone grave. "You had no time to go anywhere else before coming to us. And there is only one other resident on that floor."

She nodded, relieved to be able to tell them, whether she was supposed to or not. If Kori had still been here, she might not have said anything further, but she trusted these three with her life—and had, many times over. "It is Chuisu Ritsuro."

Dairamu frowned. "Did the flux do him in?" she asked.

Shizumi shook her head. "No. This is something far worse."

Her three Honjofu rose to their feet almost as one, dice and coin forgotten upon the floor. She half-expected them to go pounding up the stairs to see for themselves, but instead they stood at attention and saluted. "What can we do?" Genji asked.

As always, Shizumi felt a rush of gratitude for the big woman's support. "Nothing, for now," she replied, thinking fast. "Do not walk around too much. I gather you did not see anyone go past recently?" All three shook their heads. "Which means whoever did this came from somewhere else upstairs." The upper floor continued on past the section that was their barracks, but the doors at either end were sturdy wood rather than rice paper and locked securely. Only a handful of people would have keys to those, though the locks could no doubt be picked by an accomplished thief—or assassin.

Her musings were interrupted by Kori's return. Taikoro Maniko was at his heels, Itamon and another Honteno behind her, and Shizumi was once again impressed with the older woman. It was the middle of the night, yet she seemed as if she had not yet slept, nor were her eyes dulled or her posture drooped from fatigue. The tall Taikoro seemed as sharp as ever as she asked, "Where?"

"This way." Shizumi led her up the stairs, her soldiers automatically taking up guard at its base—much to Kori's consternation as the nosy soldier tried to follow them. Itamon and the other Honteno they allowed through, and so it was four of them that stomped onto the upper level. Idly she noticed as they ascended that she was the only one of them armed with nihono. The Honteno all bore ittei, and for an instant she worried that she had overstepped by carrying her blade. But this was their barracks—surely the restriction to not bear a sword within the palace's walls did not apply here? Regardless, that was a matter for later. There were more pressing concerns at the moment.

"I was asleep," Shizumi explained, leading them to the chuisu's room. "There." She pointed toward her own door. "I awoke to the smell of burning flesh and followed it here." She slid the door open to reveal the grisly scene beyond. "This is what I found. I have not entered yet—I sent for you instead."

That earned her a quick nod of thanks and perhaps even respect, though it was absentminded, for the Taikoro's eyes and attention were entirely upon the body there on the bed. "Is it Ritsuro Okari?" she asked.

"I believe so, yes," Shizumi replied. "It is the right size, the right build, what I can see of the features appear to match. If it is him, he should have a visible defect to his right ankle—he broke it once during a mission and it never healed correctly."

With a glance for permission, Itamon slid past them into the room, taking only two strides to reach the bed, and then used the tip of his yori-toki to peel back the robe that had stuck to the burned flesh at the figure's ankle. "Signs of an old break, badly healed," the warrior confirmed, straightening, his broad face wrinkled in a grimace he quickly wiped away. "It is him."

Kohori nodded. "What is that?" she asked, gesturing at something near the foot of the bed, in the narrow space between its frame and a low writing desk that seemed out of place in a warrior's room. They both watched as Itamon bent to retrieve it, coming up with a bound scroll and a handsome suzeri kabo.

"The writing box is Ritsuro's," Shizumi confirmed. "I saw it there upon his desk when I returned here." Even though he had not yet returned to active duty, the chuisu had still been her direct superior and she had felt it only proper to present herself to him. He had acknowledged her with his usual mix of chilly amusement, as if a small monkey had somehow donned deo, karuto, and the rest and learned to salute and follow orders. The chuisu had always been correct with her but had made it abundantly clear from his manner that he could not understand how a commoner like her—and a woman to boot—had ever even been allowed into the elite guard, much less promoted to gunso. Still, outwardly he had always treated her like any other sergeant, and for that she had been grateful.

The Honteno's own lieutenant was currently examining the items in his hand. "There's blood on them both," he stated, holding them up so Shizumi and Kohori could see—the other Honteno had taken up a position behind them, guarding their rear, and right now Shizumi considered that entirely prudent rather than paranoid. "At a guess, he was holding them when he was attacked." Using the scroll he gestured toward the body's neck. "Same cut we saw before, powerful but jagged, something sharp but not smooth."

"And he left the eyes again," Kohori pointed out, drawing

Shizumi's attention to her former superior's ruined gaze. "Why? Why take them from the first victim but not these two?"

"A statement?" Shizumi offered. "Some kind of message?" She frowned. "Or perhaps the first one saw something he shouldn't have, and that's why the eyes? Or did the killer need that first set for something, but now that's done and he does not require more?" She shuddered at that idea, since the first thing that came to mind was some sort of dietary restriction and a masked, cloaked figure swallowing the eyes whole. But they had to consider every possibility.

Beside her, the older woman nodded. "Any of those are possible," she agreed. "We just don't know enough." She was studying the body again, and the bed, as well as the rest of the room. "Itamon, is there blood around the body there on the mattress?"

"A little," he confirmed after checking, careful not to use his hands as he was still burdened by scroll and box. "But not much. Not as much as you'd expect from a throat wound." He checked where he was standing and scowled. "It's all here on the floor by my feet. He must have been standing when he was attacked."

"Yes, and dropped those, then fell back on the bed," Kohori said. "But that doesn't make sense either, does it? He'd have been right where you are now and if you toppled, you'd wind up across the bed, not laying on it properly." She shook her head, her gray bun whipping about. "No, he was placed there deliberately. But, again, a message? An insult? Or a last show of respect for the victim?" Her hands were clenched at her sides. "I wish I knew!"

"We do know one thing," Shizumi offered, drawing the Taikoro's gaze to her. "No one passed downstairs—my bantao were already awake down there and had been for some time. Which means the only way the killer could have gotten to Chuisu Ritsuro···"

"Is through those doors," the Honteno commander finished for her, glancing to the heavy barriers at either end of the hall. "So either they picked the locks there···"

This time it was Shizumi's turn to finish the sentence. "···or they had a key."

The older woman smiled at her, and she could feel her face stretch into a mirroring expression. It was not a happy smile, but rather a fierce one—the smile of a predator catching scent of its prey. When the killer had struck outdoors, they could have been anyone. But to kill Ritsuro here, in this hall, that required entry, and that was limited.

Which meant they had their first clue. And that meant the hunt was finally on.

CHAPTER SEVENTEEN

As usual, Maniko Kohori admired her fellow—and ofttimes rival—Taikoro's offices. Her own was stark, utilitarian, the only decorations being a handful of souvenirs from campaigns she had fought in the years before joining the Honteno—a finely crafted nihono, a handsome naritaba, an exquisitely enameled karute with one decorated wing sadly sheered clean off by her blade—alongside a beautiful carved jade fan the emperor himself had presented to her upon her elevation to Taikoro. But Fujibuki Haro, whatever else could be said of him—and she had said much, at least in her own head or sometimes out loud when out walking and sure no one was there to overhear—was a man of both wealth and taste. The scrolls and screen and the delicately embroidered silk pillows for guests transformed the space into one that was warm and inviting but most importantly handsome and refined, clearly belonging to an aristocrat of the highest order. The only thing out of place was the desk, which she remembered as having an array of small, lovely, clearly expensive sculptures and statues arrayed along its polished edge. Now it was bare save for writing utensils and, at the moment, the scroll and suzeri kabo they had found in Ritsuro Okari's quarters.

Haro had set aside a rather elegant example of utume, a tiny chest made entirely of paper but stuffed with straw, and was now studying the scroll, having unrolled it and flattened it atop his desk, showing no regard for the way the remaining droplets of blood marred the desk's smooth surface. She and Shizumi both stood at ease before him, waiting as he examined the parchment, and she was mildly amused to think that the swordswoman might seem almost a smaller, younger version of herself, with both of them standing legs slightly apart, hands clasped behind their backs, shoulders back, relaxed but ready.

"This is our annual spending report," Haro said at last, looking up from the scroll and stroking his mustache. His brow was creased in concentration. "Ever since his illness, Chuisu Ritsuro had taken an interest in our unit's finances. He was attempting to discern why we exceeded our allotment each year." For just an instant, Kohori thought she saw sorrow flicker across her counterpart's face. "It appears he found it."

"Do you think that is why he was killed?" Kohori asked, but Haro waved the comment away.

"No, it seems we have been perpetually overcharged on our purchases of rice and some other travel rations," he answered. "I doubt that would warrant such a brutal death. And how would that explain the two previous murders? This was almost certainly unrelated." He turned his gaze toward Kohori, and it was surprisingly clear, sharp, and serious. "Have you any idea who has done this yet, Taikoro Maniko?"

"Not yet, no," she replied crisply. "But this recent death was different. It was indoors, not safely out of view on the grounds. And it was upstairs, in the chuisu's private chambers, but there were soldiers awake and alert just below and they swear that no one passed by all night. Which means the killer had to come through the doors at the end of the hall."

"And those require a key," Shizumi put in. "We plan to interview everyone with such access."

"Ah, yes, good." Haro leaned back in his chair, considering. "That could indeed lead somewhere. Sloppy of the killer—but good for us." He glanced at Kohori again and offered her a formal nod that was a seated bow. "Taikoro, thank you for handling this investigation," he told her. "I am as always grateful for your dedication and awed by your prowess, and I have little doubt you will discover and deal with whoever is responsible."

"I—thank you, Taikoro," she replied, doing her best to conceal her surprise as she returned the bow with one of her own. "I am honored by your faith in me and your support, and I promise you it will not be in vain."

Now the head of the Honjofu turned his attention to Shizumi. "Gunso Misataki," he stated. "You have, as always, comported yourself with honor and devotion befitting and exceeding your station. Thank you."

She saluted. "I live to serve the Honjofu and the Empire, sir," her answer was crisp, but this close Kohori could see the shock in the younger woman's eyes.

"Please continue to assist Taikoro Maniko in this matter," Haro instructed. "I will send to Iwikaru and call Norio Shinjuru home, as we are now short our chuisu. Until he returns and I have time to consider that post, you will serve as acting lieutenant to the Honjofu, reporting directly to me except for matters of this investigation, where you will answer to Taikoro Maniko. Is that clear?" It was not said harshly, just matter-of-factly, but Kohori could guess how much the woman beside her was reeling from those simple statements. She merely inclined her head and saluted, however, to acknowledge the orders.

"Taikoro Maniko," Haro continued, drawing her attention again. "When Gunso Norio returns, he will bring with him whatever of our recruits he feels are suitable to join the Honjofu." He frowned, tapping his mustache again for an instant, then nodded. "The Honteno has been sadly depleted, entirely due to your heroic defense of the palace as per our Emperor's orders. I would like to offer you whatever recruits you desire from that pool, to fill out your ranks so that your guard can once again stand ready to protect this compound as needed."

Kohori's bow this time was lower, more prolonged. "Thank you, Taikoro Fujibuki," she replied. "That is most generous of you, and I appreciate it deeply." She did not say she was in his debt—again—though they both knew that would be the case. Still, it was generous, and she could hardly refuse. Finding decent recruits was a long, slow process, and here he was offering her soldiers who had already been vetted by the Honjofu and already put through at least basic training by them as well? It was a gift straight from the First Emperor himself.

"Then it is settled," Haro declared, and favored them both with a slightly distant smile. "Please keep me informed if there are any new developments, and anything I can do to assist further."

"Of course." Kohori bowed, as did Shizumi, and together they exited the office. Neither of them spoke as they walked along the hall, but once they were back outside and a sufficient distance away, she turned to the young swordswoman.

"That was···odd," she began, not sure how else to state her confusion, but Shizumi nodded.

"You mean how my Taikoro has suddenly become thoughtful, courteous, respectful, reasonable—and effective?" she replied. "Very."

"Did something happen while you were down in Bezenkai together?" Kohori asked. They continued moving, neither of them of the type to enjoy standing still when there was an alternative, her steps automatically taking her back toward her own offices and Shizumi keeping pace alongside. "I have seen soldiers re-evaluate their lives after facing death, especially if it was both unexpected and a near thing as to whether they would survive."

But the Honjofu shook her head. "Nothing of the sort," she replied. "We did not even encounter the resistance we'd expected." Kohori knew they had been sent to deal with the bandits who'd called themselves the Kindichi, the "kings." But that surprisingly large and deadly gang had already been removed by the time the Honjofu arrived—and, from what she'd heard, slaughtered by a single man, who she'd since heard referred to as the Butcher of the Kindichi. So a small army had marched on the region, prepared for heavy opposition—and found none.

"I suppose he could have encountered something on the way back," Shizumi mused aloud. "We parted ways in Bezenkai—I was tasked with taking my bantao and pursuing this so-called Butcher, while the Taikoro took the rest of our forces and returned here." She glanced at Kohori. "To come to your aid."

Kohori couldn't help herself—she snorted. "Yes, and I'm certain he loved receiving that request," she retorted. To plead for her rival's help had been demeaning, demoralizing, but utterly necessary. And he had arrived just barely in time—even an hour or two later and she and her remaining warriors might have been dead and the traitorous Rojiri in full control of the compound, with their own household guards arrayed to fend off the returning Honjofu. It could have meant full civil war, right there in Aihiri, and she was glad it had not come to that. With Haro's return three of the treasonous councilors had abandoned the attempt, throwing their support behind the Honjofu and the Honteno and claiming to have been loyal all along, and the remaining two had been easily defeated.

She cast her mind back to Haro's return and their brief encounter then. "When he came back, he was his usual self," she recalled. "Arrogant, presumptuous, never outwardly rude but always somehow insulting anyway."

"Sounds like the Taikoro I know," Shizumi agreed. "'Oily' is how I would describe him—and not just his mustache."

"Yes, precisely," Kohori said, matching her companion's brief smile. She forced herself to recall details. "He said—what did he say? That my loyalty and prowess did me credit, and that the Emperor would be well pleased with me."

"Like an indulgent parent praising the well-meaning attempts of a child." That was said with some venom, and from that and the twisting of her mouth Kohori could tell that the younger woman had endured such sly phrases from her superior many times. "But I arrived only a day or two later and he was different," she continued. "He greeted me fairly, even warmly. I'd disobeyed a direct order to return here, and he only commended my dedication."

"So something changed between when he returned and when you did," Kohori concluded. "Something that made him reconsider himself and his duties—and his attitude toward others. But what?"

Shizumi shook her head. "Whatever it was, I only hope it does not prove temporary," and Kohori could not help snorting again, even as she smiled in agreement.

"He *is* proving helpful, for the moment," was all she said, turning her attention back to the matter at hand. "I will work on that list, then we can begin interviewing the people on it."

"Hai." Shizumi saluted. "If I am not already nearby, just send word and I will return straightaway."

Kohori watched as the younger woman turned to go, her every movement smooth and graceful, determined but not hurried. Shizumi had swapped out her nihono for an ittei, she noted, the blunt iron tool thrust through her sash without need for a scabbard or sheath, the single tine hooked over the silk, yet she moved as if the weight did not impede her in the least. Had she ever been that dexterous, Kohori wondered idly. Unlikely. She had no illusions about her own skill, which was formidable—or about the fact that, even in her prime, she would have been no match for the swordswoman who had just departed.

It was interesting, the two of them had both been in this compound for several years, yet before this she could have counted the number of their interactions on a single hand. Yet the more time they spent together, the more she admired the young gunso.

As she continued on toward her office, Kohori admitted that, although she was still stumped by these strange murders, and still heavily concerned about who was committing them and why, she was at least grateful that, of all the Honjofu, it was Misataki Shizumi who had been assigned to help her resolve the matter.

With the two of them working together, she was confident that this elusive killer did not stand a chance.

CHAPTER EIGHTEEN

"Why," Iraku whispered, "are we going this way?"

"Shush," Ibaru hissed back. "Our master has chosen our path, and we obey." He dug in with his paddle, stabbing it down into the water and shoving it behind him with all his might, causing their tiny boat to surge through the water like an arrow shot from a bow.

"I never said I was not obeying," his younger brother grumbled in response. "I am just asking why, is all." He was rowing as well, sitting behind his brother and shoving just as hard at the water on the boat's other side, and because the two of them were so well-matched in size and strength their vessel's path was nearly arrow-straight.

Ibaru glanced up warily, but if the Silent Change noticed this exchange it did not react, and indeed gave no indication that it had heard them at all. Instead it floated forward, skipping on ahead almost giddily until it was forced to pause and then circle back lest it lose them completely. "I don't know," he admitted slowly, finding it hard to even vocalize such a mutinous thought. "But I am sure there is a good reason for it."

"Perhaps so," Iraku agreed. "But why, then, should we not know that reason? Would it not make more sense to inform us so that we might provide more focused assistance, rather than keeping us unawares and forcing us to flounder in the dark, hoping we chance to hit upon exactly what is needed from us?"

His brother shook his head, not bothering to answer aloud. In part because he realized that he had no argument for that. Why shouldn't they know their master's plans? It would indeed allow them to serve better. All they knew thus far was that the Silent had desperately wanted to cross the Wagata and Edishu rivers as soon as possible, and to reach Awaihinshi without delay.

Which then made it even more puzzling that suddenly, perhaps an hour ago, the Silent had changed its course of action. It had suddenly frozen above the water, like a hunting dog finding the scent. Then it had leaped to the right, not forward across the Wagata but down its length instead. They had followed this strange route farther to the right, along the Tonawa, almost back the way they'd come, and now they were being led to the river's far side, for—what, precisely?

A few days ago, the brothers would not have argued. They would not even have dreamed of arguing. But circumstances had changed.

They had changed.

Somewhere in the time since they and Kaemusei had reached the Tonawa, the brothers had begun to awaken again, as if from a deep sleep. They remembered everything that had happened since the Silent Change had swept over them, offering them a choice, giving them strength and power and fearlessness in exchange for color and passion and emotion, all things that seemed to be drifting back, bit by tiny bit. They had been little better than puppets at first, shadows cast by a hand moving before a fire, their every thought wrapped in cobwebs deep enough to swallow your scream and strangle your soul. As their master's focus shifted to look forward, however, evidently to plan for impending conflict, it relaxed enough for Ibaru and Iraku to find their voices again, and their emotions. They began to think for themselves, to ask questions—and to be difficult about the answers, or lack thereof.

They had begun to see themselves as separate from the Silent Change. They still believed in their master's cause, and still pledged themselves to attend and assist as much as possible and wherever necessary. But in their heart of hearts, the brothers knew that the Silent was only barely aware of them anymore, and that at any moment it might forget them entirely, or else decide it needed them for some obscure and dangerous quest. They had to watch out for themselves and each other, they realized. Certainly no one else would, not even the sentient cloud hovering impatiently above their heads.

Iraku's paddle struck the water again, and when the boat leaped forward this time its prow became stuck, for he had wedged it into the rich, muddy soil of the far bank. At last! Throwing caution to the winds he leaped from the boat onto dry land, falling to his knees out of gratitude, relief, and exhaustion. That was another detail that had astonished them, for before this, all the way back to their first encounter with the Silent, they had charged along, not feeling fatigue at any point. They had not needed food or water or even sleep, but had continued on tirelessly in their master's service, buoyed by the hate and fear and anger and despair they caused in others and then drank from them.

Why, then, did Iraku's arms now tremble from his recent exertions? Why did he feel lightheaded from lack of food, his every motion blurry, his eyelids scraping across his eyes and simultaneously weighing them down, his breath ragged and sharp-edged and uneven?

When and how and most importantly *why* had he transitioned back toward being nothing more than a poor young man again?

And in that moment, the emotion welling up from somewhere deep and dark inside, Iraku felt something else he had not known since this strange journey began. He felt hatred, deep and pure and true—

—and aimed at the nebulous creature floating a short way above, strange flashes of color sparking within its filmy confines. If Kaemusei sensed its servant's hatred, it gave no indication, which only made Iraku hate it all the more, much like any child with an inattentive parent, despising them for their indifference and their careless ignorance.

Laying upon the ground beside him, Ibaru felt shades of his brother's emotions and responded intuitively, grasping and absorbing and mirroring the feelings of his only kin, so that it was two brothers who hated their master who rose to their feet a few moments later.

And, above them, the Silent drifted forward, still uncaring.

It flowed along, its shadow gliding over the ground, as it sped down the shore, toward a dark shape that cut the ground some distance ahead. As they neared it Ibaru saw that the shape was in fact an absence, for the darkness was a deep gouge in the earth, a slice that disappeared down below into cool, calm shadows and peaceful silence.

The Silent leaped ahead like a small dog returning a ball to its master. It circled that jagged hole once, then again—before diving down into the earth there and immediately vanishing from view.

The brothers did not rely upon sight alone to track their master, however. The strange bond they had with the Silent was still intact, the tug in their own souls, and so they could feel as it descended perhaps a hundred feet, then shot forward another hundred and paused there. Even at this remove, with so much dirt and rock between them, they could feel its giddy enthusiasm. As if it had hoped for a particular outcome, and now had found it to be true. The exuberance was so overwhelming the brothers found themselves grinning at each other as they stood there beside the hole, waiting. And when first Ibaru and then Iraku shut their eyes, they found it was as if they were looking through the Silent's senses instead, seeing what that shifting cloud saw.

They saw the long, broken causeway it had drifted along. They saw the ruined towers to either side, beauty and grace evident even in those small shards and twisted fragments. They saw the wide boulevard that ran across the end of the causeway, stretching into the dark in either direction, a sturdy stone wall rearing up behind its far side—and the extensive row of towering, sturdy cages that stood there.

They watched, caught up in the majesty and the wonder and the horror of it all, as Kaemusei, the Silent Change, passed through those bars as if they were not there, dissolving the metal with its touch, and then sailed from one row to the other.

And, under its touch, the remnants left in those cages began to stir. And change.

Through their link the brothers could hear the clatter as bones rose from the cage floors and reassembled themselves, joint to joint, end to end. In many cases those bones reknit in their former pattern, while in others they clustered with former strangers to create something blended between them and wholly new. And as each shape finalized, its bones locking together, it stalked or marched or crawled or flew back down that first causeway, down the rough stone chasm beyond that, and then up, up out of the darkness and into the day, bursting upon the brothers as if wrought from the earth itself and cast out into the light.

They stared at the creatures that rose and arrayed themselves along the shore. There was one that was long and sinuous, innumerable tiny bones making up its length, longer bones forming the massive wings that swept it up into the air overhead, arcing and swooping in long, lazy circles. There was another that was massive, each bone of its thick legs wider than a grown man, its frame stooping slightly as if afraid it would brush its horned, beaked skull against the sky, rows of surprisingly delicate bone spurs running along its back. Then there was the one that looked like an oversized man until you realized that it was in fact made of tiny skeletal bodies, like a child pretending to be large by wearing its father's robes, more of them hanging down from its arms like great curtains—or bat wings.

The figures kept emerging, filling the plain around them, each one different, each one somehow monstrous, each one winged in some way, each one ultimately nothing more than old bones reanimated with the Silent's wild energies—and each one evidently waiting for its new master's commands as Kaemusei hung in the air before them all, a proud parent beaming down on its children, a satisfied general admiring his troops.

For there was no doubt in the brothers' minds that this was indeed an army, and an awesome one.

The only question was, who were they unleashing this army against? Because whoever it was, the Silent had been concerned enough about them to detour here to this strange hidden city in order to retrieve and animate these forces to throw against it.

What could be waiting for them, the brothers wondered as they fell into step at the head of this strange army, that was so powerful, so dangerous the Silent Change itself had been afraid enough to desire reinforcements?

Whatever it was, they knew they were about to find out.

CHAPTER NINETEEN

Kagiri sat upon his horse, gazing down at the village below.
Irohito. That was what Kishin Narai had said it was called.
A small, rough-hewn place, only a handful of simple homes of the stilted variety often found along the water's edge, not that dissimilar from the even smaller village where he had grown up, only these were larger and sturdier. A few homes, a barn or warehouse of some sort—

—and a long, low building, under whose wide porch sat or paced several men in conical hats, bearing poles that widened and flattened at the top.

A barracks. Built specifically to house the aiashe that patrolled this region, keeping it safe from bandits and other interlopers. And preventing such unwanted folk from crossing the Edishu and reaching Awaihinshi, which was now so close Kagiri could make out its many tiers and the thick walls that surrounded its base.

This was what he had hoped to avoid by crossing the Tonawa early instead of waiting for it to intersect the Edishu. But of course they had to traverse the smaller river regardless, and the empire was canny enough to set towns like Irohito just far enough apart to police the entire waterway. If he turned to the left and shaded his eyes against the sun's glare, he could just make out what might be the next town over. The barracks there would be able to reach Irohito in an hour, perhaps less, assuming either someone here lit a signal arrow or they had guards there watching this way in case of trouble from the east.

Kagiri knew he has to prevent such a signal from being launched. He could perhaps handle an entire chotao, though he would not want to bet his life and those of his followers on such an outcome. Two chotao would be well beyond even the Gensaiba's skills. And if they were already out on the water, unable to defend themselves from well-placed archers both here on this shore and shooting down from the walls of the city opposite?

His journey to reach the realm's capital and confront the emperor would come to an abrupt and untimely end.

"We can do this," Shito Kibi assured him softly. "A single chotao? Nothing to it. We won't even need the others—just you and I." Kibi was a master of the blade, but Kagiri suspected her words were pure optimism, of which she had an endless supply, rather than based in fact.

"She's right," Geido Shinen chimed in. "This is no problem. It will barely slow us down. Let's go get rid of them now. Then we can cross at our leisure."

Kagiri considered. He could charge down the hill and into the town. He would no doubt take the soldiers there by surprise. What sort of man would willingly ride straight into a company of aiashe, after all? It was pure suicide!

In his mind he could see the battle unfold. The three men on the porch would die first, of course. Arrows for them, fired from relatively close range, less of a challenge—even mounted—but nearly impossible to miss, and time was of the essence. Time and stealth.

Take out those three soldiers, tuck the bodies away somewhere they would not be found right away. Sweep into the barracks proper, surprising anyone even thinking of resisting, and eliminate them. Remove any and all threats. Simple.

Only, it wasn't that simple. And he knew that, even if the warriors latched onto his soul and sharing his body did not.

The first issue was they had no idea what sort of training the aiashe down there by the barracks might possess. Were they all freshly recruited, with little or no experience holding a weapon and no training in how to withstand a mounted charge? Or were they all seasoned veterans who had survived several full-on battles and would barely bat an eye at a single warrior foolishly riding out to challenge them? That, unfortunately, would be impossible to discover without actually facing them in combat, by which point it would be too late to apply any such insights.

The second issue was the one he had noted before, the proximity of potential reinforcements from both the other village and Awaihinshi itself. If they were going to cross by force they would need to do so too quickly for anyone here to raise any sort of alarm.

That type of induced silence tended to require extreme—and lethal—force, which was the other issue Kagiri had with the idea of a mounted attack. The men and women guarding the river had done nothing wrong. They were not criminals or villains. They were soldiers, serving their nation and its ruler. Why should that earn them a death sentence? Especially when he was not a rival nation and had not declared war upon this land?

The Gensaiba scoffed at this attitude. They felt it showed weakness, an inappropriate and unseemly sympathy. But their objections were muted, and Kagiri could guess at least one reason for that. Though the master warriors might talk of running roughshod over anyone who stood in their path, deep down they were all men and women of honor and discipline, which meant the notion of slaughtering barely trained, barely armed soldiers whose only crime was to be in the way must on some level be repugnant to them as well.

Still, Kagiri did need to cross the river.

He considered the matter for several minutes, studying the barracks. The building was situated right along the river's edge, the near side covered in a porch and the far side opening onto a long, wide wooden dock. Several small, fast-looking boats were tied up there, bobbing on the water, ready to be released at a moment's notice. They would have very little trouble catching any of the larger, slower ferries anchored along the village's dock a short way away.

If he stole those smaller boats—but no, that would not help. They could never carry everyone across, not without multiple trips. And claiming them would, again, require killing all the aiashe there, as he would not be able to allow even one to get loose and summon help.

No, that approach would not do, either.

Then Kagiri had a thought. And it was undoubtedly his, surfacing from his mind alone, for he could feel the Gensaiba's confusion and even condescension as the idea reached them. He ignored their responses, however, for the more he considered it, the more he liked the idea.

By the time he wheeled his horse around and made for his tent, he was satisfied that it would indeed be their best chance of success.

"This is beneath you," Nikiyu Sinchu insisted, his voice as sharp as ever. "It is beneath *us*." They were back in Kagiri's tent and he stood before his folding writing desk, his travel trunk, and the stand for his armor.

Kagiri ignored the voice, as he had the others, and instead reached for the ties holding his karute in place. When he had first emerged from the Tawasiri, he had faced off against a squad of soldiers and their mounted officers. From their bodies he had taken armor, but it had been piecemeal—a pair of suneoto here, a set of haidoto there. None of it had been made for him, or sized to him, and so none of it had fit perfectly. The helmet, for example, had been large enough to cover his head but loose enough that he'd had to be very careful, lest it slide forward and obscure his vision every time he tilted his head. When he had defeated the Kindichi, he had been able to trade out a few pieces for better versions, or at least ones better suited to him. While in Himsu he had visited an armorer and had everything adjusted so that it all fit him properly, as if it had been crafted for his measurements in the first place. Then he had had all of it enameled, unifying it visually so that it no longer looked like a random collection but instead like a single cohesive set.

He had chosen not to attach a sigil of any sort, for each of the Gensaiba had possessed one and had argued for its dominance. Nor had he allowed them to influence what color he chose. Instead he had followed his own preference, glazing the armor a deep, lustrous green that varied from near-black to almost jade but at random, each panel possessing streaks and shades but all working together as a whole. It was the most beautiful thing Kagiri had ever possessed, and the most valuable—

—and now, ignoring the protests that rose within him, he removed it piece by piece and packed it carefully away.

He had just finished tying the bakiro shut when a cough sounded outside his tent. "Enter," he called, and Shizu Yokori appeared, her sharp face carefully absent its usual look of haughty disdain.

"It is done," she told him, bowing. "Whenever you are ready." She had a garment in her hand, which she held out to him.

"Good." Kagiri accepted the simple maikiro, borrowed from Joshi, and pulled it on. The armored vest was too short for him, ending well above his waist, but it would suffice. Wrapping his nihono in a silken sheet, he carried them outside and tied that bundle and the heavy bakiro to his horse's saddlebags, then mounted, accepting the heavy wooden club and simple leather cap Buntai offered him. Then, along with the guards, he formed up behind Kishin Narai and the other merchants, following at a respectful but watchful distance as they rode down into Irohito.

Several of the soldiers had emerged from the barracks to observe the little procession, and though they were relaxed they had their weapons at the ready. An officer, a gunso, stepped forward to meet them as Narai held up his hand and their little caravan came to a halt.

"This is everyone, as I said," he informed the gunso, who was studying them all with a practiced eye. "We are returning home to Awaihinshi with our servants and our personal supplies and trade goods." The woman's gaze flicked across Kagiri, but in his borrowed vest and cap he was just one more hired guard, his club more of a deterrent than a real weapon. "Here are our credentials," Narai continued, producing a sheaf of official-looking documents and handing those over. "And this," he added, pulling a small but full pouch from his belt and tossing that to her as well, "should cover any fees."

Even with that apparent bribe the woman was thorough, insisting on poking inside each of their wagons and carts and inspecting many of their supplies and bundles. But finally she was satisfied and waved them on past, toward the docks. The ferries Narai had hired were already waiting, and it took only a short while for them to load everything on board and push off from the shore.

Kagiri did not relax until they were out on the water, and even then he faced back toward the town rather than the city ahead. But no one raised the alarm in Irohito. No one rushed out with flaming arrows ready to sink them mid-river. Narai and the other merchants were from Awaihinshi, so they had a right to return, and as far as anyone could tell they were bringing nothing dangerous with them.

The Gensaiba still grumbled within his head, but softly, barely perceptible. Hearing their complaints fade away, Kagiri allowed himself a smile. Was it an unorthodox approach he had taken? Perhaps, but he had no formal training. Others might complain that disguising himself like this had violated some sort of "warrior's code"—oddly, they would have had no objection to sneaking up on an enemy or to setting an ambush and laying in wait somewhere, but apparently felt that hiding your warrior status and, if you had them, your personal insignia, house crest, and so forth was without honor. But what did a simple boy from a small fishing village know of such things? Besides, would any code they knew still be relevant after so many centuries? Not that it mattered. His way had prevented needless deaths and would see him to the capital with no one the wiser, and that was the important thing.

Perhaps that was not how a master warrior would have done things. But it was how Kagiri did them, and he was pleased to note that he was once more the master of his own actions.

At least for now.

CHAPTER TWENTY

Noniki was meditating.

Or at least, that was what he was attempting to do.

Every morning upon waking and washing he found a quiet spot and sat, crosslegged, back straight but shoulders relaxed, hands resting loosely on his thighs. Then he closed his eyes and concentrated on breathing, slow and steady, in and out, letting his mind empty of all thought and his senses open to the world around him, exactly as the Hakara Ikibanichi had taught him. He repeated that in the evening, as dusk was beginning to fade to night, thinking upon the day's events and clearing away any questions or stress before sleep.

That had proven to be far easier among the Brothers of Many Spirits, in their secluded monastery, than it was upon the road.

When he had left Ginzai with Seikoku and Jitu Kanai, it had not been a problem. Although Seikoku had shown no interest in meditating herself, and teased him about it from time to time, she had always given him space to perform the cleansing ritual each morning and each evening. Kanai had been interested in taking up meditation himself, and after the first day had joined Noniki, the sturdy potter proving surprisingly good at emptying his mind and at sitting stock still.

It was only as more people had joined them that it had become more difficult. Some of those had also expressed interest and had tried meditating themselves. A few had quickly grown bored with it but others had stayed, and the morning and evening meditation went from two to ten in a short time, and then to sixteen. Some had scoffed at the practice but had quickly been shushed, reminded that this little traveling community was open to anyone who wished to join—provided they extended the same courtesy to others. Which included not mocking anyone for their habits or practices. "Do not meditate if you do not wish," Noniki had told several new additions over the weeks of travel, "but allow those who do the freedom and peace to enjoy it."

As the group had grown, however, Noniki had been faced with a new and different problem—people were eager to ask him questions, and many of them had trouble waiting until after he had opened his eyes again and risen back to his feet. Seikoku and Minawa did their best to intercept those, since neither of them participated in the morning ritual, but some simply insisted upon speaking to Noniki directly.

Even when they did not, it was a challenge to enter the meditative state when you had several dozen people moving all around you, carrying water, feeding animals, preparing their own food, reorganizing their gear and supplies, and just generally milling about and performing all the usual acts of waking up and getting themselves ready to face the new day.

Right now, though, Noniki was trying even harder than usual to tune all of that out and center himself, his mind, and his spirit. He desperately needed to find that inner peace and quiet—which of course made it twice as elusive. But there were answers he needed, and they could only come from within.

He had magic. That much had been proven. He had saved Kanai from the waters of the Wagata, had carried the potter to safety and then had propelled both his own raft and those of their friends across to the far bank as well. That had not been strange weather, or any other random occurrence. He had done that, himself and no other.

But how?

He had told Seikoku later that it had felt like a part of him that had always been asleep had woken up. Which it had. And, at the time it had happened, he had felt that this strange new part of him—which had perhaps always been there—would likely never go back to sleep again.

Yet it had.

Only, not exactly.

He could still feel it there. It was as if he had tasted a food like heioki that he had never tried before, and had discovered that he liked it. He did not have any more of the fried octopus balls but he now knew what they tasted like, and that if he ever had them again he would enjoy them. That was how this felt, in a way. He could tell that the part of him which had spoken to the river was still there, all throughout him, in every hair and every pore. But it was…inaccessible at the moment. Or no more accessible than, say, a particular organ. He could sense it but could not seem to use it, at least deliberately.

Which was a problem. What sort of matekai was he if he could only touch upon the magic reflexively, rather than when he wanted it and consciously called for it? In some ways, it would almost have been better to not have learned that he possessed such a gift, for now he would curse it whenever he needed it and could not use it.

That was why he wished he could meditate properly now. He'd hoped that, if he could quiet his soul, he could find this inner voice again, speak with it, somehow merge it in with the rest of him more fully so that he could access it at will.

But this morning meditation was proving particularly hard to achieve.

Which was why, when a hand came to rest on his shoulder, Noniki sighed and gave up. "What is it?" he asked, forcing his voice to stay low and even rather than snappish, which was how he felt. Calm, he reminded himself. You need to remain calm.

It was Seikoku, which was how he knew something must be wrong—she would not have disturbed him otherwise. "I'm sorry," she said, and her hurried words, along with the frown puckering her forehead, told him he was right. "I wouldn't interrupt but…we have something of a situation."

He rose to his feet. "What happened?" But even as he asked, he felt something and turned toward the south. "Someone is coming." He was not sure how he knew that, but the moment he said it, he knew it was true.

"Yes." He had rarely seen the lovely young thief look so

worried. "There are a dozen or so of them, on horse. I think they're from Jagimoto. That's the town we…got supplies from," she added upon seeing his puzzlement.

"Ah." Now he understood her concern. "All right. I will speak with them."

"Noniki, I…" She was wringing her hands, biting her lip before she blurted out, "This is my fault. I should deal with them."

Now it was his hand on her shoulder. "You did what you needed to, for the sake of our community, our friends," he reminded her. "If anything, it is these people now racing toward us who were in the wrong." He smiled. "I will try to make them see that."

Then, not wanting to argue about it any further, he turned and strode rapidly in the direction of the approaching horses.

Clearly, meditating would have to wait.

Seikoku had been close in her count, for there were fourteen in the group that rode up and came to a halt only a few feet from where Noniki waited, the lead horse close enough for its breath to warm his face. "May I help you?" he asked, glancing up at the horse's rider. He was a heavyset man, his face soft enough that flesh hung from his cheeks and jaw in thick jowls, his eyes nearly lost within the folds, but his hair was slicked back and pinned with handsome kanashi and his robes, though now dusty, were of fine silk and beautifully embroidered.

"You stole from us," the man declared, glaring down at him. "Give it back."

Noniki frowned. "I'm afraid I don't know what you mean," he replied slowly. "Who are you, exactly?"

"Who am I?" The very question seemed to affront the rider, for he reared up to his full height, which would not have been all that impressive if he had been standing on the ground himself. "I am Baniko Anahi!" he announced. "I am the master of coin for all Jagimoto!" He had a fan in his hand, its delicate panels carved and lacquered in an elegant flower pattern, and this he snapped shut and pointed at Noniki. "And you have stolen from us!"

Noniki dipped his head. "It is a pleasure to meet you, Ban-iko-san," he said. "I am Noniki. My friends and I did pass near your town recently, and several of our group bought supplies, but I hardly see how that could be considered theft"—he allowed an edge to creep into his voice—"unless you are referring to the prices your neighbors set for some of their wares."

"Do not play games with me!" Anahi roared, his face purpling with rage. "Your people bought nearly thirty gold worth of supplies from us—and the next day I discovered over thirty gold had been stolen from my counting house! Hand it over immediately!"

"Someone stole from you? Ah, that is unfortunate." Noniki shook his head. "But I fail to see what that has to do with us. Other than unfortunate timing, is there some reason you think we have your money?"

A self-satisfied smirk pasted itself upon the moneylender's face as he sat back in the saddle, arms crossed over his thick chest and thicker belly. "No one in Jagimoto would dare steal from me," he replied. "Thus it had to be you and your ragtag little group of wandering bandits."

Inside, Noniki was seething. This man, this horrible, pompous, self-important little man! He made his living stealing from everyone who crossed his path—good people just trying to survive, desperate and thus willing to pay his inflated prices—and now he was enraged because someone had had the audacity to steal from him in turn? And to take coin he did not need, when he stole from others who could not afford it? Noniki wanted to tear the man apart, or at least strand him in some distant land with no coin, no fine clothes, no fancy horse or mob of armed men, and see how he fared!

Instead he laughed. "Wandering bandits?" he repeated, keeping his tone light despite the temptation to snarl. He gestured behind him. "Do we look so fearsome, then? I have farmers, fishermen, netmenders, herbalists—but no bandits, I'm afraid. No soldiers either, so you will not need those." He nodded at the clubs the moneylender's thugs carried, save for the few bearing chokotos. "I am sorry for your loss, but I am afraid we cannot help you."

"We shall see," the fat horseman replied. He turned to his men. "Search everything," he ordered. "If you do not find the missing gold, take back all the goods instead. And anything else of value."

The thugs nodded and nudged their horses forward—only to find Noniki blocking their path. "I told you we could not help you," he stated, his temper reaching its breaking point. "Do not presume to tread upon our kindness, or our patience. There is nothing for you here. Go back to your town."

Anahi's answering smile was more than a sneer, nearly a leer, as he leaned forward to confront Noniki. "Stand aside, little thief," he warned, "Or my men will ride you down without a second thought." His little eyes sparkled as if he were excited by the notion, and indeed the fat man was licking his lips in anticipation.

"No." The single word reverberated, without and within. Inside, it echoed in Noniki's head, as if spoken by more than one voice. Outside, it echoed as well, mirrored by a sudden wind that whipped around him and then pushed against the moneylender, shoving him back so he nearly toppled from his horse.

And Noniki smiled.

I should have realized, he thought. He had been trying to meditate to find this voice again, to reawaken it. But it was not Brother Kalout, who had been in charge of the Brothers' education, or even Eldest Brother Taharo, master of the Hakara Ikibanichi, he should have been heeding here, nor even Brother Yamaki, their healer and his mentor. No, he should have been following the path of Brother Pilaru. Pilaru was in charge of the monastery's crops. He worked the fields from dawn to dusk, and often he missed meditation as a result. Noniki had asked him about that once. "Does it bother you?" he'd said. "Not being able to meditate?"

The wizened little monk had looked at him in surprise and then had laughed, for Pilaru was almost always cheerful, a smile creasing his sun-browned face. "Not able to meditate?" he'd repeated. "But I do! In fact, I am right now! You do not need a quiet room and a cold floor to meditate," he'd said, then tapped Noniki once on the forehead and once on the chest. "You only need what is here and here. Some of us think best when we're moving, rather than when we're sitting still." And he'd winked at Noniki. "Which are you?"

Sitting still, clearing his mind, Noniki had been able to cleanse himself, to calm his head and his emotions. But it was not calm that was needed here. It was passion. It was life. And for that, he needed motion, action, physical and mental activity. He needed to let his emotions flow through him, energizing him, waking his entire body to life.

Such as he was experiencing now.

"Go," he repeated, and lightning flashed in what had been a clear sky just a moment before but was now roiling with thick, dark clouds. "Go now, while you still can."

When Baniko Anahi licked his lips again, it was from nerves, not excitement. Still, he was not ready to accept the loss of his coin so easily. "Run him down!" he shouted, slapping the nearest man with his fan. "Do it now! Then tear this place apart!"

The man nodded, face set, and kneed his horse into motion— only to have a sharp wind strike him full in the side and lift him bodily from his mount, tossing him against the moneylender so both fell and landed heavily in the dirt. As if that had been a signal, the clouds overhead suddenly opened up, unleashing a torrent of hard, stinging rain so heavy it battered the men down against their steeds.

And, a few feet away, Noniki stood, dry as bone, where the rain ended in a neat line just before him, like a curtain had been drawn between two worlds.

"I will not tell you again," he stated, his words carried by the wind so that they pierced even that downpour. "Leave now, and do not look for us again."

Thunder punctuated his statement, followed by a flash of lightning almost directly above the group from Jagimoto.

That was enough to finally break their nerve. The men who were still mounted wheeled about, kicking into a gallop and racing back the way they had come. The man who had fallen staggered to his feet and helped his master remount, then fairly leaped into his own saddle and took off after the rest. Baniko Anahi started to say something, but lightning struck the ground just ahead of him, causing his mount to spook and rear and nearly dumping him a second time. When he had wrestled the poor beast back under control he tore off after his men, his face pale and his eyes wide and quavering.

Then it was over. Noniki let the storm end, the clouds thin and break apart, the sunshine return. He was no longer worried about finding the voice again—now that he knew it for what it was, life and energy and emotion, he was confident he could dip into the well as needed. Satisfied, he turned away from the fleeing townsfolk—

—and found himself faced with a slew of staring faces, all caught in various degrees of awe, wonder, delight, and even fear.

"Ah," he said. "I suppose I ought to explain."

CHAPTER TWENTY-ONE

Amani Denbi swept into the council chamber like a purple-robed thunderbolt, her face a stormcloud, lightning sparking in her sharp eyes. "What is the meaning of this?" she demanded. "How dare you insist that I attend upon you here! Who do you think you are?"

Sunao Tadazi leaned back in his chair, hands folded across his ample chest, the tips of one finger tapping the chasai thrust through his sash, and smiled beneath his mustache. "I do not *think* I am anyone," he replied slowly, enjoying how his delay infuriated his fellow Rojiri. "I *know*, however, that I am Sunao Tadazi, scion of one of the oldest houses in the Empire, one of the Emperor's own councilors, and Dogenriku of his armies. The question, my dear Denbi, is who do you think *you* are?"

Her eyes still flashed fire, but after such a calm and pointed rebuttal the woman seemed to at least accept that bluster would not take her very far with Tadazi. Instead she sank down onto the seat to his immediate left, at the head of the polished and heavily lacquered table—her customary spot, and her right as the most senior of the Rojiri. He had briefly considered taking that seat himself, just to infuriate her further, but had decided to offer her at least that much of an olive branch. For now.

"What is it you want, Tadazi?" she asked wearily, letting down enough of her guard for her public face to slide, revealing the fatigue bagging beneath her eyes and the stress tugging at the corners of her eyes and lips. To most she would still have seemed as regal and indomitable as ever, but they had known each other for many decades and he could spot the telltale signs.

"What I want," he replied, leaning forward and linking his

fingers atop the table, "is for us to decide what we plan to do about our current predicament."

"And which predicament is that?" She glanced around the room, as if the beautiful gold-leaf flower-blossom panels and handsome green-enameled ceiling tiles and heavy, metal-capped beams might suggest an answer—or pose a threat. "Have the rest of the Rogiri been done away with? Are we the sole survivors? That would be a predicament indeed!"

"You know what I am speaking of!" he snapped, losing his temper and then cursing when he saw the smirk that touched her thin lips. Damn her for always knowing how to get under his skin! "We committed treason only a few short days ago!"

"Did we?" Having evidently satisfied herself that she was still in control, Denbi sat back, one hand tapping idly on the tabletop. "I have not seen or heard any evidence of that. Kenshin did, certainly, and was executed on the spot for such a betrayal. Nagao also broke faith and is being held against the emperor's return. But only the two of them had the audacity, the impudence, the sheer gall to go against the emperor's wishes and try to set themselves up as the new powers on the throne." The smirk was back, and stronger, but no longer aimed entirely at him as she added, "or was there something I missed?"

Though his hand itched to tug free and present with a flourish the parchment tucked into his sash, Tadazi restrained himself. He had not stayed in the game so long by playing his hand too soon. "Kenshin certainly got what he deserved, the loudmouth braggart," he stated. "And Nagao is hardly any better. But"—and here he leaned in even further, lowering his voice in case the walls had ears—"the emperor still has not returned. And we do not know for certain that he will. These are dangerous times, after all."

"They are," his fellow councilor agreed. "And our illustrious ruler has left Aihiri, his stronghold, and traveled out into the world, where such dangers abound."

"Not only that, he has gone to confront the forces of Fyushu," Tadazi added, warming to his theme, his mustache practically quivering. "There is no telling what could happen when he faces those barbarians, who are always ready to slaughter in an instant, with little provocation."

"We must protect the empire," Denbi offered, her voice crisp and clear, her words ringing throughout the large chamber, off the paneled walls, tayomi floor, and tiled ceiling. "We must honor our emperor's wishes and keep his realm intact in the event that he is no longer able to do so himself."

"Precisely!" Tadazi banged his fist on the table. "That is my thought exactly! We are patriots, you and I, but we are also realists. We do what must be done."

Now his fellow Rojiri stroked her sharp chin. "And what must be done, good Tadazi? For I am at a loss. The Honjofu have returned—surely that is enough to assure the empire will continue to run properly until Hibikitsu's return?"

That earned her a snort. "The Honjofu!" Tadazi jeered, waving the comment aside with one hand. "What do soldiers know about running an empire? And Haro—well, he is from an old family, true, and a noble one, but he has no vision himself. He is too mired in trivialities and routines to recognize that we are at a crossroads, a dangerous one, and if we do not act now, swiftly and decisively, the entire nation could be lost."

Denbi eyed him carefully. "You speak of taking charge," she noted. "In the emperor's name, during his absence."

"Yes, exactly," Tadazi replied, forcing his fists open and laying his hands flat upon the table before him. "We must take charge. You and I together. We understand what must be done."

Her eyes unfocused, staring somewhere past the gilt panels. "Maniko Kohori would need to be dealt with," she said, and although her words were as bland as if she were reading out ingredients for a meal, her lips thinned to almost a snarl and her brow furrowed. "That woman does not understand her place or respect her betters." The last was said with all the bite and venom of one who had suffered a personal insult. Tadazi understood—Kohori had refused to yield when Denbi had ordered her to stand down, citing orders direct from the emperor herself, and Denbi was not one to forgive such a slap, even from the Taikoro of the Honteno.

Perhaps especially from her, for the two had butted heads many times in the past, Denbi always pushing for more control and more authority and Kohori always blocking her attempts.

"Agreed," he said, and stifled a momentary flare of guilt at the decision. Kohori was a good woman, a good soldier, a good commander. He respected her immensely. But she was utterly inflexible when it came to her duty, and they could not possibly proceed with her in their way. "I can take care of that." He was not sure how yet, but he had all the resources of the army at his disposal, as well as those of his house. He would think of something.

Denbi nodded. "Good. We would need to speak with Haro next and determine where he stands in such circumstances. I can take care of that." Which was for the best. Denbi had spent a lifetime perfecting her rhetoric and could wield it like an instrument, soothing or stirring as need be. She was capable of sounding Haro out without the Honjofu's Lord Commander ever realizing what she was about.

"What of Yatahei?" Tadazi asked. Their fellow Rojiri, who was also Dogenkaishu of the navies, had joined them in their attempt to wrest control, and like them had backed off when he had learned that the Honjofu were on their way back to assist Kohori. Like them he was a seasoned elder statesman, but Tadazi worried that his naval counterpart might have had enough rebellion for one lifetime and might be unwilling to try again, even if this time the odds were far more in their favor. He was a good man, Yatahei, but he was at his best with his boats. He had no real stomach for true politics, or the extremes to which one must sometimes go to accomplish great things.

Sure enough, Denbi shook her head, her silvery bun barely wobbling with the motion. "He will side with the winner," she stated, "and that is enough." She favored him with a small smile and a tiny nod, barely a dip of the chin. "I will admit, Tadazi, I am impressed. I'd have thought you would want no more of this, considering how narrowly you escaped the last time." They had both received news of the Honjofu's return—from Yatahei, whose sentries covered the waterways that led to Awaihinshi—and had

withdrawn their forces only hours before Haro and his Bone Warriors had come marching back in "to restore order."

He grinned at her in response, his mustache tickling his upper
lip. "This prize is great enough to merit a second attempt," he
answered, "and this is the only other chance we can hope to get."
If Hibikitsu returned before they could consolidate power, that
was that, the moment over and done and lost forever. If they were
to make this work at all, it would have to be done now, while he
was still away and his fate uncertain. Then, even if he did survive
and come home, they would be in a position of power and could
deal with the problem then. Winning the throne was the key, and
time was of the essence.

"Very well." She rose to her feet as easily as a woman half her
age and nodded to him once before turning away. "I will see to
Haro, you to Kohori. Then we shall reconvene and discuss how to
proceed." With that she swept away, clearly pleased with herself
for having taken control of this impromptu meeting. Tadazi did
not mind. Denbi was at her most amiable and accommodating
when she believed she was in charge, and he was happy to let her
assume that for now. She would learn better later.

After she left Tadazi remained seated, drumming his fingers on
the tabletop as he let his thoughts roam. How *was* he going to
handle Kohori? The woman was tough and resourceful, obser-
vant and clever, and her Honteno were almost insanely loyal. Plus,
given recent events they were all on high alert, jumping at every
sound, ready to fight in an instant, and highly protective of their
Taikoro. How to get close to her, then? He could ask for a private
audience, but that would require him to best her alone, and he
was honest enough to admit that he might not be up to such a
challenge. Besides which, if he entered her offices and then her
body was found, there would be no doubt as to who had killed her,
and if these plans fell apart he did not wish to have such a crime
placed at his feet.

He could overwhelm the Honteno by main force, of course. They had totalled barely two dozen before all this began, and the recent fighting had halved their ranks. Even with the Honjofu assisting them, Kohori's forces numbered below thirty. He could summon a chotao and crush the entire Imperial Guard in one fell swoop.

Such a move was risky, however. He would have to leave not a single survivor, for even one witness could prove his downfall if their plans failed. It was also a degree of wholesale slaughter he was not comfortable with—not that he could not order such if it became truly necessary, but he would rather find another way first. Eliminate Kohori and the rest of the Honteno would fall in line—indeed, with her gone and Haro either gone or subverted, where else could they turn for orders but the Dogenriku of the nation? It had long rankled him that both special units were outside his control, and now he could correct that error while also eliminating an obstacle. Two birds, one stone—that was sound strategy.

Which meant he would have to target Kohori alone, but he would have to be subtle about it. He could task some of his more capable aiashe to do the deed, but quickly and quietly—perhaps they could disguise themselves as bandits and thieves, to divert suspicion? No, wait, as Fyushans—it would be easy enough to claim that nation had sent spies here to attack from within. Kohori had discovered them but they had been too much for her. Perfect!

He was already running through rosters in his mind, selecting who to use for this delicate but bloody task, when a small creak caused him to glance up. What was that?

It must have grown dark out, and the lanterns at the room's corners had evidently dimmed, because the council room was now awash in shadows, making the large space seem truly cavernous with the corners and even parts of the walls all but hidden from view. But the door to the hall, had he just seen that slide shut? Was that the creaking he had heard? "Hello?" he called out, annoyed to hear his voice quaver. He was Sunao Tadazi, for bone's sake! "Who is there? Denbi, is that you?"

No one answered, and he huffed at his own foolishness.

Jumping at noises and shadows like a child! What would he be doing next, starting at the fall of a leaf or the bark of a dog? Still, he could not help but place his hand on his chasai, gripping the carved, gold-capped baton tight enough that he could feel the lacquered wood creak beneath his fingers.

Still, he heard nothing else, nor saw anything, and after a moment he relaxed and returned to his planning.

It was only then, when his attention wavered and his head drooped, that a shadow disconnected from the rest, gliding forward without a sound. It had reached the table's edge when Tadazi chanced to glance up again. His eyes widened as he took in the apparition before him, a shadowy shape whose very edges bled off like smoke, whose every feature was inky black—save for its eyes, which flared with crimson light.

"Who are you?" he managed to stammer out, shoving back in his chair and struggling to his feet, his hands tugging at the baton that was both a symbol of his office and his only weapon. "Help! Guards!"

The chasai was only halfway clear of his jeweled sash when the figure lunged forward, its one arm sweeping around in a fast arc, the shadows from its hand jutting out and tapering off into a spike or blade of the same darkness. That vaporous edge sliced across his throat and Tadazi's knees buckled as pain shot through him, radiating outward from that wound. His hands rose from his weapon to clutch at his neck and he stumbled, slamming his stomach into the table's edge and reeling backward, toppling his chair and then falling across it as he struggled to draw breath past the jagged, throbbing agony in his throat. Tadazi hit the ground hard and thrashed about, struggling to stand again but unable to rise as his limbs spasmed, his breath coming in rattling gasps now, his vision starting to blur, his limbs beginning to go numb.

The last sound he heard was the stomping of feet nearby and then the clatter of someone's mailed hand shoving open the chamber door.

CHAPTER TWENTY-TWO

Suda, Chimehara was pleased to note, sat still as a statue. She had worried that the girl might fidget, but should have known better. Though the child still had difficulty with a great many things and often did not follow correct behavior in public, one thing she excelled at was going still and silent. She could sit for hours without moving, her eyes fixed on a single point, seemingly dead save for the faint movement of her chest as she drew slow, steady breaths. Exactly as a hunter eyeing its prey.

At this moment, of course, they were not hunting. Though Chimehara did have a target in mind, that would be for later. For now, clad all in white as the rest of their house was, they simply sat patiently, watching as Master Eijiri and Madam Ponsoi approached the front of House Chohu's private temple, moving in slow and stately steps down the tiled floor until they reached the large stone tablet set there, leaning against the two coffins upon their low platform. A basin of water was brought for each, and they rinsed their hands, then produced small packets from the folds of their robes. Acting in almost perfect concert, the master of the house and its true mistress—for even though Master Eijiri was married with children, no one could dispute that it was Madam Ponsoi who was the most powerful and influential female within these walls, having knowledge of everyone and everything that happened here, such that even Eijiri often bowed to her judgment—extracted a pinch of incense from their respective packets. Crouching, they set the incense in the burners there before the tablet, then bowed, rose, and retreated to their seats in the front row, tucking the rest of the packets away in their left sleeves.

Once that was completed, the rich scent of the incense rising and wafting across them all as it filled the vaulted space, the priests rose from their own seats along the same row and, stepping forward and turning, they began to chant the start of the funeral service.

Chimehara paid close attention to those around her, as did Suda. Neither of them had ever attended a proper funeral before. Death was cheap in Suranmui, after all, and to waste time mourning was to leave oneself vulnerable to those less inclined to distraction. Now they were among civilized folk, however, and were expected to behave accordingly, observing all the minute customs that made up polite society.

Still, Chimehara had had to assure her young charge several times as they prepared for this day that no one would attempt to stab them in the back while they sat in prayer, or poison them at the ceremonial tea afterward. Those warnings had been half for herself, too, and she had not argued when Suda had requested to bring her knife. After all, there was civilized and then there was careless.

She had been able to acquire a description of a funeral ceremony from a bookseller she knew, and she and Suda had studied that carefully, so now they were able to stand when expected, sit when required, and mouth the appropriate responses at the right times. She did feel that it was all a bit excessive, and more than a little foolish, but at the same time there was a certain grandeur to the entire process. How nice to think that, after you died, you could be laid out in your finest kitoro and jewels, painted as if for a formal dinner, for all to see and admire and mourn. That was so much finer than dying alone and unremarked in a ditch.

The ceremony seemed to last forever, though Chimehara knew it was in truth only a few short hours. Not so much time to surrender in order to remember a life—or, in this case, a pair of them. Afterward, the bodies were carried out on the shoulders of the most senior men and women as well as the deceased's closest kin, to be taken to the house's private funeral chambers. There they would be rendered down, the flesh boiled away so that only the bones remained. Those would be extracted from the rest using long metal chopsticks reserved for this purpose and placed in a pair of urns, which would be kept by the family for forty-nine days. After that the urns would be placed in Master Eijiri's care, their contents added to House Chohu's bone repository, preserved there for the house to use as its master saw fit, the better to help them survive and prosper.

While that was being attended to, however, everyone else rose and removed to the gardens, where a light repast was served in honor of the deceased, with much tea, food, and rice wine. Many toasts were made in the deceased's memory, and many stories were told about their life.

Chimehara participated in several such toasts in order to not seem ungrateful or uncaring. After that, however, came the moment she had truly been waiting for.

"You have my deepest sympathy," she stated, having left Suda in Yuni and Rataru's capable hands—the girl continuing to charm the cleaning ladies and receive many sweets in return—and entered the small covered structure that had been erected at the garden's far end to bow deeply to the small, hemp-clad figure seated there. "Your parents were fine people and they will be sorely missed."

"Thank you," Ruisoki replied, dipping his head in an answering bow. "I appreciate your kindness and I know that my parents would be grateful for your high opinion of them." His voice was leaden, his posture slumped, his head lowered, his hair loose and falling around his face. He was the very picture of filial grief, a small child whose parents had been taken from him far too soon and who was now struggling to contemplate a life without them in it. He would not be alone, of course—House Chohu looked after its own. He would continue to live here and be cared for, clothed, fed, educated, and would eventually take his place among the house's many workers, at whatever task Eijiri felt him best-suited for. But never again would he feel the warmth of his mother's embrace or the cheer of his father's proud gaze.

Chimeharu had no idea what those must have been like.

"Your mother was a kind woman," she commented, lowering

herself to sit opposite the boy. She was not the first to assume such a position today—he would sit here from dawn until dusk, mourning, and during that time any member of the house might visit him to extend their sympathies. For some that meant only bowing and offering a few words, while others would sit and talk with him for a more extended period. "I felt almost as if she were a mother to us all," Chimehara continued now, keeping her voice soft so that no one beyond the tiny pavilion would hear, and her tone light and conversational. "Almost a mother to thousands."

Beneath his loose-hanging hair, she saw the boy's eyes dart toward her, though his face remained slack, a perfect mask of grief. Still, she had been watching for that look, and had to resist crowing in triumph and delight.

And, now that she was sure of her prey, she began to slowly, carefully close the trap around him.

"I believe she was good with plants, was she not?" she asked. "I would often see her here in the gardens, admiring the many flowers. Do you share her passion for such things?"

"I am afraid I do not have a good touch with green things," Ruisoki replied, his voice still coarse with sorrow. "I fare best with books and scrolls, old dusty words from long ago."

"Ah." She nodded. "One can learn so many things from books, can one not? I am often in awe. Histories, languages, customs, medicines—so much is available given the resources and the time and determination to look through them properly." She paused, tapping her lower lip with a forefinger. "Why, I believe if I read a treatise on plants it would tell me not to touch certain flowers, for fear they might prove poisonous. Some are so deadly they can kill in an instant, did you know that? Others take a great deal longer, and repeated exposures, but slowly wear away strength and stamina, leaving you weak and sickly, until eventually your body can no longer support itself and you die, seemingly of natural causes." She leaned forward until her forehead was nearly touching his hair. "But, if reminded, those who knew of such things might suspect foul play here. Especially given the presence of the Senoha-a around this very garden's edges."

Senoha-a, whose name meant "Mother of Thousands."

The boy tilted his head so he could regard her, eye to eye. His were cold, as she had noted when she had seen him walking behind his parents that day, and utterly calculating. There was not a shred of sorrow in them, not a hint of remorse, not a touch of grief. "What do you want?" he asked, his words barely loud enough to hear.

"Was it in their tea?" she replied instead of answering directly. "Or mixed into their food?"

"Tea at first," he admitted, clearly aware that there was little point in dissembling now. "Later, as they grew weaker, I added it to their broth as well." His lips twisted for an instant. "I was the dutiful son, bringing them their meals. They never thought to question." He said that last with disdain, as if disgusted by his own parents' lack of suspicion.

"You used the leaves, did you not?" was Chimehara's next question. "The flowers would have been too potent, and their flavor too noticeable. The leaves would take a good deal longer to be fully absorbed through the body but they would be much more subtle."

"Precisely. It took months," he confirmed, a faint, satisfied smile touching his wide, thick lips for an instant before he remembered himself and banished the expression, once more donning the appearance of grief as if it were a convenient robe. "Months in which they got weaker, day by day, hour by hour, and never understood the reason why. How did you know?"

"I did not, not for certain," she answered. "Not until just now. But seeing you behind them that day in the gardens—you should have been more upset. In more shock. Your parents were both gravely ill and you looked sad, but to a child who truly loved them it would have been heartbreaking. And you were only stiff and distracted, barely concerned at all." She waved a hand at the gardens beyond. "Senoha-a grows in abundance here, and even a small child learns quickly never to touch its flowers or buds, but few realize the entire plant is poisonous. It was a clever choice, since even if someone discovered what had made them ill you could have passed it off as your mother accidentally ingesting some of the pollen from her time in the gardens, then passing it along to your father when they were intimate." She had sat back while stating all of this, but now leaned in again. "But why?" she asked. "Why kill your own parents?"

"Why?" Now his face did twist, but not with grief. Instead it was anger that wrenched at his broad features, that blazed across his cheeks, though it never touched the ice in his eyes. "You have no idea what they were like!" Though his words were still low, they were laced with hatred, hot and heavy. "Master Ryoto and Mistress Etsuki! The perfect couple! So kind, so sweet, so useful! Only, not so kind to a boy who was no good with gems, whose eyesight could not perceive the difference between two pearls, who was better with musty old texts than with people and conversations and bargains!"

His eyes squeezed shut for a moment. "They never hit me," he continued, his tone leveling out now, becoming almost monotone, as if reciting facts. "That might have been easier to bear. It was just their constant disappointment, like I was a failure but they would love me despite that. I couldn't bear it." He sighed and blinked his eyes open again to study her, showing none of the lust she saw from most males, only a detached, almost resigned curiosity. "What will you do now?" he asked. "Will you turn me over to Master Eijiri for discipline?"

Chimehara tapped her lip again. "I could," she replied. "Certainly, by any normal standard, you would deserve that. Murdering your own parents—that is surely a serious offense."

Now the boy's head tilted and his eyes narrowed slightly, considering. "You say that as if it were something you had read about, rather than knew personally," he commented with the insight of someone far older. "As if you were outside it all. And you do not seem horrified by what I have done."

"Horrified?" She nearly laughed, but remembered the occasion in time and merely smiled. "No, Ruisoki, I am not horrified. I grew up without parents, so I have no sense of the normal attachment one should feel toward theirs. You found living with them unbearable, and so you took steps to alter your situation. Clever steps, careful steps, steps that only someone familiar with such methods might have noticed." She paused to see if that sank in, and was gratified when his eyes widened. "You are a clever boy," she told him, not to compliment him but because it was true. "You have a quick mind, and a certain…willingness to do what must be done in order to achieve your goals."

Now he was studying her carefully. "You are beautiful," he told her bluntly, also just stating a fact, "and you know it. You use it. It is a weapon for you, isn't it? But you are clever, too. You have many more weapons than most people realize." He hesitated before adding, "and you are also…willing to do what must be done."

She favored him with a nod and another smile, "I think we are of a similar mindset," she agreed. "And because of that, I would like to make you an offer. I could train you, Ruisoki. Teach you not to make such mistakes again. Teach you to use your gifts and grant you several others. Prepare you for a life where you can get what you want, no matter who stands in your way."

"And for this you will not reveal what I have done?" he asked.

Now she did laugh, only a single short chuckle, low enough that no one else would hear. "I will not turn you in regardless," she assured him. "Consider it a mark of respect from one craftsman to another. No, you can continue on your own if you'd prefer. But there are things I can teach you that you will not find in books. And there are things you will know that I do not, that can help me as well. It would be to both our advantages, I think." She offered him another smile. "And you would be with someone who appreciated what you can do, what you are capable of, rather than people who judged you by what you could not."

The boy considered that a moment, then nodded. "Yes," he stated. "I believe I would like to learn from you. Thank you." And he dipped his head, the bow of a student to his teacher.

"Excellent. I will wait a few days, as is proper, then speak to Master Eijiri," she said as she rose to her feet, bowed, and backed away. "I will see you soon, Ruisoki."

She had no doubt that the head of the household would agree

to her request. Though they were honorbound to care for the orphaned boy, having him living here would only remind everyone of his dead parents. If she took him, he would still be raised by House Chohu and thus their debt would be fulfilled, but he would not be constantly in their sight, and no one else would have to be responsible for his upbringing. It was a kindness upon the house and would be gratefully accepted.

And for her part, she would now have two children to train. Suda, who was eager and quick but rough—and soon Ruisoki, polished and cold and methodical.

Between them, they were the perfect killer. And both of them would be beholden to her and would do her bidding.

CHAPTER TWENTY-THREE

"This is not what I expected," Otokai protested, his strong, capable hands holding a braided leather whip between them. It was the mark of his trade, both a tool and a symbol, and he had a tendency to fidget with it whenever he was agitated, Seikoku had noticed.

Right now the horsetrader was twisting the whip as if it were a chicken whose neck needed to be wrung.

Minawa laughed, the old woman's sharp bark cutting through the murmuring. "You did not expect our leader, our teacher, our guide to turn out to be a matekai filled with wondrous magic?" she asked, warping her lined face into an expression of surprise. "Why ever not? I thought nothing could have been more obvious! I am only surprised it took so long!"

That brought some laughter but also more muttering, not all of it amused, and Seikoku realized she had best step in before things got ugly. "Yes," she agreed, raising her voice to cut through the chatter, and was gratified that the crowd ringing their nightly fire fell silent to listen. "You are right, we did not expect this. How could we? There have been no matekai since the Schism! This is wholly unexpected, and new, and even a little frightening. It is beyond anything we have experienced, and so of course you are right to be concerned and cautious."

She turned slowly so that she could take everyone in before she continued. "But think about it—is this not exactly what Noniki was speaking of just the other day? We are the first of a new day, the dawn of a new era in Rimbaku. We are learning new things, new skills, new trades, without the help of aishone. We are becoming something new and wonderful!" She raised her hands, then lowered them with a rueful shrug. "And what is newer and more wonderful than magic?"

For a moment, everyone was silent, and she imagined she had won them over. But of course it was too good to last.

"How do we know he will not turn on us?" Ratal asked. He glanced around at his fellows, his voice rising. "How do we know the magic will not change him, warp him into something monstrous, something that sees us as the enemy—or as prey? What if he becomes like the akatai, filled with malevolence and mischief, and we become his playthings, for him to torture whenever he grows bored? What then?"

That brought more mutterings, much of it dark, until Kanai cut in. "What if he becomes a donkey and offers us rides upon his back?" the potter wondered aloud. "I will be first in line!" The mutterings turned to chortles and giggles, and Seikoku could have hugged the man. Good old Kanai! He might not be the quickest thinker, but his good nature and good heart often led to just the right words at just the right time!

Now Kuma spoke up. "I do not know anything about magic, save the old stories my auntie read to me when I was a girl," the washerwoman offered. "But I know Noniki. I have followed him since Madam Ushi and I met him in Shakomi and heard his words and saw his heart. That has not changed. He is still the same man and I will follow him still, whether he is a matekai or an akatai or the First Emperor himself!"

That brought a ragged cheer, mixed with claps and stomps of approval, and Seikoku smiled. Nor did her relief fade as Isoro stepped forward, clearing her throat before saying, in that soft voice of hers, "I agree with Kuma. Noniki is a good man, a kind man. I do not know what to make of this magic of his, but I know what to think of him, and that is enough. You should always be wary of a sword's edge, but as long as it is wielded by a good man you should never have cause to fear it."

There was little more to say after that, and the impromptu post-dinner meeting broke up as people finished their food and began washing dishes and packing away supplies and readying for bed. But Seikoku caught up to Otokai before he had wandered too far from the fire. She was less worried about Ratal, especially after Isoro's words, for she knew he and Amon worshipped the quiet herbalist. But Otokai tended to keep his own counsel, and when he did speak his words carried some weight around the circle.

He paused as she approached him and held a hand, though there was a smile on his long face. "I know what you would say, Seikoku," he told her, "and there is no need. I did not say that I was afraid of Noniki, or that I no longer believed in what he said, or that I meant to leave. Only that I was surprised and concerned." He tapped the whip's handle against his leg. "I appreciate that our little community affords me the opportunity to express such concerns without censure or ridicule. There is nothing wrong with a healthy discussion, as long as all opinions are allowed to be considered."

She nodded. "You know Noniki, above all others, favors such fairness," she reminded him. "That is part of why I am not concerned. Though," she grinned, "I was certainly surprised, myself!"

Otokai shook his head. "If so, you took it in stride far better than I," he told her, a twinkle in his eye. Then he dipped his head and turned away toward his cart and the two horses who drew it but were currently grazing beside it.

Seikoku watched him go. She did not think he would cause trouble, but perhaps Noniki should speak to him privately, just to reassure him further. With that in mind, she went looking for the matekai himself.

She found him beside the small stream near their camp. He was seated upon a large boulder there, though she did not remember there being such an object when they had first paused here for the evening, and studying the water. It was not a deep stream but its waters were quick and lively, clear and very cold, and they created a musical trickle as they rushed past.

Only most of the stream's contents flowed normally, however. As she approached, she saw Noniki reach out his hand in a cupping motion over the water. A narrow current rose, arcing high enough to spill into his hand before falling back over it and down to rejoin the rest. He leaned forward, taking a sip of his captured treasure, and Seikoku burst out laughing.

"Is this how the mighty matekai uses his magic, then?" she asked, stepping up beside him. "To keep from having to bend down to dip his bowl?"

He was smiling when he turned to face her. "It seems that way, doesn't it?" he agreed lightly. "Who knew matekai were so lazy?"

"Well, certainly the only matekai I know is far from that," she replied teasingly. "He is one of the hardest-working men I know and would never treat something so grand so frivolously!"

That brought a chuckle from him as well. "He sounds very noble," he commented, then gestured behind her. "Would you care to join me?" There was a strange sound from her shadow, as if rocks were grinding together, and glancing back Seikoku watched as the ground shifted, sloughing aside to allow a large boulder to surface like a cork on the water, bobbing to the top and then settling more firmly into place just behind her legs.

"Thank you." She sat, a little gingerly, but the rock proved to be well planted now and offered a stable seat. That explained the other boulder, at least!

"How did it go?" he asked then, tilting his hand and looping the remaining water in a ring around it, which he then flicked upward, only to catch again. "Should I be worried that they might stone me, or try to drown me, or at least run me off with torches and clubs?" Though he was not looking at her, and his antics seemed to indicate a light heart, she could hear the concern in his tone. Besides, she knew him well enough now to recognize how much other people's good opinion mattered to him.

"There were a few concerns," she admitted, not wanting to lie. "But there were far more speaking in your support, and even those who had expressed worry seemed convinced that there was nothing to fear." She bit her lip. "You should speak to Otokai, though," she blurted out. "And maybe Ratal, too. Just let them see that you're still the same you as ever."

"Am I, though?" Now he did meet her gaze and she was surprised to see tears there, glistening but unshed. "What if I *have* changed, Seikoku? What if I'm not who I was? I have this...gift now, this power, and we've both seen what happens to people with power. What if that happens to me?"

"It won't," she promised him. Leaning forward, she took his free hand in both of hers. "Noniki, it won't. You're a good man, and that won't ever change. That's who you are. This magic, it's just a tool, a talent. It's not you." She squeezed his hand. "Besides, I'll be here to kick you into shape if you start misbehaving."

"Will you?" Letting the water ring disperse into droplets that rained back down into the stream, he added his other hand to hers, leaning in so close she could see the stars reflected in his eyes. *Still handsome*, she noticed. Maybe even moreso now as this serious, thoughtful young man than he'd been as that brash boy, though when he smiled or laughed she was happy to see that sense of exuberance still lived on as well. "Will you stay by me, Seikoku?" he asked now, his face intent on hers. "Will you keep me from going astray?"

Her heart leapt, her own vision blurring, and for an instant she could not reply, for her throat seemed to catch. When she did answer, her words were husky. "Of course," she promised, stroking the backs of his hands with her thumbs. "I'm not going anywhere."

They sat like that for a second, so close she could almost feel the air shift against her face every time he blinked those long, thick lashes of his, their mouths not more than a few inches apart, his breath warm and sweet against her lips, their breathing the only sound save the rippling of the stream and, somewhere, the call of a bird.

It was Noniki who finally pulled back, his face flushed, and released her hands, setting his own upon his thighs. "Who would have guessed we'd be here, eh?" he asked, his voice thick, his eyes still bright. "A poor fisher boy and a graverobber, on their way to see the emperor!"

Seikoku blinked, gulped air, then laughed, nodding. "It does sound like something from an old tale," she agreed, her words all tumbling out in a rush. "But shouldn't there be an evil wizard somewhere, or a dragon, or a horrible old witch?"

"Oh, there should, there should!" Noniki said, rubbing his hands together with glee. "And we are the only ones who can stop

him or it or her in time! It falls to us to save the kingdom!" He
laughed, that giddy boy surfacing again, and she laughed with
him, the brief awkwardness of the moment before fading back
into the easy, affectionate camaraderie they shared.

She sobered slightly, though, as her thoughts turned to that
tiered city they could see in the distance, growing closer by the day.
"Do you really think he will grant us audience?" she asked quietly,
winding her fingers together. "What if he does not? What if he
turns us away, after all this?"

"He won't," her companion assured her. "We will see him." He
raised his hands, and light gathered around them, as if the stars
had descended from the heavens above and wreathed his fingers
with their brilliance. "After all, who can refuse the matekai of
Rimbaku?" For just an instant, the way the light shadowed against
his features made him look almost sinister. Then he giggled and
it was only Noniki, tracing his fingers in the air between them to
draw first his name, then hers, then crude images of a cat, a dog,
and various other ill-made animals.

Even as she laughed at his antics, though, Seikoku could not
help but feel that he was right about one thing. She never would
have believed she would be here, on this journey, with him or any
of the others. A year ago, less, she had been a thief and a koshitsu,
beholden to none, surviving by her wits and her stealth, stealing not
just to stay alive but for the thrill of it, the sheer joy of outwitting
others and making off with that which did not belong to her. Now
here she was, one of the leaders of a small community, on the verge
of completing a trek halfway across the nation to reach the capital and demand audience with the emperor. And her closest friend
was this young man who grinned as he sketched what might have
been a snake in the air with the light from his fingertip, the first
matekai since their nation had been broken apart, the stuff of leg-
ends reborn, and one of the kindest, sweetest men she had ever met.

She told herself that it was only the sparkle of that snake that
caused her eyes to tear up again, and she laughed and smiled with
Noniki as she brushed those away.

CHAPTER TWENTY-FOUR

Kohori barreled down the halls, her knees protesting the pace with each pound against the tiled floors, but she refused to slow down. There were few people in the hall, and those who were there started and hastily got out of her way, which she took as a sign of respect and acknowledgement. The fact that she was still carrying her yanoi slung across her shoulder like a fishing pole, the glittering blade bouncing behind her and the long shaft with its polished endcap preceding her by several feet, surely did not factor into anything.

Despite her speed she still reached the council chamber behind Shizumi. The younger woman was conferring with Manari, and although the tall, thin Honteno towered over the Honjofu, Kohori could see how he deferred to her in the way he bent to better hear her words. Both of them glanced up as she skidded to a breathless stop beside them, a flicker of guilt quickly chased away by relief on her warrior's face and, surprisingly, nothing but relief and pleasure on Shizumi's as well.

"I was hoping you would get here soon," the young swordswoman began, raising her hand in salute and dipping her head as well. "I wanted to wait for you, of course, but I thought we should examine the scene as soon as possible."

"Agreed," Kohori wheezed out, then thumped her chest to get the air flowing again properly. "Sorry. Has anyone else been in there?"

"Only me," Manari answered. "I was nearby and heard what sounded like a shout. I rushed over, slid open the door, and—" He paused, gulping, his eyes wide, face pale. "Forgive me, Taikoro. It was not a pleasant sight."

She nodded. She had certainly seen enough of those herself, of late. "What did you do next?" she urged gently.

"I closed the door and placed myself here, before it," he answered, giving her a grateful look as he regained his composure. "Linai appeared—she had heard the commotion as well—and I sent her to fetch you." He bowed to her, then nodded to the Honjofu beside them. "I remembered your orders from the previous night and told her to fetch you both."

"Good." It was Reiko who had pounded on her door, shaking it almost to pieces before she'd had a chance to yank it open, so Linai must have encountered the chuisu first and relayed the message, then gone to find Shizumi. It was smart thinking—if she had insisted on locating them both herself, it would have taken twice as long. "And I take it no one has entered or exited since you arrived?"

"No one," Manari confirmed, his throat moving visibly as he swallowed. "Do you need me to…go in there with you?" he asked, his voice hoarse.

"No. Gunso Misataki and I will handle it," Kohori replied, taking pity on the usually stoic soldier. "Maintain your post here and do not let anyone enter." He saluted and she handed him her yanoi, then nodded for Shizumi to precede her through the beautiful gold-leaf doors.

They stepped inside, sliding the door shut again behind them, then paused to take in the scene. Kohori had been in here before, when asked to confer with the Rojiri about some matter of household security, but she was always impressed by the room, with its high, vaulted ceiling, the dark wood crossbeams linked by bronze caps and framing those beautifully decorated ceiling tiles; its lighter, stained wood columns separating the gold-leaf wall panels; its sliding wall panels that could be closed to split the vast space in two, framed by another heavy crossbeam with an ornamental railing above it that connected via narrow columns to the ceiling beams above; and of course the long, beautifully lacquered conference table that filled much of the floor, with its irregular outline and smoothed edges, the rings visible just below the surface proof that it had once been the cross section of a single massive tree. Elegant high-backed chairs were placed all around it—except in the spot diagonal from them, where a gap called out for them to investigate further.

Edging around the table, Kohori saw the blood first, staining the tayomi mats in a spreading circle, the woven fibers soaking up the crimson so quickly they barely seemed wet.

Then the body came into view.

She knew him at once, of course, with his thick hair that was still a glossy black despite his age, not a single strand of white or gray visible there or in his well-trimmed mustache. At his breast, where his purple robes had fallen open, she could see his kisoni, embroidered with the black bear crest of his house. She had often considered him a bear himself, gruff and intimidating yet a coward at heart, but now she felt only pity for him, and a touch of sorrow. Whatever else could be said of Sunao Tadazi, the Dogenriku had given his life to serve the empire.

Such a man deserved better than to be found stretched out on the floor like a battered fish, his back arched in anguish, his face twisted into a rictus of pain, his eyes wide and staring up at the ceiling as if he might find some release there.

Shizumi had moved carefully around both the body and the damaged portions of the floor, and now crouched on his far side, leaving Kohori free to approach from this angle. "His throat was cut," the younger woman pointed out, indicating the jagged tear with her forefinger. "Sharp but jagged, like the others." She frowned. "But he is not burnt like them. And he still has his eyes as well."

"Ritsuro Okari had his eyes," Kohori reminded her, squatting down to look more closely herself. "But you are correct. It is almost as if whoever is doing this is diminishing their attack rather than escalating it—from burnt and blackened and blinded to just burnt and blackened and now to just murdered." She frowned. "That makes little sense, though. I would expect them to grow bolder and more elaborate with each additional death. Not more hesitant and more simplistic."

"Perhaps the change is not one of choice," Shizumi suggested. She frowned, tapping her cheek in thought. "Ritsuro was just down the hall from me. That meant the killer had less time than before if he wanted to escape notice. This chamber is even more visible, plus there are guards roaming about, as Manari's presence demonstrates." She moved her hands to her knees, balancing perfectly on the balls of her feet. "He said he heard the noise and came running. What if he interrupted the killer? Perhaps this is not as elaborate because it is incomplete."

"So he meant to burn Tadazi-sama, but ran out of time and had to flee." Kohori nodded. "That does make sense. But it begs the obvious question—where did he go?" She gestured all around them. "There is only the one door and Manari has not left it. Is our killer a spirit, able to walk through walls?"

Her companion shot her a look that was a mixture of gravity, concern, and no little fear. "I would not rule out such a possibility," she admitted quietly. "We are seeking a killer who seems capable striking anywhere in Aihiri and disappearing into thin air, while the bodies he leaves behind burn to cinders and the eyes vanish with him. Given all that, is it so far-fetched to think it is an akatai—or worse?"

Kohori started to reply but was interrupted by raised voices outside the door. The panels were thick enough that she could see nothing through them, but as she rose to her feet the door began to slide open. She quickened her pace, hurrying back around the table, and was able to catch the door before it could open far enough to let anyone enter—only to find herself face to face with Amani Denbi.

"What is the meaning of this?" the senior Rojiri demanded, sneering at Kohori as if she were some washerwoman who had just spilled nightwater on her bed. "These chambers are for Rojiri only. Get out." The old woman's sharp eyes flicked toward Shizumi and narrowed slightly, no doubt upon noticing the black armor denoting a Honjofu, but her sneer never wavered.

Kohori was having none of it, however. "With all due respect, Madam Councilor," she replied, straightening to her full height and peering down at Denbi. "You cannot be in here. Please leave at once or I will have you escorted out." She bared her teeth just long enough to reveal that this was no idle threat.

The councilor sputtered in outrage. "How dare you?" she spat, her face mottling. "You may think yourself important, Maniko Kohori, but in the grand scheme of things you are still just a poor little soldier girl. And you had best stay out of my way." She moved to step around Kohori—and found Misataki Shizumi blocking her path. "Stand aside, Honjofu," she demanded. "I am Rojiri, and speak with the voice of the Emperor himself."

Shizumi dipped her head in a formal bow. "I regret that I cannot, noble Rojiri," she replied, her tone perfect, her face placid. "I am under strict orders from Taikoro Maniko and Taikoro Fujibuki, both of whom also speak with the voice of the Emperor." A glint appeared in her eye as she added, "And there are two of them, to the one of you."

Denbi opened her mouth to utter some vicious retort, but Kohori interrupted her. "When were you last in these chambers, Rojiri Amani?" she asked formally, crossing her arms over her chest.

"What? What business is that of yours?" the old woman snapped. She frowned. "What has happened?" Whatever else one could say about Amani Denbi, she was no fool.

"When was the last time you were in here?" Kohori repeated, willing her face to stone so that it would not give anything away. Possession of the details was one of the few advantages she had at the moment, and she was determined to hold onto that as long as possible.

Something about her tone or expression must have convinced the councilor that this was indeed something serious, for the woman replied with only a touch of asperity, "Perhaps half an hour ago. I met with Dogenriku Sunao to discuss some concerns." Her eyes widened a fraction. "Has something happened to him?"

"Was anyone else present for this meeting, or nearby when you left?" Kohori asked next.

Denbi shook her head, her silvery bun as tidy as ever. "No, no one." For once the arrogance dropped from her tone. "Is he all right?"

"Thank you," was the only reply Kohori gave. "I will have

someone notify you when these rooms are once again available
for your use." She reached past the councilor to rap on the door
with one knuckle, and Manari slid it open at once, then stepped
aside to allow Denbi to leave. Which she did, wrapping her dignity
around herself once more, head held high, eyes sharp and hard.
But she glanced back once before she departed, an unusually vulnerable gesture for one so fierce and proud, and Kohori nearly
broke and told her. Nearly.

"Ash!" Shizumi exploded as soon as the door had shut again.
"That woman is like a quisuin, sharp and deadly! I'd rather face a
dozen men with swords than try to bar her path again!"

"She is dangerous, and sharp," Kohori agreed. "And most
likely the last person to see Sunao Tadazi alive."

"Save for his killer," Shizumi corrected. "Unless you are
suggesting..."

That earned a bitter laugh. "No. If Amani Denbi wished
someone dead, she would never be so crass as to have them killed
moments after she had seen them." Kohori looked back across the
table, to where she knew the dead nobleman lay. "Whoever did
this was quick, deadly, and able to sneak in and out without being
seen." Tadazi might have been a pompous fool and a coward, but
as a young man he had fought in battle and had still retained
some of those old instincts. The fact that his chasai had still been
at his side meant he had never had the chance to wield it.

"Unless..." Shizumi turned away then, circling around the
table once more, and began tapping the wall panels, one after
another. She would tap, listen, then move along and try the next.
On the fourth panel, she straightened. "Here."

Kohori joined her and listened as she tapped again. Sure
enough, there was an echo behind the gold-covered paper. "It is
hollow," she agreed. "Which means there is a passage there."

They both began feeling around the edges of the panel and
along the columns there. It was when Kohori reached up to the
bronze joint at the top that a spot on that flattened metal pressed
inward. There was a faint click and the panel popped open along
the near side.

Peeling it back, Kohori and Shizumi studied the long, narrow corridor beyond. Clearly this was how the killer had entered and exited unseen. Only—

"Whoever did this knew about this passageway," Shizumi stated, saying what they both were thinking. "But how?"

"Knew of this—and had a key to the upper passages," Kohori added. "Or had the skills to pick those locks."

They exchanged a look, clearly thinking the same thing. Stealth and the ability to open locked doors was one thing—those suggested a thief or an assassin, someone from outside who had snuck in and was now attacking the compound's residents. But knowing where to find certain people, and now knowing secret tunnels even Kohori had never seen before, meant someone with inside knowledge.

Which meant most likely the killer was someone they knew.

The other question, beyond "who," was still "why," and Kohori growled in the back of her throat at that one. She was no closer to an answer there.

Except that one thing was clear. "First a caravan guard who did not even belong in Aihiri," she stated, as much to herself as to the young woman beside her. "Then a new Honteno. Then the Honjofu chuisu. Now a Rojiri, and Dogenriku of the armies."

Shizumi nodded. "He is growing bolder," she agreed. "And his circle is narrowing in, closer and closer to the center."

That was what Kohori had discerned as well. This killer was testing their defenses, their responses, at the same time that he was striking greater and greater targets. And after the Rojiri there was only one person placed even more highly—

The Emperor himself.

For the first time, Kohori found herself hoping that Hibikitsu took his time returning home.

CHAPTER TWENTY-FIVE

t was with a strange mix of reluctance and impatience that Hibikitsu stepped from the *Aio-akeo*'s fine teak deck onto the weathered oak planks of the dock which jutted out of a small, sheltered cove that butted up against the side of Awaihinshi. After weeks away, he was home.

Which meant, of course, that he was no longer just one of the dozen or so aboard the sleek takeneburi, tacking the sail and swabbing the deck and hauling in the nets when the boat's captain commanded. No longer was he just one of the many crowded in the rear at meals, eating and drinking and laughing with everyone else, listening to coarse jokes of a type he had never heard before he had embarked on this strange journey and which he still was too uncomfortable to attempt himself, but which made him guffaw along with the rest. No longer was he dressed in only ponmei and hosode, barefoot so that his toes could find better purchase on the slippery deck, a broad, loose-woven straw hat atop his head to block the sun's glare.

No longer was he free to relax and just be.

Now it was Hibikitsu, Echo of Victory, ruler of all Rimbaku, who stepped forth, resplendent in his gold-chased armor, imperial crest waving atop his karute, hair once again tamed and combed and pinned into a proper warrior's knot, jade kanashi sparkling in the early morning light. It was the emperor who nodded regally at the guards that had stepped forward, ever vigilant, as this unfamiliar vessel pulled up to the dock reserved for the royal family, the imperial councilors, and the nation's generals, and who accepted their swift obeisance with a practiced nod.

At least that answered one question, and the most urgent one at that. For if the Rojiri had succeeded in their attempted coup, it would be their own household guards who would have been holding this dock, and he would not have found nearly so warm a welcome. That meant that Kohori had succeeded in blocking the attempted rebellion, though at what cost remained to be seen.

That led to his next concern. "What news from without?" he asked the chuisu there, a hearty-looking woman with a crescent-shaped scar puckering one cheek. "Has the city been approached?"

"No, sire," she answered quickly, her voice as direct as her gaze was circumspect. "But the sentries indicate they are close." She frowned but did not lift her eyes. "This morning there were new reports, as well, of some sort of disturbance across the Tonawa. It may be that one of the two groups has split in half, to approach from two sides at once. We do not know."

Hibikitsu nodded. "Send word at once if there should be any news," he instructed. "Oh, and see that Daiso Futoba is paid well for her efforts to bring me here." The *Aio-akeo*'s captain, who had disembarked just behind him and now stood off to the side, nodded her thanks.

A whinny interrupted his thoughts, and he turned back just as Diritan and Nioko led Shisi off the boat. The black stallion reared his head once, glancing about, then seemed to accept that he was back home and settled. He nickered at Hibikitsu as the emperor stepped up beside him, rubbing his hands gently along Shisi's jaw and over his nose, and nudged him back. A moment later Hibikitsu had swung into the saddle and was riding majestically down the dock, toward the city walls. After so much time on the water it felt strange to be on horseback again, but comforting, too. Much like his homecoming in general.

The guards stationed at the dock's end pulled the door open before their emperor reached it, and Hibikitsu passed through without pause. Diritan and Nioko were several paces ahead of him, hands on sword hilts, and Ganema and Kenso and the others followed so close behind he wondered how Shisi's tail did not batter their faces.

From there, the ascent was swift. Awaihinshi's gates were

staggered so that, even if an invader breached the outermost walls, they would have to not only traverse that lowest level but then circumnavigate it to reach the second gate, and repeat the process with the next level and so on. But the Imperial Channel, as it was known, allowed a more direct route. Each segment was a long, covered walkway, the roof latticed for both light and air, and led from one gate to the next. The whole was wide enough to allow three riders abreast, but here it was only Shisi and a dozen Honjofu, two ahead and the rest in pairs marching behind, so they had ample space. Honjofu stood at each gate and saluted the second they saw their emperor approach, opening each portal and allowing him and his entourage to pass through without challenge or comment. Thus it was that, only an hour later, Hibikitsu passed through the final gate and emerged onto the back lawn of the highest tier, Aihiri, the Imperial compound.

His home.

He saw at once that the entire space was on high alert, for it took only a minute before a bantao was marching toward him, weapons not drawn but ready. They released those and saluted instead once they recognized him, dropping to their knees on the grass and bowing until the brims of their helmets scraped the ground.

"Rise, my faithful Honjofu," he assured them, raising a hand in benediction, for their black-enameled armor was unmistakable, and indeed he recognized several of them. "I am well pleased to see that you have kept my home safe while I was away." He glanced around. "Where is your Taikoro?" he asked. "And where is Taikoro Maniko?" He hoped the Honteno's Lord Commander was still alive, but assumed the guards would have mentioned already if she was not. Besides, he expected she was too tough to die—she would view that as a dereliction of duty.

"Taikoro Fujibuki is in his study," one of the soldiers replied. "I believe Taikoro Maniko is in the Rojiri's chambers."

"Oh? He frowned, wondering what she was doing there, for there was no love lost between Kohori and the Rojiri. Especially now, though he assumed those who had rebelled had been dealt with accordingly and were not still debating with their former fellows. Still, if she and they were all in one place that served his purpose nicely. "Instruct them to attend me in my throne room," he directed. "We have much to discuss, and plans to make." Then he nudged Shisi to a faster pace and rode past, letting the horse have his head as the stallion unerringly sought out his own stables.

"You should all take some rest," he told Diritan and the other Honjofu as he dismounted, letting the stablemaster take charge of Shisi, who welcomed the horse like a dear, long-lost friend. "I may have need of you again soon, and I would have you at your best." He realized how that sounded, and bit back a wince. "Thank you for all that you have done for me," he continued, trying to thaw his icy demeanor while still maintaining clear control. "I am grateful for your support and your recent companionship."

Diritan opened his mouth, most likely to argue, and Nioko elbowed him in the side. Taking her hint, the burly warrior just nodded, then offered a firm salute. Hibikitsu could not help but feel that a part of him went with them as they left. Would he ever know such freedom again?

This was not the time to worry upon such things, however. Not with two unknown but potentially hostile forces about to descend upon the city and a third mystery beyond them, plus whatever unrest remained here after the attempted coup. He would focus on those, on restoring the peace and maintaining it, before he gave himself the luxury of bemoaning his responsibilities or the restrictions they caused.

Less than an hour later, Hibikitsu stood within his throne room, pacing the dais there, hands clasped behind his back. His gaze strayed about the room as he moved, taking in the wide columns that lined the large chamber, with their beautifully carved sides; the tiled floors with their intricate patterns of gold and precious stones inlaid among the marble; the rich silk banners hanging along the walls; the fierce war masks hanging along the back wall, peering down over his throne; and the delicate traceries of colored glass high above sending shimmers of light down to him. It seemed so long ago when he had last stood here, and he felt almost a different man than he had been then.

Would that Hibikutsu have sailed the sea, laughing as the salt water sprayed his face? Would he have dug a grave with his own hands, leaving them bleeding and blistered? Would he have ordered the deaths of his own citizens, to protect all the rest—and then taken full responsibility for that action, without any attempt to shirk the guilt that came with it? It felt so foreign to be back here now, wearing once again those fine, jewel-encrusted robes he had once taken pleasure in but now found gaudy and stiff, to feel soft silk beneath his feet rather than the hard leather of traveling boots. To have nothing but silk and stone to protect himself with, though at least his sword, Kosshiki, was thrust through his sash as always. It was almost a relief when the throne room doors creaked open, forcing himself to turn from his musings and face the real world and their very real concerns instead.

The pair that entered were in some ways a study in contrasts, the one tall and broad-shouldered, with gray hair and crimson armor, the other shorter, slender, with inky black hair and armor of almost the same hue. But in other ways they struck him as very similar, and certainly both were capable warriors. He also had no doubt of either's loyalty and allowed himself to smile down upon them as they approached and prostrated themselves at the base of the dais.

"Your Imperial Majesty," Kohori declared, her voice as strong and clear as ever. "Thank the First Emperor you have returned to us safely."

"Thank you, Kohori," he told her. "It is good to be back." He nodded. "You may rise. You as well, Misataki Shizumi." He almost laughed as she started slightly, much as Ganema had once done. Why was it so strange that an emperor would know the names of his own elite warriors? "I am pleased to find you both here and both hale." His tone soured slightly. "You must tell me of what occurred while I was away—and who was responsible." For he had not failed to notice how few Honteno there were now, the Honjofu clearly filling in for their household brethren.

"Whenever you desire, sire," Kohori confirmed, straightening. She seemed about to say more but others were filing in behind them, and so instead she saluted and stepped to the side, pivoting to place herself just beside the corner of the dais. Shizumi took up post on the opposite corner, the two of them flanking Hibikitsu like a pair of armed statues. Although they had obeyed the usual strictures and entered the hall armed only with ittei, still he took great reassurance at their presence.

Two of the Rojiri came next, Watane Yatahei and Orito Sadachi, with two more at their heels, Yoshino Nanami and Domo Haruta, all in their customary purple kisoni. But where were the rest? Where was Etsuya Kenshin, short and belligerent, or Sunao Tadazi, old and wily, or Ieyuki Nagao, smooth and oily? For that matter, where was their leader, the most difficult of them all? Where was—ah, but here came Amani Denbi, sweeping in with her usual poise, head held high as if everyone had been waiting upon her. She brushed past her fellow councilors, each of them unable to stop her, and approached the dais, dropping into a graceful bow, her white hair gleaming in the light.

"Your Imperial Majesty," she intoned. "We are so relieved to see you home safely." Similar words to those Kohori had used, but without the Taikoro's warmth—or, he suspected, sincerity.

"Thank you," he answered anyway, keeping his face blank. "We are happy to be home." He let the frown form now. "But where are your fellow Rojiri? What is keeping them?"

Denbi opened her mouth to answer but was cut off by the figure that appeared next, his black armor edged in gold. Though not a councilor, he was an important figure, and though Hibikitsu felt no love for the man it would be necessary to include him in this conversation.

"Your Imperial Majesty!" Fujibuki Haro, Taikoro of the Honjofu, marched to the front, stopping just shy of the dais, and sank to his knees, bending forward until his forehead touched the floor. "Praise to the First Emperor that you are returned!" Rising at Hibikitsu's nod, Haro leaned forward, his head and shoulders now angled past the vivid red rails around the dais. "I have urgent news, sire," he stated, keeping his voice too low for most of the others there to hear. "And it concerns some in this very room. May I have your leave to approach that I might convey this information to you and you alone?"

Hibikitsu frowned. Gone were the other man's usual affectations. Now he seemed entirely serious, and more than a little worried. "Very well," he stated. "You may approach."

"Thank you, Your Majesty." Haro set a booted foot on the dais's outer edge and levered himself up to step over the low railing. He was now standing upon a polished, inlaid wood mosaic that no one but the emperor had touched in generations. "It concerns the recent events here in Aihiri, which I was witness to firsthand," he explained softly, stepping in closer and keeping his face respectfully tilted toward the ground.

"Oh?" Hibikitsu stepped closer. "What about them?" Out of the corner of his eye he thought he caught a flicker of movement, and had that been a gasp? But he was too intent upon the conversation to let that distract him.

"Here is the heart of the matter," Haro began—then lifted his head and grinned. Only it was no longer the Taikoro of the Honjofu grinning. The face that leered at Hibikitsu now was longer, thinner, more angular—and, as he watched, the color seemed to leech out of it, the skin darkening, hair as well, until he looked as if he had been carved from shadows. Only his eyes stood out, for they almost glowed. "Now you die, and your kingdom dies with you!"

Then the man that had been Fujibuki Haro lunged for him, a long, smoky dagger in his hand, its jagged blade already sweeping forward for Hibikitsu's throat.

CHAPTER TWENTY-SIX

"Hai!" Shizumi leaped, arm at full extension, weapon outstretched—and the ittei's blunt, hexagonal iron shaft rang as it took the full force of that strange dark dagger, stopping the weapon mere inches from the emperor's throat.

A part of her was still reeling in shock. She had known that her commander was acting oddly, not at all like himself, but trying to kill the emperor? How did that make any sense? There had been little doubt in her mind, however, that he was up to something when he had insisted upon mounting the dais, and she had seen Kohori's eyebrow rise and her lips tighten as the older woman clearly thought the same. They had not even needed to glance at each other before they had each abandoned their posts and vaulted the railing, moving quickly to flank their ruler. Shizumi had barely seen Haro draw a weapon before reacting on instinct, yanking the ittei free and charging forward to block the attack.

It was a good thing she was wielding that instead of her nihono, too! Her sword's blade, though sharp, would have snapped like thin wood from the force of the blow. The ittei's sturdy shaft was designed to block swords, however, and though she felt the jolt all the way up to her shoulder, that smoky edge did not reach the emperor.

Haro turned her way with a hiss of annoyance, and she blinked, her mouth dropping open. This was not her Taikoro! The creature before her looked to be crafted from shadow itself, as dark and wispy-edged as its blade, all features gone save its glowing eyes. And its teeth, which gleamed white and sharp in a nasty grin.

"That was unwise," it warned, its voice chillingly low and cold, more of a rumble than a true utterance. "You are only ensuring that you die first."

"I think not," Shizumi replied, taking two quick steps forward to regain her balance and pivoting to put herself bodily between the emperor and this creature, this shadow assassin. "But I am willing to test my skills against yours, in defense of my emperor."

She attacked then, her second hand wrapping around the ittei's base as she slashed her opponent's chest. The blunt rod did nothing, however, only its rounded tip even grazing the figure's dark torso. Oh, for the proper reach and edge of her nihono again!

He laughed at her, then, tilting his dark head back. "Is that truly the best the Honjofu have to offer?" he asked, giggling in a shrill way that made bumps break out all across her skin. "This will be a simpler matter than I expected." He advanced—and broke off, cursing, as something slammed against the side of his head, sending him staggering back toward the dais's edge.

It was Kohori. The Honteno commander had struck him with the butt of her ittei, reversing the weapon in her grip to use as a short club, with devastating effect. Shizumi quickly flipped hers over, then drew her yori-toki from her belt and reversed that as well, so the short, thick blade jutted from below her clenched fist.

Now better armed and balanced, she struck for the second time, moving in close. The assassin swung at her but she blocked with her dagger, then swung the ittei in a backhanded arc, its sharkskin-wrapped handle slamming into his jaw. He stumbled and she followed up, moving in to strike again, this time clubbing downward and catching him in the temple. Kohori appeared on his far side, bashing him across the back of his head, and he staggered, nearly colliding with Shizumi as she ducked away, catching him across the jaw for a second time.

"I will end you all!" he howled, slashing about him with his dagger in wild motions she easily sidestepped. Kohori tugged the emperor back out of the way as well, giving Shizumi more room to maneuver up there on the cramped dais.

I'm standing on the imperial dais, she thought, but quickly shoved that away before it could overwhelm her. She could consider all that once she had taken care of the immediate threat.

The shadow assassin had clearly realized that being trapped did not allow him much space either. Rather than striking at Shizumi or going after the emperor again, he turned to the side and dove over the rail, flipping in midair and landing on his feet, crouched amid the councilors and attendants who had all remained frozen in place at the spectacle unfolding in their midst. A quick sweep of the knife and several of those toppled, screaming, right in Shizumi's path as the assassin backed slowly away, eyes darting back and forth to make sure no one was lying in wait along the path of his escape.

Shizumi know she could not let him reach the throne room doors. If he did, he would disappear, and they would never know when he might try to strike again. She had to keep him from getting through that portal. With that in mind, she flipped her yoritoki so that it spun upward, catching the base of its handle as it rotated around, the blade now pointing skyward. Then, in a single fluid motion, she whipped her arm downward, releasing the weapon at the peak of her swing and hurling it forward, a small, glittering missile—that buried itself in the fleeing figure's lower back.

Letting loose a cry of pure anguish, he jerked, spasming, and fell, limbs splaying out, the hard, polished tiles of the floor catching him in his chest and his chin.

She was already racing along the dais and leaping over the far corner, sprinting for him, ittei in hand. Kohori was right beside her, the older woman's longer legs making up for any loss in vitality. Rojiri and other attendants scattered like startled birds in their path, many of them now shaking off their paralysis enough to scream and cry and wring their hands.

Useless, the lot of them, Shizumi thought as she darted past, but her attention was on the shadow stretched out between the courtiers and the throne room's massive double doors, which were still open.

The assassin was stirring, pushing himself up on his hands and knees, shaking his head. He had dropped his knife somewhere, or it had vanished, but his fingers were long as talons, she noted, and tipped with cruel barbs. Best not to let him get too close.

As if hearing her thoughts, the shadowman turned and glared at her—then smiled slowly. "You think to disarm me," he taunted, his voice echoing as if they stood within a cave. "But you cannot. For I am never without my shadows—or my fire!"

And, where his hands still rested upon the floor, fingers splayed, flames began to lick up, swaying like dancers summoned to perform.

Ash! Shizumi had planned to bash him across the back of the skull with her ittei, but now she adjusted that strategy mid-motion. Lowering the weapon, she crouched, bringing herself closer to the ground—and hurled her entire body at him instead. Taken off guard by the crude maneuver, the assassin straightened in surprise, which only meant Shizumi's shoulder caught him square in the stomach rather than in the arm or chest. The force of her flight knocked him off his feet a second time, sending both of them careening into the far wall, where his head and back slammed up against one of the massive pillars there.

Behind them, just as she had hoped, the flames vanished, unable to sustain themselves without their master's presence.

The assassin was shaking his head, clearly dazed from the impact. Unfortunately, Shizumi had knocked the wind out of herself as well. She took great gasping breaths, struggling to restore strength to her limbs in time to act, but already he was pushing her off him, trying to give himself enough space to stab or slash with those claws—

—and a long, glittering blade thrust forward, gliding just above her shoulder to take the assassin full in the chest. It sank in deep, gleaming steel vanishing within shadowy skin, and he let out a gasping sigh, then a rattling breath, his body tensing before going limp.

Shizumi glanced up and nodded at Kohori, who stood over her, the yanoi in her hands. She had clearly taken it from one of the guards stationed at the doors, then had doubled back and put the long spear to good use.

"Bones!" The explosive utterance came from the dais, and Shizumi shifted to look over as the emperor himself stepped down and crossed the room toward them. Kohori moved to block his path, ever vigilant, and Hibikitsu, Echo of Victory, stopped a few feet shy, a rueful smile touching his lips. His eyes were wide and his cheeks pale.

"What was that?" he asked, directing the question to Shizumi and Kohori. "Did the head of my own elite guard truly just attempt to kill me?"

"No, Your Majesty," Shizumi answered, accepting a proffered hand from Kohori and rising to her feet, then saluting. "I think we will find that Fujibuki Haro is already dead." The faint stirrings of grief over that surprised her, for she had never been fond of her commanding officer and the only times she had felt any respect for him had apparently been for this imposter instead. She nudged the body beside her with her foot—in death, the shadows were beginning to fade, washing away like ink in the rain, leaving an unfamiliar figure behind, a slender man with a long, pinched face. "This man, whoever he is, evidently killed him and took his place."

"Who is he?" Hibikitsu asked, eyes intent upon the would-be assassin. "Some sort of demon?"

Kohori shook her head, crouching down to check over the dead man's body. With the shadows gone he was revealed as wearing hakami and a sort of tight hantien, both black, both close-fitting. "A darakada, I think," she answered absently, and the part of Shizumi that could still observe such things noted how casually the Taikoro answered her emperor, speaking as she might to Geniji or Akino rather than to the ruler of all Rimbaku.

"I have heard of such, though I believed them only tales designed to frighten us," the older woman continued. "They have something akin to aitachi, only it works very differently. They absorb their victim's very flesh, taking face and form as their own. But in order to do so, they must consume something more...vital than mere bones."

"The eyes," Shizumi blurted out, flushing as the emperor turned her way. "That's why the eyes. He needed them to take the shape."

"I think so," Kohori agreed, plucking a small pouch from inside the dead man's right sleeve cuff. Tugging the little bag open, she upended it over her hand. Several gems fell out, valuable even to Shizumi's untrained eye.

And with them a signet ring. The carved black stone, with its image of a winged serpent reared back ready to strike, was unmistakable.

"Yatamoro!" Hibikitsu fairly spat the name of the nation to their east. "I might have known! If it is underhanded and vicious, it is likely from Yatamoro." The emperor was clenching his fists, his jaw tight, eyes blazing. "How many?" he asked. "How many died so he could get this close to me?"

Shizumi was not sure she should even answer that question—how would knowing it help any? But it seemed Kohori was more obedient. "Five that we know of, Your Majesty," the older woman replied bluntly. "A caravan guard, which is how he got into Aihiri. Fujibuki Haro. Umibuki Nihiro, a new recruit to the Honteno. Ritsuro Okari." She paused for only a second before adding, "and Sunao Tadazi."

"Ah." The emperor shut his eyes, a pained expression forming on his face, part grimace, part scowl, and part mourning. "I had wondered why he was not here." He sighed, then opened his eyes again, fixing both women with his intense, brilliant gaze. "I am grateful to you both," he told them, and to Shizumi at least he seemed both surprisingly young and almost painfully sincere. "I owe you my life and much more. What can I do to reward you for your loyalty and your service?"

Kohori dipped her head and saluted. "I live to serve the Empire," she stated proudly.

Shizumi followed suit. "I live to serve the Empire," she echoed.

For an instant, the emperor frowned, as if put out that they refused to ask for rewards. Then he got an odd look in his eye and smiled. That expression transformed his face from stern to amused, from fierce to handsome—and a touch mischievous.

"Then serve you shall," he declared, a grin beginning to form. "Misataki Shizumi," he announced, his voice ringing across the room. "In recognition of your loyal service, your valor, your skill, and most of all your honest devotion, we hereby appoint you to the role of Taikoro of our Honjofu. As we can already see how well you and Taikoro Maniko work together, we trust the two of you will have little difficulty restoring both forces to full strength and protecting both this compound and all of Rimbaku."

For an instant, Shizumi just gaped at him. Had she just heard what she thought she had? A subtle cough from Kohori snapped her out of it, and she bowed deeply, hand to chest.

"You honor me, Your Majesty," she told him, keep her eyes lowered out of respect. "I will do my best not to disappoint you, and to live up to your faith in me."

The squawk that arose might have come from a barnyard chicken—but instead emerged, rather improbably, from the throat of Amani Denbi.

"Your Majesty!" the Rojiri called out, pushing her way forward to reach their little tableau now that the danger had passed. "You cannot be serious!" She spared Shizumi only a single baleful glare before turning back toward Hibikitsu. "Need I remind you that the position of Taikoro Honjofu is and always has been hereditary? The title and office must pass to Haro's nearest male relative." Her tone was harsh, scolding, that of a teacher disappointed with a once promising student.

When the emperor turned toward his seniormost advisor, Shizumi could swear she felt the temperature in the room drop. "Oh?" he asked in the type of voice a mamusha might be imagined to use right before it struck, its fangs already dripping venom. "Must it? How good of you to inform us of what we must do." He grinned at the councilor, baring his teeth, the fierceness in full evidence once more. "We are the emperor. We determine the rules. And we are long since tired of promoting the scions of the same few families, regardless of actual ability. Taikoro Misataki is immensely capable and we have every confidence in her."

"But—" Shizumi did not know Rojiri Amani well, but she had always imagined the woman carved of ice, so flawlessly smooth and cold had she seemed. Now, however, the councilor stamped her foot like a small child denied a sweet. "She is a commoner!" The accusation rang across the room.

If her face was normally ice, Hibikitsu's now turned to stone, a living statue chiseled in an expression of near-volcanic rage. "Is that all that matters to you?" he demanded. "Rank and title and house? Not loyalty and skill and service? Just whose ultimate forebears were richer than whose?" He shook his head. "We have spoken, Denbi," he warned, his voice soft enough that Shizumi barely made out the words. "It would be wise to stand down."

Amani matched him glare for glare, and when she spoke again her words were glacial once more. "It is my sworn duty as Rojiri to offer you advice, Your Majesty, even if you choose not to take it. Especially when I see you about to do something so foolish it would destroy generations of history and tradition."

Rather than calm him, however, her careful, cool words seemed only to enrage the emperor further. "The First Emperor take tradition!" he snapped turning and leveling such a scowl at the silver-haired councilor it was a wonder she did not burst into flames on the spot. "And the First Emperor take titles and houses, as well!"

"Your Majesty!" Amani looked genuinely shocked, but it was clear to Shizumi from the frenzied look in her eye that the old woman just could not keep from pushing for control. "You cannot mean that! Perhaps recent events have unsettled your mind—you should retire and leave these matters to us." Her tone was exactly that of a mother attempting to soothe a recalcitrant child back to bed.

The emperor was no child, however. "Enough!" he declared. "I am sick of your constant prattle, your desperate need for elevation, always more elevation, as if you could ever rise high enough to wash away the stink from when your ancestor stole horses—and whatever else he could find." A sharp, nasty grin showed on his face a moment before reverting to simple anger. "Perhaps," he said slowly, "I should simply grant her Sunao Tadazi's lands and titles. Or Fujibuki Haro's. Both must have adequate stature for a Taikoro, even in your eyes. And they certainly no longer need those trappings."

"You would not dare!" The look of dawning horror on her face told Shizumi that Amani Denbi had not meant to call the emperor out so blatantly, but now the die was cast and of course she was too proud to ever admit to having made a mistake. She simply raised her chin, preparing to meet the devastation face-on.

Nor did she have long to wait. Hibikitsu was silent for almost a full minute, which was far more terrifying than any shouting or cursing. Finally he nodded once, a single sharp gesture. "You are dismissed," he told Amani Denbi. "You are no longer Rojiri. None of you are. Instead we name you jigekugi—and be grateful we did not strip away all titles and exile you to Sakiriti or lower. Which we will certainly do," he added as Denbi opened her mouth, clearly intending to object, "should you continue to press your hopeless suit." That finally shut the former councilor up, though her eyes continued to flash in defiance.

"You may leave us," he instructed loftily, and the men and women who had been the emperor's closest advisors up until a few minutes before filed out, heads bowed. Many of them looked like they would still be arguing and pleading if not for fear of his carrying through on that last threat. Jigekugi might be the lowest form of nobility, mere bureaucrats, but they were still nobles, at least. It was a chastened, cowed group that departed, leaving only Shizumi and Kohori with their emperor, the man who had been sent to kill him still stretched out dead at his feet.

CHAPTER TWENTY-SEVEN

"I do not enjoy this!" Iraku shouted, having to yell himself nearly hoarse for his words to not be whipped away completely by the wind that tore at his clothes and hair and skin, tugging him this way and that like a leaf on a vine.

"Nor I!" his brother agreed at the same volume, for though they were only a few feet apart they could barely hear one another, or anything else. They were near enough that they could have clasped hands, in fact—if they both had not been clutching desperately to the limbs above them in sheer terror and holding on for all they were worth.

This final leg of their long journey had proven to be short and swift, for all of the skeletal figures in their strange undead army possessed wings of some sort. Only the brothers lacked the ability to fly, but that problem had been solved by the simple expedient of ferrying them like so much baggage. Expedient, but terrifying.

Iraku glanced down and immediately wished he had not. The ground seemed almost impossibly far away, as if they were somehow above the Heavens themselves, looking down upon the very stars and clouds. Instead he forced himself to settle his gaze forward once more, staring at the tiered city that was rapidly growing larger until it nearly filled his sight.

Awaihinshi. The City of Polished Light. When they had been little, he and Ibaru had dreamed of coming here someday, of finding a way across the country to this capital and here finding fame and fortune, growing rich and powerful and well-respected. The "how" had always been unclear, but it was the destination that had mattered. The capital of the empire and its jewel. Home to the emperor himself, and many of his richest and most powerful subjects. Awaihinshi, with its six tiers, each surrounded by high walls of a different color.

From up here he could see all of them with perfect clarity. It was the city's residents he had trouble making out, for they seemed the size of ants as he and Ibaru raced toward them, caught up in the massive talons of that strange horned skeleton, its rows of tiny wings working in concert surprisingly well to move it along so smoothly and so rapidly. Several of the tiny figures had gathered along the walls, most likely soldiers, and this assumption was borne out as miniscule slivers lanced from those positions, growing in size and definition as they approached until it became evident they were in fact heavy spears, their sharp metal tips gleaming. Most fell short, while a few clattered against a skeletal frame or passed harmlessly through where muscle and flesh might once have been. Still, the aerial army pulled back slightly, placing more space between itself and the city walls.

All the while, the Silent Change hovered slightly above and slightly behind them, as if it were stepping aside to let them lead the way.

Only, Iraku had certainly never been here before, nor had Ibaru. And he was not sure the skeleton army all around them had either, even before they were fashioned into their strange new forms.

Still, he expected that the higher the tier you lived in, the more important you were. Which meant that the very top, with its walls of pure white, was reserved for the emperor himself.

Therefore, that was where they must go.

As if reading his thoughts, their monstrous mount angled higher, its many small wings all working in tandem. It soared upward—

—and a well-aimed or simply lucky spear passed through its ribcage, shattering several of those bones in its flight and clipping a few of the wings as it exited as well. The skeletal creature began to list to one side and to drop down jerkily, its remaining wings struggling to compensate.

"It is no use," Ibaru pointed out. "We must find some place for our skeletal steed to land, then work our way upward on foot."

Rather than waste time replying, his brother began scanning the streets and buildings below them. "There," he said at last, indicating one structure. It stood two stories high, its walls made of sturdy sand-colored stone, and more importantly its squared roof was flat, with a hatch leading back inside. "Land us there," Iraku instructed, freeing one hand to bang on the creature's leg. "Land, please," he tried again, waving his hand at that roof. "Over there."

There was no grunt of acknowledgment, no nod, no indication that it had heard at all—but the creature did begin to bank slowly, straightening out once it was facing the building in question.

Iraku tightened his grip on the leg and squeezed his eyes shut, swaying and swinging as the creature began to slow down, dipping lower and lower as that roof drew closer.

His feet were still dangling a short ways above the roof when the bone-bird suddenly flexed its talons, releasing its hold on the brothers, and they fell from the sky like twin thunderbolts, slamming into the roof hard enough to snap their ankles had their master not left them some of its vitality. As it was, both brothers dropped to their knees, heads bowed, as the strange creature flapped those little wings and flew off again to rejoin its equally bizarre brethren, wobbling but functional.

After a moment to collect himself, Ibaru rose to his feet, his younger brother doing likewise. They brushed off their clothes, though the dust and travel stains were more or less permanent now, and then stepped over to the rooftop's edge to see what they could see.

From this vantage point, with pale rose walls behind them and peach-colored firmaments ahead, the brothers admired their new location and gave thanks to the master who had brought them here, the same master that hovered above them now as always, its inky black center surrounded by its usual brilliant flurry of agitated swirls. Down below, some folk were running and screaming and shouting, while a handful kept their heads and waited to see what would happen next and how they could be most useful. Where the cloud's murky shadow fell across people, they invariably grew pale and narrow, the color fading from their skin and hair and clothes even as their emotions were released to run wild. Observing all of the chaos below, the brothers were pleased.

The Silent Change had come to Awaihinshi at last.

CHAPTER TWENTY-EIGHT

"Welcome to my home," Kishin Narai announced, bowing and gesturing for Kagiri to proceed him across the rough but masterfully fitted stone of the terrace and into the house. "I hope you find it pleasant, and will treat it as if it were yours."

Kagiri glanced around, admiring the fine carving on the heavy wooden beams and corner posts and door frames, the thick, rich rugs upon the floor, the beauty and delicacy of the painted wall panels. Through the open door ahead he could see into the house's central garden and hear the bubbling of a little brook. "It is beautiful," he admitted, gazing at the expensive furnishings, the wide hall, the large, airy rooms. He had never seen such luxury before. Small wonder Narai and the others could afford to hire him and his brother for that ill-fated trek to the Tawasiri!

The rest of the merchants trailed behind them both as they toured the house. They each had homes here in the third level of the city, Motohiri, where the most powerful merchants lived among the meanest nobles. They could have all returned to those abodes. But it seemed none of them were willing to miss even a moment of what Kagiri might do next.

For now he led them out into the garden, selecting a spot upon a wooden bench beside the little stream and seating himself there gracefully, legs folded under him, hands resting loosely on his knees. The others quickly arrayed themselves before him, standing ready to receive instruction. "You have done well to get me here," Kagiri told them. "And now we are but a stone's throw from the emperor's compound itself." He frowned, stroking his chin. "But now I must confront the emperor himself, face to face," he warned his followers. "How can we make that possible?"

The merchants exchanged glances. "He rarely grants an audience to any but the most powerful nobles," Shizu Yokori warned. "Even all of us together would only rate time with one of his jigekugi." They each bore frowns, grimaces, or glares of varying degrees and Kagiri realized this was a sore spot for them, that for all their wealth they were not considered important enough for the emperor to see in person.

For himself, he simply wondered how anyone who could not be bothered to speak with his people directly could possibly think himself fit to govern them? What did this emperor know about the bakers and the fishermen and the potters and the tailors and all the rest? Had he ever even met anyone who had not been born and raised a noble?

He was certainly about to. Provided, of course, that Kagiri could reach him.

"Get me into Aihiri," he stated, pounding both fists gently atop his knees. "Once there, I will do the rest." He smiled at the idea, his hand falling to the scabbarded nihono that lay across his legs. He did not expect anyone stationed in the imperial compound to pose much difficulty.

"You will not be able to bring that with you," Jiro Masute pointed out, indicating the sword. "All blades are forbidden within the walls of the imperial palace. Which is where you'll find His Imperial Majesty Hibikitsu, the Echo of Victory." He shrugged, which sent his long, silky hair floating about him like an angry cloud, and a nasty smile touched his narrow face but failed to brighten his sharp eyes. "It seems the echoes have faded a great deal. I can barely hear them."

The others laughed and Kagiri joined them, but deep down he was not entirely comfortable mocking their nation's ruler. Surely such an exalted position deserved respect, if not the man who held it? "Do not worry about that," he assured the men and women who had hired him and tossed him into that ancient tower specifically hoping to create a weapon to turn against their emperor. "I will not let anyone take it from me." He frowned, considering. "How soon would we be able to gain a meeting with these jigekugi you mentioned?"

Narai opened his mouth to answer but stopped as a shadow fell across them. A shadow out of place against the clear blue sky above. Kagiri glanced up, as did the others, and only the cumulative experience of the Gensaiba enabled him to keep from gaping and gasping as the merchants did, staring up at the strangely shaped bone creature flapping high above them. It resembled nothing so much as an eel with wings, he thought, if an eel had been divested of flesh and blood and bone, leaving only its narrow, needle-spined skeleton behind. And although it appeared no longer than his arm, he had the impression that a significant distance stood between that odd figure and him, which meant that it had to be enormous. How did something like that even exist, he wondered as he rose to his feet. And why was it here now?

A strange sound rang out from somewhere, vibrating across the garden. It was deep and resonant and he frowned, trying to place its origins. "What is that?" he asked after a moment, when it became clear that no one was about to volunteer the information freely.

"It is the gong," Fujiko Oritano explained, her usual humor having been replaced by fear. "It indicates when the city is under attack." Her eyes were wide, her face nearly bloodless. "We need to find shelter somewhere safe!" She darted a look up at the monstrosity overhead. "Now!"

"My study," Narai replied, sounding far calmer than Oritano. "It is the sturdiest room in the house, and the most defensible." He turned back toward the front, and the rooms between there and here. The other merchants were quick to follow.

They paused, however, when they realized that Kagiri was not among them.

"We need to go," Yokori urged, her usual sharpness buried beneath barely controlled terror. "Now!"

"Go," Kagiri agreed, absently waving them away. He had carried his bakiro in with him and now crouched beside it, untying the knotted drawstring. Once that was done he reached in and began drawing out the pieces of his armor. "I will make for Aihiri."

"But the attack—" Masute began.

"Means the city's guards will all be distracted," Kagiri finished for him, shedding his concealing maikiro and tugging on his deo in its place. "Perhaps the emperor's as well. If they are not"—he shrugged— "at least the commotion will cover any noise I cause as I make my way to the throne room. And if they are"— he grinned— "then I will be able to enter unopposed." He saw no downside, either way.

Narai evidently did not either, for the sturdy merchant nodded, then bowed deeply. "Good luck, Kagiri," he stated. "We will be here, awaiting word from you."

"I will send it," Kagiri promised. He finished donning his armor and rose to his feet, pleased to be properly outfitted once more. Then, thrusting the sword back through his sash, he turned and hurried toward the front door, leaving the merchants behind. He would leave their guards as well, and all the rest who had followed him here. They would only be in his way for this, and he needed to keep his wits about him.

After all, he had an emperor to kill.

CHAPTER TWENTY-NINE

"I can't believe we made it!" Ratal exclaimed. A few of the others laughed as hands among them reached for the sides of the docks, and after a second Ratal laughed with them. Though still surly from time to time, the fisherman's general attitude had certainly improved the closer they had come to their goal.

And why not? Noniki wondered as he helped steady the raft he was on, then waited while Seikoku leaped forward, easily bridging the gap between boat and dock. She turned and offered a hand to Jitu Kanai, pulling the potter up beside her. Then they each began to haul others onto the wide wooden causeway. Noniki waited until the last, using his magic to calm the waves that lapped up against the thick pilings, keeping their little collection of boats steady so that everyone could affect the transition more easily. In a few cases, like Isoro's cart, people dragged the watergoing vessel up as well, but most of the rafts they simply left to bob there in the Edishu, carrying their supplies on their backs and in their arms. Noniki had no idea if they would need to come back for the rafts, and if so how soon. He had no idea if they would get to see the emperor, or even be allowed through the front gates. He had little idea of anything right now, but he did know one thing—

As Ratal had said, they had made it.

Standing on the dock at last, he took the time to gaze up at Awaihinshi, admiring the gleaming stone walls that rose before them. Back in Ginzai there had been a shop that had specialized in elegant desserts, well beyond the few coins he and his brother got tossed for their backbreaking labor at the Happoa Kappua, but he had sometimes gone and admired the food there, drooling over the delicate little rolls and clever little spun-sugar figures and carefully decorated stacked cakes. This city resembled that last one, a confection of glittering, sparkling colors, one atop the other in a perfect array that rose effortlessly toward the pure white layer at the top.

That, he knew instinctively, was where he had to go.

Now the only question was, how would they get there?

The walls at this lowest level were blue, shading from dark to light as they rose, and set in their base spanning nearly as wide as the dock itself was a pair of massive iron doors carved with the higeibara, which had been enameled a deep, brilliant crimson. The doors stood open at the moment, leaned back so they pressed up against the stone to either side, and through them Noniki could see a wide, tidy street, with buildings crowding close on both sides.

To reach that welcoming sight, however, they would first have to traverse the full length of this dock—and that meant passing through the sturdy wooden outpost that was set roughly halfway along. Its peaked roof rose a good ten feet above, covered in tiles the color of a summer storm, and wide windows on either side hung open to admit air and light, just as the doors fore and aft were swung wide.

The guards stationed at both entrances, however, looked a good deal less friendly.

Dressed in the standard maikiro and jingaso of the army, the guards carried long yanoi, with clubs or swords stuck through their sashes. Four of them were facing Noniki and his friends, and he could see another four beyond them at the outpost's far side, with four more blocking the gates to the city proper. This was not a gauntlet he had anticipated, and he was momentarily paralyzed by the question of what to do next.

It did not help that all the others, including Seikoku, Kanai, and Minawa, had turned toward him, waiting on him to guide them past this newest obstacle.

"Noniki?" Seikoku asked quietly, for she was right beside him, as was often the case, her presence and her warmth and the faint flowery scent that was her all serving to bolster both his spirits and his resolve. "Any ideas? They look...fierce."

Indeed they did, but Noniki knew he had to appear confident for the others. "Fiercer than those bannin back in Ginzai?" he asked her, summoning up a grin. "I fail to believe it!"

That wrung an answering smile from her, and a little laugh. "No, perhaps not," she agreed, though her gaze and her tone told him she had not fallen for his trick. Not completely. Still, she did not ask anything further. Everything about her told Noniki that she trusted him to find a solution to this for them all.

He just wished he knew what it was.

Well, perhaps the easiest answer might suffice. Sometimes that was the case. So he strode forward, his friends parting to let him pass as he walked down the dock, his sandals slapping against the rough wood as he approached the outposts and the guards waiting there. When he was still a short distance away—near enough to speak without shouting, far enough to show respect for their weaponry—he stopped and bowed.

"Good day," he began. "My name is Noniki. My friends and I have come a long way to visit your lovely city, and I hope that we will be allowed to enter. We do not mean anyone any harm."

The guard on the far right, a big, burly woman with pale eyes and a scar curling down from the left one like a crescent moon, opened her mouth to reply. He could already tell by the set of her shoulders and the cast of her lips and brow that it would be some form of "I am sorry, but we cannot let you enter." But before any words could emerge a shadow fell across her and him and all of them.

They all glanced up as one.

"Bones!" That burst from the guard as she scrambled back beneath the roof's overhang, seeking shelter from the strange shapes swooping down from above. Nor could Noniki blame her. For himself, he dove to the side and just in time, as something shaped much like a tree frog, with powerful back legs, spindly front ones, a wide, stout body that grew directly into a wide head with an enormous mouth, and vast staring eyes, leaped down onto the dock, splintering the sturdy wood where he had stood just an instant before. Yes, it looked like an enormous raeteru—

—if one of the ubiquitous tree frogs had been flayed, its bones stripped clean and dry.

And if it had enormous bat wings. And long, vicious claws curving from both its hind legs and its forepaws, plus twinned rows of needle-like teeth filling its gaping mouth.

The creature turned toward Noniki, those huge empty eye sockets seeming to lock in on him somehow, and it took a short, half-hop, half-flying step toward him, those arms extended, the claws like rakes ready to tear him to bloody strips—

—when a spear came hurtling at it from the side, aimed straight for its head.

Noniki reacted without thinking. The spear was set to scrape across the creature's front lip, doing little harm. Instead the wind caught the thrown weapon, straightening it, steadying it. Aiming it.

It pierced the creature's cheek, shattering its jaw, and continued through the other side, shattering that as well so that the entire lower jaw toppled to the ground.

That barely even made the creature pause in its attempt to swipe at him.

But the attack had given Noniki time to catch his breath and regain some poise. Now he clenched his fists—and lightning flashed down, obliterating the creature in a burst of light and a cloud of bone dust. A second, softer wind swept that out over the water before it could reach Noniki. He had turned his back on the aitachi—he was not about to accidentally inhale aishone now!

Seikoku was at his side in an instant. "Are you all right?" she asked, hugging him quickly and then pulling back to wrap her arms around herself instead.

"I am fine," he assured her. A quick glance told him that the others were all crowding up behind them, and that everyone looked to be accounted for. "What—" His question was interrupted by a loud, deep, reverberating sound he recognized as a gong, much like the one the Hakara Ikibanichi had used to summon everyone to meals. This one, it appeared, had a different purpose, as the guards turned their backs on the docks and ran for the gates.

Halfway there, the guard with the scar glanced back, as if only just now remembering they were there. "Come on!" she shouted, waving for Noniki and the others to follow. They did at once, not even needing to discuss it, and charged through the gates right behind the guards—and mere seconds before those same massive portals were hauled in, slamming shut with a loud and decisive clang.

"Well, that solves one problem," Seikoku commented. "We're inside. What do we do now?"

Noniki shook his head. "Ash if I know." He grinned. "But things seem to be working in our favor so far."

As if on cue, another shadow passed overhead. Then another. And another. He looked up, and stared at the flock of oversized, misshapen, skeletal beasts descending upon the city.

"You had to say it, didn't you?" Seikoku muttered, shoving his shoulder with her own. "What are those things?"

"I don't know," he admitted. "Not natural, I'd wager. But I may be able to get rid of them." He shut his eyes and started to concentrate, pulling the magic in around him.

"Don't." That startled him enough to blink and gape at her. "The guards can handle...whatever this is," she continued, waving at the creatures overhead. "We'll stay and help. But you, you need to go find the emperor."

"What? No." He shook his head. "I am not leaving any of you behind. We will all go see him together, once this threat—whatever it is—has passed."

But Seikoku regarded him with a serious look in those big, beautiful eyes. "And what if there is another threat after that?" she asked. "Or if this one turns out to last for years and years? Or if the entire city collapses and the emperor is spirited away to some remote island for his own safety? You don't know what's going to happen, Noniki. None of us do. But right now you're here, he's here, and these things are going to keep most people occupied." She favored him with a wry smile. "Every good thief knows—if you want to sneak past overhead, create a distraction on the ground. This is the same thing in reverse." She put a hand on his shoulder. "You may never get a better chance. Don't waste it. For all our sakes."

Noniki wanted to argue with her, but as usual she was smarter than he was. "Fine," he said finally, though he had to force the word out through gritted teeth. "But I'm coming back after."

"You'd better." She studied him a second, then hugged him quickly. "Now go."

Squaring his shoulders and refusing to glance back, blinking away sudden tears, he went. Behind him, he heard Seikoku calling the others together, instructing them to find a good place to seek shelter while they waited for him to return.

He vowed not to make them wait any longer than necessary.

CHAPTER THIRTY

Shizumi stood there, not sure what to say. She was saved further uncertainty by a commotion without, which heralded the
arrival of Itamon. The chuisu rushed into the throne room and
quickly dropped to one knee, fist to chest and head nearly to the
floor. He was red in the face and gasping for breath, she noticed.

"Forgive me, Your Majesty!" he declared, head still down. "But
I bring grave news! Awaihinshi is under attack!"

"What!" Hibikitsu gestured impatiently for the Honteno to
rise. "Who is it? Is it the Butcher of Kindichi?"

She started at that, but before she could ask about the unexpected question Itamon was already answering. "No, sire, though I
wish it was," the warrior replied between gulps of air. "That would
be straightforward, at least. This is...there are strange creatures,
sire. Winged skeletons, but not from any animal I have ever seen.
They are attacking from the air." The man was very nearly trembling, she saw, only his extreme discipline preventing him from
breaking down. She could only imagine how terrifying the sight
must have been, if it could affect him in such a way.

The emperor was frowning, stroking his chin as he digested
this information. Kohori did not hesitate, however. "Your Majesty," she stated, stepping forward and saluting. "Allow me to see
to our city's defenses."

"Hm?" He glanced up, met the tough old commander's gaze,
and nodded, straightening himself. "Yes, of course. See to it."

She returned the nod and turned—but not to go. Instead she
closed on Shizumi. "I leave the emperor in your care," Kohori
instructed. "See that you keep him safe."

"What?" Shizumi sputtered, but in confusion rather than

outrage. "You should stay with him," she argued. "You are Honteno, I am Honjofu. You are far better equipped to defend him than I."

"And do you know where our defenses are?" the Honteno commander countered. "Or, for that matter, the gong to signal their use?" She shook her head, her steel-gray chonmage barely twitching from the motion. "No, I will see to that. You stay here." She smiled, then, to take any sting from her words. "Once this is past I will show you those things, and next time it will be as you say."

There was nothing to say to that, nothing to do but salute and accept the charge as the older woman strode from the room, Itamon snapping to and all but trotting along behind her.

Which left Shizumi alone with her emperor. A man she had only spoken to twice before, both times here in this very room within the past hour.

But she had a job to do, and no time for nerves. "Is there a place you will be safe, Your Majesty?" she asked him. "Preferably some place small and hidden close by?"

He scowled at that. "I am no child, Taikoro," he reminded her sharply. "I am a warrior in my own right and can defend myself ably." His hand rested upon the hilt of his sword as if he were eager to prove that point.

She would not allow herself to be dissuaded, however. "I know that to be true, sire," she assured him. "Yet which is more important, your pride or your life? If I am to keep you safe, that would be easiest with you in a location I can defend." She glanced pointedly around the throne room, with its high, arched ceiling, its wide, open floor, its heavy columns casting shadows along the wall.

For a moment, they locked eyes and wills. Then Hibikitsu sighed. "Yes, I take your point," he admitted grudgingly. "Very well." Moving back toward the dais, he stopped at a column roughly midway across the room and reached up to press a particular flower that was part of the carving there. She heard a muted click and a panel popped open. Approaching it slowly, Shizumi saw that the column was hollow, its interior a small compartment with a bench big enough for a grown man to sit upon comfortably. From the inside she could see that there were holes placed throughout the carvings to allow air and light, and even for the occupant to be able to see what occurred beyond.

"That will be perfect, Your Majesty," she told him. "We can hope that, if the First Emperor smiles upon us, no threats will breach Aihiri's walls and you will be able to emerge again shortly, none the worse for it." She left unspoken the rest of that thought, that if something did reach the compound he might survive, provided he stayed hidden.

"Let it be so, by all means," he agreed. He looked her up and down, clearly unhappy, and for an instant she was taken back to every commander who had ever judged her for her height, her build, her gender, her upbringing. What he said, however, was, "Where is your sword?"

"Back in my quarters, sire," she replied, struggling to hide a smile. "It is forbidden to carry blades in your presence."

"Ah." He actually had the good grace to look embarrassed about that. "Well, I believe we will make an exception this once." And, tugging his own nihono free from his sash, he presented it to her. "I trust that, if you need to draw Kosshiki, you will acquit yourself well with it."

Shizumi's breath caught in her throat. Her hands reached out of their own accord, accepting the fabled blade. Even sheathed, she could tell that its balance was exquisite. Still unable to speak, she bowed deeply. Then, tugging the ittei from her sash, she set the iron rod on the ground and slid the sword into its place.

Without another word the emperor stepped into the tiny space inside the pillar and tugged the panel shut behind him. With it closed, Shizumi could not tell it was there.

Now she had only to wait and hope that her precautions would prove unnecessary.

Her gut told her, however, that she was unlikely to be that lucky.

Kagiri stalked the halls of Aihiri. He had encountered only a few guards and those he had dispatched easily, stunning rather than killing them since it had cost him nothing to be merciful and their deaths would simply be a waste of resources. As he had hoped, most of those who should be here were on the walls instead and he could hear cries and screams and shouted commands from the city's other levels, with the occasional thrum of a bowstring, all undercut by the odd whistling of airborne skeletons swooping and diving as the wind breezed through the gaps in their strange frames. At some point, if the city's defenders did not manage to deal with those creatures, he knew he would be forced to step in. After all, there was little point in seizing control of this place if he then allowed it to be reduced to an empty ruin. But for now, his main concern was finding and dealing with the emperor.

Up ahead he spied a wide doorframe, the largest he had seen in the palace thus far. The massive doors it held were currently open, a large man in armor standing before each, yanoi in their hands. Oddly, one man wore the red Kagiri knew was the armor of the Honteno but the other had on the black of the Honjofu. Regardless, they settled into defensive positions as he approached, those long spears pointed in his direction. "Halt!" the one in crimson declared. "The throne room is off-limits by order of the emperor himself!"

"Why, is he within?" Kagiri asked, gliding to a stop just shy of the spears' reach. "If so, I would speak with him. It is a matter of some urgency."

Neither guard batted an eye. "Turn back," the one in black warned. "Or we will be forced to stop you."

"You will try," Kagiri corrected. "And you will fail."

He read it in their eyes, the slight widening and then tightening as they were about to act, and reacted before they had actually begun to move, taking several quick paces forward so that he was now inside their reach and too close for them to hit without adjusting stance and grip. Reaching out with both hands he grabbed hold of the yanoi himself, tugging them behind him so that the shafts flew from the guards' hands. A quick upward thrust brought the butts crashing into the two men's chins, sending them reeling back against the doors behind them. The one on the right collapsed immediately. The one on the left was still staggering, so Kagiri struck him again with the spear. That was enough, and he dropped the two yanoi atop their owners, stepping past them and through the doorway into the throne room itself.

It was a magnificent space, he saw at once. The floor was delicately tiled, marble mixed with other stone and metal and wood in an intricate pattern. The ceilings were high and arched, supported by heavy, carved pillars that marched down either side. There was stained glass arranged in a pattern at the peak to create a majestic skylight, and banners hung along the walls. At the room's far end was the dais, a low platform of enameled wood with gold fittings and a low railing blocking access to the curtain-ringed pavilion where the emperor held court, massive war masks peering down from the wall at his back.

Only the pavilion was currently empty.

The room was not, however. A single figure stood just before the dais, hands behind his back. His armor was black enamel, with the higeibara crest and a single tsodami petal overlapping the edge, and at his slim shoulders were gold bars, marking him as an officer despite his apparent youth and small stature. A sword jutted from the sash at his waist, which Kagiri found odd since it contradicted what Jiro Masute had told him. Still, it was no matter. One man would not be sufficient to slow his progress.

"Where is the emperor?" he asked as he stalked forward, closing the distance to this stranger. "I would speak with him at once."

"I am afraid that will not be possible." The stranger turned, and the features thus revealed confirmed what the voice had already suggested, that Kagiri was not facing a young man at all. "Perhaps I can assist you, however. My name is Misataki Shizumi, and I am the Taikoro of the Honjofu."

"You?" Kagiri studied the woman, who seemed only a few years older than him at most. Had someone so young truly attained such an exalted rank, or was that just a ruse to distract him from his quest? Did she even know how to use that handsome nihono at her side, or was she another spoiled noble whose only talent was an accident of birth? "I think not," he answered. "But if you tell me where he is I will spare your life." In truth he had no desire to kill her, but she did not need to know that.

Instead of cowering from this threat, her eyes narrowed, her chin rising. "I live to serve the empire, and the emperor," she declared, settling one hand upon her sword hilt while the other grasped the scabbard, ready to tug it free. "I will gladly give my life to protect him."

Kagiri sighed. "So be it." And, with a quick stride forward, he drew, his sword flashing out and up in a classic first strike.

She had her sword out in time to block easily and reversed the blade's direction just as fast, sweeping downward in a crossbody cut, her second hand releasing the scabbard and moving to grip the chahito. Bringing his own sword down quickly to knock hers aside, Kagiri backpedaled a step, reevaluating. Clearly she was no idle lady, not with skills like that!

Nor did she wait for him to reset himself, instead advancing with a quick downward thrust that would have skewered him through the throat had he not blocked it, followed by an interesting backward sweep that nearly knocked his blade from his grip. Impressive!

"Your aishone is very good," he complimented, using his longer legs to good advantage by retreating and circling slightly, keeping well away from the door and putting enough space between them for him to pause and shift his grip and his approach. "Where did you obtain it?"

She did not answer, only glaring in response and tightening her grip on her nihono. Perhaps it was not one of her ancestors, and thus a sore spot.

Moving to the attack, Kagiri brought his blade down once, hard, directly toward the top of her head. Instead of blocking she sidestepped, exactly as he'd expected, but the twist he put on his weapon, freeing one hand to sweep it suddenly sideways at her head, did not take her by surprise, as planned. Instead she crouched, her lesser height enabling her to duck below his swing, and then jabbed suddenly upward, attempting again to catch him in the throat, which was one of the only places his armor did not cover. He could not bring his sword back around in time and blocked with his forearm instead. The sword scraped across his hanketo, but the armor plates there protected both his arm and his neck. He kicked out, but she twisted away so that his boot only caught her in the side rather than full in the stomach. It still knocked her back several feet and drove the wind from her lungs, leaving her gasping for air as she brought her sword back in line, both hands placed perfectly on the silk cords of the handle.

"I am impressed, truly," he told her, circling slowly, his blade twirling almost idly in his hand. "I have never faced anyone your equal. Whose aishone is it? I must know!"

Still she did not answer, other than to raise her sword slightly.

Her stubbornness was beginning to annoy him, and he was also growing tired of the delay. *Time to end this,* Kagiri decided. This time he hammered her with a series of blindingly fast blows, left and then right and then left again, forcing her to give ground with each block and never giving her time to rally and strike back. He feinted for her head and, when she moved to parry that, kicked her in the knee instead, causing her to gasp and nearly buckle, though she was able to bring her sword back around in time. A moment later he tried the same trick, then, as she pivoted to avoid his kick, punched her full in the face instead. He nearly lost his hand to that, as her sword came leaping up reflexively, but the blow stunned her and she staggered back, bumping up against the wall and sagging back, eyes unfocused.

"Tell me whose aishone it is," Kagiri insisted. He batted her sword aside, grabbed her wrist with one hand to pin the blade in place well away from him, and laid the edge of his own across her throat. "Tell me or die."

"Enough!" someone cried out, and he glanced up to see a man emerging from within one of the columns across the room. A man who, though still in the shadow of the pillar, was clearly young and tall and richly attired, his hair caught up in a golden higeibara comb.

At last!

Hibikitsu had watched silently as the stranger, tall and lean and fearsome in his emerald armor, had stalked into the throne room like a tiger hunting prey. He had seen Shizumi stand up to the man and trade a dozen blows with him, any one of which Hibikitsu knew would have left him carved up and bleeding upon the floor. He had heard the stranger demand to know her aishone and had silently willed her to answer, her own words coming back to him: her pride or her life? When it had become clear that she would not give in, however, he had decided he could wait no longer.

"Taikoro Misataki!" he called out now, having left the safety of the column, though still the width of the room separated him from the emerald assassin. "Tell him your aishone!"

She shook her head, though carefully due to the blade at her throat.

"Tell him!" Hibikitsu ordered. "We command it!" Then, more gently, "we would not lose a warrior of your prowess, or your loyalty, for something as trivial as pride."

Shizumi sighed, though she stayed still as a statue. Finally, she spoke.

"There is no aishone," she answered, so softly he could barely hear. "There is only me."

"What?" He knew he was staring but he could not help it, feeling her words sink in like a thunderbolt. "Are you saying that you—"

"Yes." She raised her chin, daring either him or the stranger to find fault with her or her words even as she declared, shattering his entire world, "I am Mukanichi." Untouched. No aitachi at all.

Which meant, as she had said, all her skill, all her talent, all her martial mastery, that came from her and her alone.

CHAPTER THIRTY-ONE

"What?" She felt the blade loosen at her throat, shifting away an inch—barely any distance at all, but enough that she could breathe unrestricted again and shift her head to regard her captor. She was under no illusions about renewing their battle, however, especially since, as he took a single step away, he released her wrist—and plucked the emperor's sword from her hand as easily as she might have pulled a blade of grass. Ash, he was strong! And fast. And remarkably skilled, for all that his eyes behind the green menatu seemed so young.

And currently so wide with shock. "What?" he repeated again. "No aishone? No aitachi at all? But—how?"

"How?" Now disarmed, with anger fueling her and clearing her head from the blow she had taken there, she pushed away from the wall and he backed up further, allowing her to stand freely—and to turn on him. And on the emperor, who was even now crossing the room, stopping only a few paces behind this man who had clearly come to kill him and who now held both their swords. Fool! But she would deal with that after she answered his question, finally free to do so after so many years of hiding.

"How? By waking up every morning hours before everyone else and training. By staying up after them and training more. By practicing every second I could steal away. By reading every scroll on swordplay I could find, watching every warrior with good aishone, listening to every instructor willing to train a common girl."

She was almost spitting the words at them and it felt good, so good, to speak the truth after so long. "I would have had to work twice as hard as anyone else, even if I'd had aitachi. Without it? Ten times harder. Twenty." She reached to her throat, pulled up her aishone pouch, and tugged it free, clutching the worn-soft leather in her hand. "This? Dried chicken bones, ground fine. I had to swallow that each and every time, pretending it did anything more than make my throat itch." She tossed the bag aside. Her chin rose and she glared at them both, these men who could not possibly understand what she had gone through. "But I did it. Me and me alone. No relic bones to help me, no ancestors to lend me their strength and their skill. Everything you see, everything you fought, that is all me."

She had just signed her own death warrant, of course. Mukanichi were casteless, the lowest of the low, barely allowed to live in most towns, and she had lied and cheated her way not only into the military but into the Honjofu and now to its very top. She had faked aitachi to the emperor himself! Surely that was a crime punishable by death.

But—if that was the case, why was he smiling?

"That—is amazing!" Kagiri sheathed his sword absently, though he was still holding hers, this incredible woman who had nearly fought him to a standstill. Him! "You are incredible!" And the way she faced him now, unafraid despite being unarmed, not cowed in the least—he had never met anyone like her before.

Except that, in a way, he had.

Only, they lived inside him now.

"Will you agree not to fight me again?" he asked her. "I would very much hate having to kill such a noble opponent." She considered for an instant before nodding—and her eyes went wide as he reversed her sword and offered it back to her, hilt first. Taking it, she sheathed it with the ease of a warrior born. Which she was. Far moreso than he had been.

Truly if anyone was worthy of being a Gensaiba in this day and age, it was not him but this woman standing before him, daring him to judge her for her confession.

Pondering that, what it meant for him, for her, for the nation as a whole, he slowly remembered that there was someone else there, someone who was now only a few feet behind him and slightly to one side. Twisting around, Kagiri turned to look full upon the emperor for the first time—and, seeing the ruler of all Rimbaku's features plainly in the light from the skylights above, his jaw dropped as memories came flooding over him.

Memories that were not his own.

"Segei?" he whispered. "Is it really you?"

Hibikitsu was still reeling from his new Taikoro's admission. She was Mukanichi! Astounding! And she was magical with a blade, nearly the equal of the demon in green who currently stood between them—a demon who had acted honorably, even nobly, by not only accepting her surrender but returning her sword. Which was his.

The same demon who had just turned to him—and called him by an old, old name.

"I—no," he replied, and had to laugh at the incongruity of it all. Here he was in his throne room, with no one but the head of his Honjofu—who was Mukanichi!—beside him, and he was being confused with someone who had been dead and gone for centuries! Who was this stranger in green? "You mean Taido Segei, yes?" he asked now, barely able to keep from giggling, no matter how inappropriate that was given the current situation. "He was my ancestor. My forebear." He gestured around him. "He built all of this, after the Schism. He was the First Emperor."

Pushing the fit of laughter down, he focused on this tall stranger who had just fought the greatest swordswoman in the nation and won. "And who, exactly, are you?"

"Me?" Kagiri shook his head. That was the one question he had so often struggled with himself. Who was he, really? Was he still himself at all? Or was he Geido Shinen, Shito Kibi, Onyoku Jeizen, or any of the others?

But, considering that question, tossing it out into the vault of his mind, he was surprised to discover that it echoed in a nearly empty chamber. The Gensaiba, they were gone!

No, not gone. They were still there, as evidenced by his recognition of the man before him, who was the exact image of his long-gone ancestor. But though he could still feel them, Kagiri could barely hear them, and then only as whispers. They had faded, somehow. Merged into him. There was no longer any battle for control.

Now, there was only him. A different him than before, influenced by all of them—and the benefactor of all their skills—but one mind, one set of thoughts.

"My name," he replied, reaching up and unhooking the menatu, removing the face plate so they could see his face fully, "is Kagiri."

Shizumi shook her head. She had been bested by a mere boy? How was that even possible?

Though "boy" was perhaps unfair. He was nearly her own age. It was just that his face was still boyish, barely lined at all, his eyes bright and his jaw firm and smooth. But he could fight like he'd been blessed by the First Emperor himself—the same historic figure he had just confused with Hibikitsu.

What was going on here?

Kagiri was still trying to figure that out himself. "Your ancestor," he told the emperor slowly, "was one of the Gensaiba matekan. The wizards' warriors. There were seven of them, right before the Schism. One for each." He rubbed a gauntleted hand along his jaw, piecing things together from the memories of those within him. "He was not in the tower, though, when the Cataclysm occurred—the tower you know now as the Tawasiri. His wizard had refused to attend the moot and so they were not present. After the Schism, when the magic fled, he must have taken charge to keep the empire together."

The emperor—who was no older than him, Kagiri saw now, and his eyes were deep and thoughtful—nodded. "The kingdom had fallen into chaos," he confirmed, eyes distant as if reciting an old tale. "Taido Segei stopped the fighting, forced everyone to work together. He built this city and declared himself the first Relicant Emperor." His gaze sharpened. "Who are you, to know so much of his past that you confuse me with him?"

"I—am Gensaiba," Kagiri answered, tapping his chest. "The rest of those warriors live within me." He smiled and bowed. "And they would never forgive me if I were to kill the descendant of their good friend and comrade at arms." He had almost said "permit," but had known instinctively that it was no longer true. Though they still existed within him, the Gensaiba could no longer control his actions. His body was his once more, and his alone.

"I—" The emperor, who Kagiri had assumed would be cold and heartless, a true tyrant, broke into a grin and laughed. Laughed! "I am very pleased to hear that," he stated, clapping Kagiri on the shoulder as if they were old friends. "I am very interested to hear your tale, if you are willing to tell it." He frowned, though that only lasted a moment. "You said you came to kill me. I hope we can find some other way to resolve whatever dispute may have pointed you toward that goal."

Looking at this man now, Kagiri had to nod. This was not the emperor he had expected to find. The Gensaiba had still been influencing him when he had settled on this path of conquest, but with their influence waning he saw other options. And something about this emperor, who grinned and laughed and did not seem horrified at hearing his own Taikoro's secret, was appealing. And hopeful.

Hibikitsu allowed himself to relax just a little. This stranger—Kagiri—had sheathed his sword and seemed willing to talk. His story must be fascinating! All this talk about the Tawasiri—he had to be the one who had broken into that ancient monument, which meant he most likely was also the one who had killed the guards stationed there. Having seen him fight, Hibikitsu could well believe it, and there would be a reckoning for those lives, but the circumstances were unclear and he would withhold judgement—and punishment—until he knew all the details. But here was a man who carried in him the living past! What details about the land from before could he reveal? And what would knowing about those elements from the kingdom before it followed the Relicant Touch do for his own goal of moving them past that dependency, helping them out of their slump and back onto solid ground once more?

The fact that Shizumi did not use aishone at all—that she had no aitachi—was both a marvel and, he hoped, a sign of things to come.

He was still thinking these things through, having reflexively accepted Kosshiki back from Shizumi and returned the sword to its place at his side, when one of his Honteno rushed in. "Your Majesty!" the woman called, but skidded to a stop upon seeing Kagiri standing there, armed and armored.

"It is all right, Linai," he promised, recognizing her. "There is no danger here." He fervently hoped that would prove true. But she still looked concerned, agitated—and not because of Kagiri, he realized. "What is it?"

"There is—" she was winded from running and had to take several quick breaths before she could continue. "Someone is coming, sire. He—we cannot touch him, cannot reach him. He is like a force of nature!"

"Hm. Who is it?" His thoughts cast back to a conversation from what seemed like months before, back in Furukotai. "Is it the butcher of Kindichi?"

Beside him, he felt as much as saw Kagiri start, and even Shizumi looked surprised. "What did you say?" the green warrior asked.

"The Kindichi were bandits," Hibikitsu explained quickly, not taking his eyes from Linai. "They sent their finest warrior, the Butcher, here, it seems." But now all three of the people near him were shaking their heads.

"The Kindichi are gone, slaughtered," Shizumi was saying. "By a single man, from all reports." Her eyes widened as they turned to Kagiri, who seemed so calm and innocuous now with his sword sheathed and his face exposed.

Still, he nodded. "Yes, that was me. They were murderers and thieves, and I do not regret disposing of them."

Ah, now Hibikitsu had it, and he had to laugh again. "*You* are the Butcher of Kindichi!" he stated, chuckling at his own misunderstanding. "Not *their* butcher but the one who butchered *them*! Oh, I owe you a debt, then, my friend!" Which brought him back to Linai, and a sobering question. "But then, if it is not you who approaches, who is it?"

That question answered itself as a sudden wind swept through the room, racing from down the hall and pouring into the throne room like a small storm. It carried several guards with it, tossing them about like so many leaves in the breeze, to slam up against walls and pillars.

And at its center, buoyed but clearly in control of himself and his limbs and the chaos around him, was a young man. Stocky, with a broad, handsome face and close-cropped hair, dressed in simple, sturdy clothes, armed only with a stout walking stick, yet the sense of power emanating from him was so strong Hibikitsu could feel it. The wind deposited the newcomer just inside the doorway and he stepped forward, even as additional gusts battered both Linai and Shizumi away. Then he moved closer, the light catching his features—

—and, still at Hibikitsu's side, the Butcher of Kindichi gasped. "Niki?"

CHAPTER THIRTY-TWO

Kohori hoped, as she raced along the tunnel, that she had done the right thing.

Technically, Shizumi had been exactly correct—as commander of the Honteno, safeguarding the emperor was Kohori's direct responsibility. But so was protecting this city. If it had been Haro, Kohori wouldn't have even considered leaving—she would have directed him to oversee the defenses and stayed by Hibikitsu's side. But then, Haro had never been even a fraction the warrior Shizumi was. While the young woman, though a natural leader from what she'd seen thus far, was not yet the commander Kohori knew herself to be. So it made sense to leave the Honjofu there to protect the emperor and rally the various defensive formations herself.

Still, it felt like she had abandoned her post.

I don't have the time or the luxury for second-guessing, Kohori reminded herself as she ran, her long legs eating up the distance from one gate to the next. Itamon and Manari were right behind her, one slightly to her left and the other slightly to her right, in classic triangular formation. They were trailed by several aiashe they had pressed into service when they'd passed through the gate to Motohiri, since from the brief reports she'd received thus far Kohori gathered the heaviest attacks were down in Mazihini and beyond that in Suranmui, around the outer wall. Why anyone capable of flight would concentrate their efforts there instead of simply going to higher ground—and more critical targets—she had no idea, but she was grateful for their poor strategy, at least.

Of course, she still had no idea how she would deal with these creatures when she got there. What did she—or anyone, truly—know about fighting off winged skeletons?

Well, she would simply have to make it up as she went along.

"Shhh," Chimehara urged, and beside her Suda went still. They had exited their building and were now tucked neatly into an alley some distance away, only the far wall did not back up against a home or a shop or one of the nobles' compounds. Instead, the wall there traversed not only the alley but the street beyond, and though a mere ten feet high it was completely roofed over, with a decorative iron pattern across the top. A pattern that allowed light and air into the space beyond.

It was a tunnel. She had noticed it on her first walk around Motohiri, back when she had just been accepted into House Chohu and had decided to familiarize herself with everything she could about this elevated tier where she now lived and worked, with its outer walls of warm peach. The tunnel cut from that outer wall all the way to the pale-yellow wall ringing Atsani beyond. And, when she had ventured down into Sakiriti, she had located an extension of that same passage crossing that district and presumably connecting it to Bejinuri below that.

She had known at once what they must be. For anyone walking the streets, entrance to each tier was through a set of wide gates manned by several aiashe, though they did not interfere with people provided they looked like they had some reason for being there. The gates were not one after the other, however—that would have been advantageous for anyone bridging more than one level but also would have allowed any attacking force to charge straight across and up, from the outer gates all the way to Aihiri. No, instead the gates' placement was staggered, one on the west side and the next on the east and so on, so that if you were invading you would have to move in a long, looping path, allowing defenders many opportunities to whittle away at your forces.

But if the defenders needed to move quickly, they would want a straight path up and down. One that was covered, protected, and guarded.

A path just like this one.

When she had heard the gong, Chimehara had known something serious must be happening. The last time the gong had sounded had been almost ten years ago, when a storm of unprecedented size and ferocity had blown in from sea and still had enough force to crash down upon Awaihinshi like the wrath of some forgotten god. Hundreds had died, businesses had been destroyed, and much of Suranmui had simply washed away. She had hoped never to hear the gong again, yet she could not deny that any such chaos could present an unparalleled opportunity, one she would be foolish to pass up.

Which was why they were here now, listening.

Sure enough, she heard the sound of heavy feet running, several sets of them, most likely armored from the timbre. Those raced past, heading from Atsani toward Sakiriti. Given that the few screams and shouts she'd heard had also been from down below, Chimehara considered it likely that whatever had required the alert was taking place on one of the lower levels, well away from here.

That also meant that all eyes would be turned that way. Perfect.

"Come," she told Suda, and they returned to their building. It was a fairly standard nahiya, only three stories tall, with the first floor occupied by a clothier who worked in the front and lived in the back. The second and third floors were broken into two apartments each, and she and Suda occupied the left-side space on the top floor. It was a lovely place, quiet and peaceful, but once Ruisoki had passed beyond his period of mourning and she made arrangements for him to come live with her, Chimehara feared it would not be enough.

Which meant it was time to expand.

Reaching her apartment door, she unlocked it and slid it open, stepping inside. Then she turned just within the entryway, barring Suda from following. "Do it now," she instructed the girl. "Just as we practiced."

The girl nodded and, backing away, pivoted and skipped the few short steps across the hall to the door on the far side.

"Hello?" she knocked once, twice. "Hello? Is anyone there?" Chimehara eased her own door shut all but a sliver, peeping through that narrow gap.

After a moment, the other door rattled slightly. There was a click, then it slid open to reveal Madam Ione. "Yes?"

Chimehara had found it ironic when she had learned that the slender, almost emaciated-looking Ione owned a bakery. Did the woman never consume her own wares? That seemed a poor recommendation for such a place! She was not terribly friendly and tended to return late from the bakery and leave early, but over the months Chimehara had managed to catch her in conversation a few times—enough to ascertain that the other woman owned the apartment outright and that she did not have any family here in the city.

It was too good a chance to pass up.

"I'm sorry," Suda was saying to their neighbor now, blinking up at her with those big eyes and long lashes, her lower lip trembling slightly. "Do you—have you seen my cousin? I can't find her anywhere!"

"What?" Ione's eyes flicked to Chimehara's door, but from there it would appear to be shut completely. "She is not home? Did she go out?"

The girl nodded, trembling a little. "Just a little while ago. She said she was going to the store. Then that gong started and— I'm scared! What if something's happened to her?" Chimehara thought that might be overplaying a little, but she was not about to interfere. Not unless things seemed to be getting away from her young apprentice.

The baker's eyes were wide and perhaps a little moist, though that was difficult to tell from here. "Let us go find her, then," she declared. "Wait here." She ducked back inside and returned a moment later, shrugging into a flour-dusted hantien. Then she locked the door and, taking Suda's hand, started for the stairs.

The girl let the woman tug her along but kept just a pace or two behind. Which positioned her perfectly to draw her dagger and stab up through Ione's rib cage just as they reached the top step. The woman stiffened, a sound like a hiss escaping her lips, then fell forward. But Suda's hand was still held tight, and the falling baker was about to drag the girl down with her!

Chimehara raced from her room, grabbed Suda around the waist, and yanked her free, falling back on the floor with the girl in her arms. They righted themselves and listened to the thump-thump-thump as Ione toppled, banging against the wall and floor and railing as she tumbled to the bottom. There were raised voices down below and the sound of more doors opening as the lower neighbors rushed to investigate.

"Are you injured?" Chimehara asked. Suda shook her head, the dagger already wiped clean and back in its sheath. "Then let's go." She let the girl give her a hand back to her feet and then the two of them ventured down to express shock and dismay and horror at Madam Ione's tragic misstep.

With all the blood and bruises such a fall would cause, no one would notice the stab wound that had truly killed her. Chimehara would wait a few days before offering to buy the dead woman's apartment—most would consider it bad luck to live where someone had so recently passed, so she did not expect any competition for the space. And then she and her growing troupe would have ample room to live and work.

She still did not know what the city-wide alert was for, but she thanked the First Emperor for it nonetheless.

"Keep together!" Seikoku instructed and Minawa and Kanai nodded, passing the message along. The guards had led them into the bottommost tier—Mazihini, they'd called it—and then had run off, presumably to assist others in defending from those flying terrors. With Noniki gone to seek the emperor, it had fallen to Seikoku to keep their friends safe. Unfortunately, she did not know this city at all, but when in doubt she felt the best plan was to find a sturdy wall and put your back against it. At least then you knew you had one direction covered and could focus on watching the rest.

She spotted a wall up ahead that looked like it might serve admirably. It ran across the boulevard, cutting the section off completely, and was ten feet of smooth, whitewashed stone, with an iron lattice for a roof. Was there some sort of compound beyond? She had no idea. All she cared about was that the wall looked sturdy and had enough space for them to all pile up against it, carts included.

They had nearly reached it when a small iron-bound door near the center opened and a trio of armored figures emerged. Several more followed, but while the latter wore the garb of standard military, complete with jingaso, those first three had proper armor, and all of it enameled a deep red.

"You there!" the one in front, a tall, broad-shouldered woman with gray hair and a commanding appearance, called out, spotting her. "What is happening here?" Strange that she would not know!

But Seikoku answered anyway. "Winged skeletons," she replied, pointing up to where several were swooping overhead. "They appeared from nowhere and started attacking." Fortunately the strange creatures did not seem well-organized—they had only struck a few times, and that haphazardly at best. "Guards have been harassing them with spears and arrows, but—" She shrugged. "No flesh."

"Hm." The woman frowned, glaring skyward as if her gaze alone could knock the creatures from the sky. "Yes. Hammers would do better."

"No leverage," the one beside her, a tall fellow and thin, with a long face, pointed out. "Not unless they want to come down here."

"I'd rather they didn't," the woman snapped, her tone and the way the two men deferred making it clear she was in charge. "Crowded enough as it is, and if they land they could hurt a lot of people." Her gaze flashed back to Seikoku again. "You should get inside somewhere. It isn't safe out here."

"Probably true," Seikoku agreed, "but we don't have anywhere to go. We only just arrived and we don't know anyone here." She watched as one of the soldiers unstrapped an umi from his back and, fitting an arrow to it, fired up at something that resembled a flying bull, complete with horns. The arrow passed clean through its chest, not even drawing the creature's notice. "You could use those better," she suggested.

"What?" the other woman glanced where she was looking. "The bows? They can't do much against bone."

"They could if you attached something like a metal ball to the arrow, instead of a tip," Seikoku pointed out. "There are your hammers, but with enough range to reach."

The older woman nodded. "Yes, that would do the trick." She turned to the other man with her. "Itamon, see what you can do with that." Then she returned her attention to Seikoku—and bowed, one fist going to her chest. "Maniko Kohori, Taikoro of the Honteno, at your service."

Seikoku didn't know what the Honteno were, but it sounded impressive. "Seikoku," she replied, dipping her own head in return. "Of...this group here." She waved her hand to include the others. "Happy to help."

That drew a smile from Kohori. "Why don't we see if we can get you and your people someplace safe?" she suggested, striding forward until she was standing companionably close. "And then I'd love to hear any other ideas you have on how to deal with these flying menaces." At this distance Seikoku could see the warmth in the other woman's eyes, which somehow didn't seem at odds with her grim, warlike demeanor, and she found herself nodding.

"I don't know how much help I can be," she admitted, "but I'll do what I can."

She knew that, even if it meant leaving the others for a time, Noniki would approve. She hoped, wherever he was, he was faring as well or better.

CHAPTER THIRTY-THREE

Noniki stared—not at the emperor, for he had no doubt that was the handsome young man with the sharp features, the beautiful, jewel-crusted kitoro, and the golden higeibara rising from his chonmage like a flame. No, his eyes were riveted to the tall warrior beside him, clad all in gleaming emerald armor like the play of sunlight across a river bottom—save for his face, which was bare, and as familiar to Noniki as his own. It was a face he had believed he would never see again.

"Giri?" He stumbled forward, his winds retreating as he crossed the expansive room, leaving a loud silence in their wake. "Is that really you?" Now that he was closer he could see without a doubt that it was indeed his older brother, who he had thought dead in the cursed Tawasiri. Kagiri looked a little older, his face a little thinner and with a few more lines that made him seem even more serious, but now a grin broke out across that face and any doubt vanished. With a cry, Noniki sprinted the last few feet, his arms wide, and engulfed his brother in a crushing hug. Kagiri returned the gesture and the two of them spun around, alternating lifting each other off the ground, laughing and crying until they had to pause for breath.

"I take it," the emperor cut in, his voice laced with amusement, "that you two know each other?"

Up close, Noniki could tell that the emperor was probably Kagiri's age or perhaps just a little older. He stood between them in both height and build, and his features were sharp and clean, matched by the clear intelligence in his dark eyes. Was this truly the man Noniki had come to remonstrate with? He had expected someone a good deal more boorish, more crude, with a cloudier gaze and a grimmer demeanor.

It was Kagiri who answered first. "My apologies, Your Majesty," he said, pulling one arm free so that he could turn them both to face their nation's ruler, their other arms still wrapped around each other's waists. "Allow me to introduce my brother Noniki, who I last saw outside the Tawasiri. The winds," he added with his usual wry humor, "appear to be something new. Niki, this is His Majesty Hibikitsu, emperor of all Rimbaku."

Noniki could see that there must be a story here, judging by the way the emperor's eyebrow quirked, but that would keep for now. He disengaged from Kagiri and bowed as best he could. "A pleasure, Your Majesty. I have traveled a long way to speak with you."

"Oh?" Hibikitsu folded his arms across his chest. "What about?"

"About the Relicant Way, sire," Noniki replied bluntly. "I think this nation desperately needs a change if it is going to survive."

"Hm." The emperor frowned, but after an instant of panic Noniki judged the expression to be less displeasure at him than thoughtfulness—and perhaps a dislike of the situation he spoke of? He had no experience reading rulers, but the man's stance did not seem combative, at least. "I would very much like to hear what you have to say," he stated at last, and that sounded genuine. "Though first there is the small matter of the creatures menacing my city. I trust those are not yours?" That last was said with an edge to it, and Noniki was glad he could honestly deny that.

"Not mine, no," he said firmly. "But I would be happy to help rid the city of them, sire." That brought a smile to the emperor's face, which Noniki felt himself returning. Ash, had he actually considered shouting at and threatening and even possibly deposing this man?

And what was Kagiri's role in all this?

He turned to ask his brother that very question—and stopped, the words dying in his throat, as Kagiri's gaze sailed past him, locking onto something well behind. His brother's face tightened and he shifted his weight slightly, pivoting and sliding one foot forward, hand going to the nihono at his side—a weapon he wore as if born to it. Clearly, they would have some tales to exchange.

For now, however, Noniki turned to see what had captured his brother's attention so completely—and beheld a pair of the strangest men he had ever seen, striding into the room.

Kagiri locked away his joy at finding his brother alive and well—and possessed of some strange power. He tucked down his growing respect for this young emperor who greeted them both with more curiosity and interest than fear, and who seemed genuinely open to new ideas. He hid any concern about the strange winged creatures flying about outside.

Right now, his entire focus was upon the pair who had just entered the throne room.

They were shorter than him, perhaps Noniki's height, and slight. Their clothing was in tatters, mere rags and pale, the color all washed away. But more arresting was their skin, which was as chalk-white as their hair, and their eyes, which were black from tip to tip but seemed to shift somehow as he watched. Neither carried anything, weapon or otherwise, but he could sense, perhaps from the sneer on their lips or the angry glare of those odd eyes, that they were more dangerous than anyone he had faced yet.

Which was why, rather than wait, he charged.

Nor was he alone. The warrior who had delivered the message was back on her feet and also ran at the strange pair, as did Misataki Shizumi, though she had no nihono now, only a yanoi she had presumably plucked from one of the dazed guards.

Not surprisingly, given the length of her weapon and the fact that she had been closer to the door, she reached them first.

There were no niceties here, no formal challenge—she stabbed forward, the long spear blade glittering as it sailed toward the taller of the two men—

—and Kagiri was near enough to see the gleaming metal head essentially disintegrate on the spot, crumbling to rust and dust the second it came in contact with that pale skin.

The messenger warrior was there next, her sword flashing out in a clean arc to remove the other man's head from his neck—

—and the nihono fell apart as it struck, the blade dispersing into a puff of particles.

The man glanced her way and then reached out and, as she stood gaping, rested a pale hand against her cheek, almost tenderly.

And she screamed, her skin wrinkling and drying out, her hair graying and then shattering in a cloud, her body shriveling as she felt to her knees with an audible crack, then toppled sideways to the ground, a shriveled husk where a vibrant woman had stood an instant before.

"Don't touch them!" Kagiri shouted and tackled Shizumi, who had been about to attack again, with only her yori-toki this time. "Niki, do something!"

The answer was immediate. The wind returned, whipping past him as he forced Shizumi to stay down. It struck with the force of a full-on gale, ripping the two strangers from their feet and hurling them from the room the way a man might toss aside a small pebble from his boot. There was an opening to the compound beyond—Kagiri had not seen such a direct entrance when he had found a way in here and something told him that it might not have been there, but he was happy to see it now, as the pair were slammed out through the opening and disappeared.

"Done," Noniki answered from behind them. "They're still in Awaihinshi somewhere, but at least they are no longer here in the palace. If they even survived that, we'll have time to find them and deal with them—carefully."

"I believe," Shizumi offered, her voice slightly muffled by the fact that Kagiri was still pinning her to the floor, "that we may have a more pressing matter." Her eyes were focused on the door and reluctantly Kagiri glanced that way as well—and froze as what appeared to be a small, whirling cloud of colorful sparks and swirls floated into view.

What now?

Hibikitsu's head was whirling. First, the Butcher of Kindichi arrived, dispatching or disabling his guards with ease and then defeating Shizumi in a duel, only to turn out to be a pleasant if serious-seeming young man interested in social reform. Then a stranger with control over the wind flew inside, only to reveal himself as the first man's brother and also a would-be reformer. Next a pair of ghost-pale men arrived, their touch deadly corrosive, and were tossed out by the apparent matekai. And now a cloud of light and color was here in the throne room? What was next, a visitation from the First Emperor himself, only riding a winged quisuin or a horned raeteru?

"What is the meaning of this?" he demanded, stepping forward, his eyes locked upon this new apparition. "Are you here with a petition? If so, you will have to wait—I am not hearing requests at this moment."

The cloud had paused in the center of the room, almost directly beneath the skylight. Though lacking a face or any other clear features, he felt that it was looking for someone. Then it began to move again—only, not toward him.

Instead it appeared focused on the young wind-master named Noniki.

"Get off me!" Shizumi snapped, shoving the tall warrior away and rolling to the side so she could find her feet. She was up again in an instant and looked around for a weapon, any weapon. The yanoi she had used was gone, destroyed somehow by that strange pair, along with Linai's nihono and Linai herself. Ah, Linai. Shizumi had not known the Honteno long, but she had liked the earnest young woman. She would grieve later, however. Now she had more pressing concerns. Specifically, the strange apparition hovering in the air less than a good spear-toss away—and the emperor only a few feet past her, completely exposed should it choose to attack.

Unfortunately, even if she had been properly armed again she was not sure what she could do here. How did one strike down a cloud?

Still, she would not be guilty of failing at her duty. The two guards had recovered from their tumultuous entry into the room and were now standing again, still looking confused and uncertain. "Back to the door!" she ordered, making them jump to attention. "Re-equip and take up guard positions! Do not let anyone through without my order!" Both men saluted and hurried to comply. "And find me a sword!" she called after them.

Then, lacking anything more substantial than her yori-toki, she stomped across the floor and planted herself in front of the emperor, legs apart and slightly bent at the knees, arms crossed. Anything trying to get to him would have to go through her first.

"You!" Noniki growled, for he recognized the small, color-filled cloud now headed his way. Though he had been only a disembodied spirit at the time, he could never forget that sensation of leaving his body and soaring over the world—or of being sucked in by a glowing, coruscating cloud that had attempted to rip his soul to shreds and swallow every last scrap of it. He had fought free then, however, and he was a good deal more focused, more concentrated now.

Not to mention his other gifts.

Accordingly, he hurled a torrent of air at the cloud, intending to send it flying from the room the same way he had those two pale men—and had they been connected in any way or was it just coincidence that both had appeared now, much as he and Kagiri had? But instead of being flung aside the cloud···swelled. The wind disappeared into it, expanding its glowing edges, and the colors within it began to swirl even faster.

That did not seem good. Not good at all.

"Do something!" Kagiri shouted. "Get rid of it!"

"I just tried that!" Noniki yelled back. "It didn't work!"

"So try something else!"

Fine. He had been using wind because he was comfortable with that, but that was certainly not the only arrow in his quiver. Concentrating, Noniki raised his hand, the room around him darkening as all the light was pulled toward that limb, gathering around it. Then he gestured toward the cloud, palm outward, and the light erupted from his grasp, blasting the cloud with a column of pure brilliance.

The cloud drank it up like a thirsty plant being offered water. It grew even larger, the colors it contained far brighter, and now they appeared less random, more defined. And were those images within the washes of red and green and gold and others?

"I'm just making it stronger!" he shouted. How was he supposed to fight this thing if his magic only helped it grow?

Kagiri cursed under his breath. He had no idea how Noniki was doing any of that with the wind or the light but his brother was right, it was not working. The cloud was clearly bigger and brighter now, and instead of random splashes of color it seemed to be displaying vague shapes, like an image slowly coming into focus as you approached it, the fuzziness giving way to detail. Like that, there. It was a mound of some sort, but with shapes thrust up at intervals across its length. There was something familiar about it, in fact. He squinted, staring, trying to dredge his memory—and then it clicked.

"It's the Tawasiri," he whispered. Now that he knew what to look for, the Tower of Ghosts was unmistakable.

But what did that cursed spire have to do with this strange being?

Noniki heard what he'd said. "The Tawasiri? Are you sure?" But his mind was already racing, trying to put the pieces together. "The home of wizards," he said softly. That's what one of the merchants—Master Kawatai, he believed—had said of it. Was that where this thing had come from? And was that why it seemed fixated on him? Because he was a matekai himself now, or at least in the process of becoming one?

"That's right," Kagiri agreed. "It was. Well, not so much a home as a council chamber. It was where the matekai met to deliberate. And their Gensaiba, their sworn swords, would be there as well, waiting for them to finish." He tapped his chest. "I have the Gensaiba inside me—they died there in that tower, all of them at once, and were trapped within it until I stumbled in and absorbed them all. But the matekai—Geido Isami, Shito Daiko, and the rest—I have no idea what happened to them."

His brother had let out a gasp, however. "Say that again," he demanded. "Just the names."

With a shrug, Kagiri complied. "Did you see?" Noniki asked. "Watch the cloud and name each of the matekai in turn. Do it!"

Kagiri did—and stared. Because as he recited each wizard's name, the cloud flickered, changing to a single color overall, like someone cycling through patterns and associating each one with a particular term or name.

It was definitely responding to the names. Which meant he was not entirely surprised when his brother blurted out, "I think— I think those might be the matekai themselves!"

Noniki was sure he was correct. The way the cloud responded to each name in turn, it clearly had a connection to those long-gone wizards. And it had shown the Tawasiri, where Kagiri said the matekai had congregated. If they had died at the same time as their Gensaiba, perhaps they had been trapped as well? But they hadn't been found by Kagiri—and Noniki would want to hear more about that later! They had escaped on their own, but not in or with anyone. Might that be why they were an unformed cloud?

Which meant perhaps he had an idea now on how to remove them—or at the very least stop them from being a threat.

"Giri," he called out, extending his hand. "I need you to tell me about each of the matekai in turn. Everything you can remember about them. Take my hand and think about each one, really picture them in your head."

His brother didn't question him. Instead, a second later he felt an armored hand clasping his own, tightly but not painfully. And then, as he reached out with other senses he was still learning to control, he felt the comforting presence of his brother's mind linking with his. Kagiri's mind, his essence, had a strange quality to it, as if there were too many layers, too much complexity for so few years, but it was still clearly him, his soul shining clear and bright, and Noniki took comfort in that even as he opened himself to the images his brother began providing, using each one as a focus for his newfound magic.

"Geido Isami," his brother intoned, and the image that emerged was of a tiny woman, birdlike, with bright eyes and sharp features but a surprisingly warm smile. She hated bullying of any sort, loved flowers almost to distraction, and dressed in drab and dark clothes when in public but wore the brightest, most garish attire when in private. He took those images, that encapsulation of the former matekai, and pushed it at the cloud, not an attack but a lifeline, a pattern for it to latch onto. The cloud turned a soft rose red—and a portion of it separated from the rest, shaping itself into a face.

The same face Noniki had just seen in his brother's mind.

"Shito Daiko." She had a broad, open face, warm and appealing. Quiet but when she spoke it was sharp and clear, incisive. Hated bugs of all sorts but had a soft spot for cats and, oddly, snakes.

The cloud turned a warm, rich yellow, the color of the sun— and her visage separated to hover above the rest, right beside Geido Isami.

"Onyoku Ebima." A handsome woman with strong features and expressive eyebrows over a ready smile. Chilly in person, however, difficult to get to know—but steadfastly loyal to those who won her trust. Her hue was a cool blue with hints of gray like the onset of a mild storm, and she looked down on them with a friendly but slightly distant gaze.

"Bushiki Honei." He had wide features and a mouth that already twitched in a smile, with dancing, laughing eyes. He loved to dance, in truth, and to laugh and joke, but never meanly—he merely felt that life was too valuable not to appreciate to its fullest. His color was spring green, warm and lively.

"Komu Juroji." Large eyes dominated a long face, rendered even less attractive by thin, colorless lips and a high, peaked brow. He preferred books to people but could be friendly enough with those he respected, though that number was few indeed. His visage as it broke free was a dusky violet, pale and almost dour.

"Nikiyu Bezaitin." Slender, with a narrow face and narrow features, brow permanently arched as if laughing at everyone but lips pursed and clearly unwilling to share the joke. His color was dark amber, rich and deep and as complicated as he was—

—and that was the last of the cloud, the final matekai's face shaping the remainder so that now, instead of one big, inchoate mass, there were six faces peering at them, each a different shade and hue.

And each, to some degree, alive.

At least now, however, they were no longer all jumbled together. No longer insensate.

No longer mad.

The question was, what to do next?

Hibikitsu had watched—from over Shizumi's shoulder, which had amused him no end, not that he would let the fierce swordswoman know that, lest she feel slighted or unappreciated—as the two brothers had somehow separated that strange undulating cloud out into a half-dozen faces, unweaving it much the way a seamstress might unravel a snarl of thread, sorting it into its strands so that it might be used again. But how to use these, who had been wizards and rulers before this realm had formed?

Perhaps, he reasoned, it was not a question of use, but merely one of respect. One ruler to another.

"Noble matekai," he called out, setting a hand on his Taikoro's shoulder and gently nudging her to the side so that he could step forward. He did his best not to flinch as all six sets of eyes turned to regard him, each glowing softly in its chosen hue. "I am Hibikitsu, inheritor of Taido Seigei, the first Relicant Emperor. My ancestor served as one of the Gensaiba, alongside the men and women who served you. As his descendent, I salute you, who governed this land before me. I thank you for your efforts in protecting it and guiding it. But that time has long since passed. It is a different world now, and one unsuited to receive your gifts. You have done more than your duty. Now it is time for you to rest, with all our gratitude."

Those faces studied him, handsome and ugly, smiling and severe, plain and glamorous. Then one of them, the one that was a warm green, broke into a sunny smile. He nodded once, a clear mark of respect—and then he vanished, popping like a soap bubble, leaving only a faint afterimage and a fading scent behind.

Next was the one in violet. Then the one in blue. Each disappeared in turn, until the last, he of the amber hue, allowed himself to go, leaving the throne room feeling oddly empty but also refreshed, much like the air after a cool rain.

"It is over," Noniki declared. "They have gone." He released the breath he had been holding and smiled. "And I believe you will find that they were the cause of that strange cavalcade in the skies, so I suspect that threat has now vanished as well."

They had won.

CHAPTER THIRTY-FOUR

"That's it!" Kohori shouted. "Wrap it up tight!"

Her troops—a mix of the few Honteno she had brought with her, a handful of Honjofu who had caught up with them, several aiashe she had pressed into service, and that young woman, Seikoku—hurried to comply. One of the Honjofu, a woman named Itami Kane, was known to be an exceptional archer, but she had also proven to have excellent aim with almost any thrown object, including the weighted chains they had borrowed from a stables just inside the main gates. Flinging one of those, she had managed to snag it around the legs of a creature as it swooped past—then several of the others had latched onto the trailing end and pulled, yanking the creature to the ground. Now they were tossing heavy nets on top of it, pinning its flailing limbs in place and keeping it from escaping or from ripping through them with its long, clawed hands.

Then Itamon and Manari set upon it with the ganabo they had liberated from the guardhouse. The heavy iron clubs pounded down, turning bone to powder with each swipe, until soon there was nothing but bits of dust blowing away down the street and gritting up their armor and boots.

This was the third skeleton they had disposed of in this manner, and she had dispatched squads to the other tiers with the same instructions and comparable equipment. With any luck, they were having similar success.

Unfortunately, the number of creatures circling the city appeared to be nearly endless, so she wasn't sure how much good they were actually doing. But she had to keep trying.

"Here comes another one!" Seikoku shouted. Though smaller

and lighter than any of the soldiers, the young woman had sharp eyes and quick hands—she had taken on the role of spotter and was often the first to manage netting whatever creature they'd brought down. Sure enough, a new monster sailed into view, its body a strange mix of jointed limbs and cylindrical torso, as if someone had married an eel to a crab. The problem was its wings, which were also jointed, almost bat-like—and spanned wider than the street.

Ash, Kohori thought. *How are we going to get a net around that?*

Then the sky shook.

That was the only way she could describe it. The entire horizon seemed to vibrate for an instant, almost like they were inside a bell that had been struck, though there was no sound she could hear. Everything shuddered slightly, the skeletons most of all—

—and then they began to drop from the sky. Not in the previous way, when they'd swooped and dived to attack. No, they were simply falling. They were not even moving, no flailing at all. It was as if whatever had been animating them had suddenly vanished.

Which Kohori took as a very good sign, even as she shouted, "Scatter!" and dove to the ground right before the crab-eel hit the paving stones and shattered, sending bone shards in every direction.

"What just happened?" Seikoku asked once they'd all dusted themselves off and were back on their feet. Manari had a shallow cut along his cheek where a bone shard had caught him, and one of the aiashe had taken a piece in the leg, but no one else had been hurt.

"I don't know," Kohori admitted, wiping the sweat from her face with a cloth. "But if we're no longer under attack I need to make sure the emperor is safe." She studied this stranger she had only just met, making a snap decision. "You are welcome to come with me. Things would have gone significantly worse if not for your aid, and I am sure the emperor will wish to thank you himself." *Assuming he survived,* she reminded herself, but shoved that thought away. She refused to believe Hibikitsu was not fine.

Especially with Shizumi there to protect him.

"Thank you," Seikoku replied. "I need to check on my other friends, but then I'd be happy to. Our leader, Noniki, was actually headed in that direction when all this started, so I'm hoping we will find him along the way." Her furrowed brow suggested she was more worried than she cared to admit, but Kohori chose not to press her on that. They had only just met, after all. She could hardly blame the young woman for not wishing to share everything about herself or her friends. Still, there was something about the way she had said "leader" that made Kohori frown and wonder if she should hope to meet this Noniki—or to never catch sight of him.

"There, you see?" Chimehara said, patting Suda's head. "That dreadful gong has stopped. Everything is fine again."

The girl nodded, not taking her eyes from her task. She was currently copying a list of poisons one could cultivate from local plants, including name, effect, method of cultivation, amount needed, time for full potency, and antidote, if any. It was hardly Suda's favorite assignment—in fact, it might be safe to say that it was her least favorite, as was anything involving reading and copying—but it was important information, and it also allowed her to practice her writing, which was still atrocious.

She was diligent, however. She might pout and glare and grumble, but she never turned away from any assignment Chimehara set for her, and she did her best with each and every one of them.

Still, Chimehera could not wait until they were able to add Ruisoki to their little enclave. Why, the boy might even be able to teach her a thing or two about poisons!

Though she would be very careful never to let him near the tea or the food. At least at first.

Ibaru groaned and sat up. "Iraku?" he called.

"Here," came an equally weak voice from somewhere nearby. Something stirred, and then a head and shoulders emerged from the wreckage.

"Are you intact?" Ibaru asked. He was taking stock of himself but though every part of him ached, he did not seem to be broken anywhere.

"I believe so," his brother agreed, performing a very similar check. They had grown up being beaten for being Untouched, and so had many years of long practice testing to see what was merely bruised or sprained versus actually broken. At the moment, he could find none of the latter.

Part of that, he knew, was thanks to the gifts their master had bestowed upon them. When that man had somehow flung them from the palace and from Aihiri itself, he had assumed they were doomed. They had plummeted at least one level before finally colliding with a roof of some sort. But its tiles had crumbled upon contact, lessening the impact, and they had fallen through to the ground, which was heavy stone but had also worn a bit at their touch. Otherwise, he doubted they would have survived.

He pulled himself to his feet—and nearly toppled again as something passed through him, like a heavy cloak being torn from his shoulders. It was a weight that had lifted, a tight feeling inside that had loosened—but also a protective robe that had been ripped away. He staggered and rested a hand against a nearby wall to steady himself—

—and the wall stayed standing.

"Ibaru!" Iraku rushed to his side. His little brother looked as battered and dusty as he felt, but otherwise uninjured. "Are you well? What was that?"

"Our master," Ibaru answered, straightening. "He is gone." And it was true. He knew it in his bones. Somehow, Kaemusei was no more.

His brother gasped, and at first he thought it was in response to that statement. Then Iraku pointed a trembling hand at him. "Your face!"

Ibaru felt, but it seemed normal enough. The sight of his hands, however, made him gape. For, even as he watched, the white was leeching away, as if a thin layer of makeup was being washed clean. Beneath it, his normal skin color waited, seeming dark and grubby after so much time spent pale as an infant's tooth.

Nor was he alone in this transformation. "Yours as well," he said, watching as his brother's face resumed its old coloring. His hair, too, was turning dark. Within seconds it was a dusty but inky black once more.

"What has happened to us?" Iraku asked.

"Our master is gone, and with it much of what he lent us," Ibaru replied. He pressed his hand against the brick wall and concentrated. After an instant his skin there seemed to pale, and the brick began to crumble. "Much, but not all." He smiled. "And now we may walk amongst the people of this city, with no one the wiser."

Iraku smiled at that, the sharp, hungry smile of a prey turned predator. "They will never see us coming," he declared. "We will avenge the Silent Change."

"Yes," Ibaru agreed. "We will."

CHAPTER THIRTY-FIVE

s soon as she was sure the threat had passed, Shizumi rounded on her emperor. "What in the First Emperor's name were you thinking?" she demanded, stepping so close her boot tips nearly trod on his delicate silk slippers. "You put yourself in danger! How am I supposed to protect you if you shove me to the side like that?"

Hibikitsu studied her for a second—and then he laughed. She was beginning to get the impression that the ruler of all Rimbaku laughed a great deal, though she did not remember seeing him so much as smile in the previous glimpses she'd had before he'd left Awaihinshi. It seemed his travels had changed him, and for the better, as far as she was concerned. Though she did not much appreciate being the source of his humor right now.

"I am sorry, noble Taikoro," he told her, dipping his head ever so slightly, as befitted a ruler speaking to one of his officers. "You are correct, of course—I should not have stepped past you in that way. I hope you can forgive me." His lips quirked into a smile, however, and he added, "But I must ask—exactly how had you intended to protect me from that cloud?"

"I do not know, precisely," she grumbled, arms across her chest. "But I'd have thought of something!"

He nodded, sobering instantly. "No one can fault your courage, or your loyalty," he assured her. "Which only confirms to me that I was correct in promoting you to Taikoro. Truly, you have my thanks."

There was little she could say to that, so she saluted and bowed, her anger dissipating. Though only a little.

Instead she glanced about and found another target, the young man in green. "And you!" she snapped, approaching him with such fury he backed up a pace, hands raised in surrender. "You tackled me like I was a runaway pig!"

The third man, the shorter one, laughed. "Have you known many runaway pigs?" he asked, causing the taller one to guffaw as well. Lovely. This was exactly what she needed right now, she fumed—a bunch of men standing around laughing at her.

"No one asked you!" she told him, which only made him laugh harder. "You tossed me about like a stray cloth!"

"I did," he agreed, taming his grin, "and I apologize." He bowed. "My name is Noniki, by the way."

"Misataki Shizumi," she replied, returning the gesture. At least she could not fault his manners. And, in truth, his demeanor was so open, so friendly, she had a hard time taking exception to his mirth, even if it was aimed at her.

"Yes, what was that, anyway?" Kagiri asked his brother. He unbuckled his karute, easing it off his head with a sigh of relief and scrubbing at his hair with one hand. Bones, that felt good! "I don't recall you having such tricks before," he teased Noniki, who grinned in reply.

"No?" His little brother made a point of eyeing his armor. "And I don't remember you being garbed like a warrior, and moving like one, too." He eyed him closely, his face going serious for a moment. "You said you'd absorbed all the Gensaiba. Did you use aishone to do it?"

Kagiri frowned. "Not...exactly," he admitted. "It's complicated. They weren't even bone anymore, not entirely, but they were everywhere, and I was breathing them in, and now they're part of me." He sighed. "For a while, I could hear them, practically see them, each one as a separate person, like I was a boat and we were all packed into it together. But now they've faded. I can still draw on their knowledge, their skill, and if I concentrate I can see some of their memories, but it's less like I'm borrowing what they have and more like...like they've given it into my keeping." He shrugged. "I don't know how else to explain it."

But Noniki was nodding. "I stopped using aishone," he declared, glancing quickly at the emperor and his warrior as if to check their reaction to that bold statement. "After you— after I lost you, I wanted nothing to do with any of it anymore. The Relicant Way is what brought us there, and without it we'd have been better off. So I left it all behind." He grimaced. "Not easily, mind. But I had help. And after I cleared my head, and cleansed my body and soul...I felt better. All that was left without the bones was me. But I decided that was enough."

"And then you found magic," Kagiri pointed out.

His brother nodded. "And then I found magic." He grinned again. "Giri, you would not believe some of the things I've seen!"

"What?" Kagiri asked him. "Like a cloud filled with angry colors that turned out to be the remnants of the last wizards of the land?"

Noniki laughed. "Yes, all right, fine, I suppose you've seen some things, too."

"I have," his brother replied, his eyes staring off into somewhere else, a dreamy smile crossing his face. "I saw a dragon once. It was beautiful, all water and ice, long and silvery and blue."

"What?" Noniki stared at him. "I saw that, too!" He wondered if his brother was jesting with him again, but his surprise looked genuine.

And it only increased when a third voice interjected, "I think I have, as well." Both of them turned to face the emperor, who was staring at them now. "It was just as you described," he said. "Silver and blue, long and sleek, dancing in the water." He gulped, looking younger than ever. "And I saw a waterspout that reversed itself, from spinning down into the depths to arcing high overhead."

Noniki frowned. "That's...not possible," he stated slowly. "I caused that waterspout when I saved my friend from drowning.

But that was on the Wagata, nowhere near here."

"I was on the ocean," Hibikitsu admitted. "Heading back here. But I did see it."

"What else did you see?" Kagiri asked them both.

"I saw a creature in a cage," Noniki answered, turning the ring on his thumb. "It looked like a tree but moved like a man."

Kagiri stared at him. "I saw that too," he said softly. "It was in Horohaba, the City of Beasts. But it is nothing but ruins now—the Gensaiba showed me how it had been and that was one of the creatures along the Avenue of Beasts, back when they were still alive."

All three of them stood there, gaping at each other. What to make of this, Noniki wondered, twisting the ring again. Was this some other magic of his? But it didn't feel like he'd had anything to do with it.

Then his brother's eyes went to his hand, and the band there. "Where did you get that?" he asked.

Hibikitsu was confused by the sudden question. What did it matter where the younger brother—Noniki—had acquired some bauble? But Kagiri seemed very interested, almost intent, and he was already beginning to realize that the young warrior was not the sort to be distracted by inconsequential matters.

"It was a gift," Noniki answered, pulling what looked like a thick jade ring from his thumb and offering it for inspection. "Why?"

Kagiri accepted it, holding the item in the palm of his hand—then laughed. "I know what this is," he said. He lifted it up for them all to see. "It is not meant for your hand, you know. It goes in the hair, to hold a queue. This is part of a set, one ring and one kanashi. They were worn by the matekai and their Gensaiba, and allowed them to communicate one to the other through their dreams."

Startled, Hibikitsu's hand went to his own chonmage, and

the one item stuck there beside his golden higeibara. "A kanashi like this?" he asked, extracting the ancient jade from his hair and offering it for inspection. "It and my sword are the only two items I have that belonged to my ultimate ancestor, Taido Segei himself."

Held together, it was obvious the two items were indeed matched. "This is why you dreamt or saw the same things," Kagiri pointed out, returning the ring to his brother and the hair stick to Hibikitsu. "As long as you wear those, you are linked."

"And what of you?" Hibikitsu asked. "Two items but three people."

The swordsman laughed. "Niki and I have always been close," he pointed out. "When we were young we could practically tell what each other was thinking. His magic may have enhanced that. Plus I have the rest of the Gensaiba within me and you are the descendant of their friend and peer, so in a way, we are connected as well."

Hibikitsu nodded. It was as good an explanation as any, and did answer why he had seen the waterspout when no one else had. And perhaps it was a sign as to what he should do next, for a certain idea had just come to him and the more he considered it, the more it appealed. "I have need of new Rojiri," he said slowly, glancing at these two young men he had only known a short while but already liked and was beginning to trust. "Since I seem to have demoted all my old ones. I am hoping the two of you might consider becoming the first of a new type of councilor, one appointed on merit rather than birthright."

"Us?" Noniki looked surprised. "I came here to tell you we needed to change if we wanted to survive!"

"And I came to depose you, since I felt you did not know enough or care enough about your kingdom and its subjects," Kagiri put in. He smiled. "But now that I've met you, I begin to think I was mistaken."

"You were not," Hibikitsu admitted heavily. "I was all those things and more. But I have changed. And I think our nation needs to change as well. Help me determine how, so that it is for the better."

Kagiri considered, then nodded. "I will be your Rojiri," he stated, offering his hand.

"As will I," Noniki added.

Hibikitsu clasped hands with them both—that was not something emperors did, perhaps, but then again, perhaps he was becoming a new kind of emperor. A better one, he hoped.

"Your Majesty!" Two women appeared at the door, Kohori and a slender, very pretty young woman in practical traveling clothes. "Are you all right?"

"Yes, we are fine, thank you, Kohori," he answered, waving her in. "We—" He was cut off, however, as the young woman saw Noniki, screamed his name, and raced forward to grab him in a fierce hug, which he returned happily. "Is there anyone you don't know?" Hibikitsu asked the matekai drily.

"I am sorry, sire," Noniki replied, blushing as he disentangled himself. "Allow me to present Seikoku. A very dear friend."

"Your Majesty." The bow she swept into was not practiced but her natural grace and beauty more than made up for that. "It is an honor."

"We met defending the city, sire," Kohori cut in, favoring the young woman with a quick smile. "Seikoku's resourcefulness saved a good many lives." Her gaze then came to rest upon Shizumi, who stiffened into attention, but all the older Taikoro said was, "Good work. I knew I could trust you to keep him safe."

"No thanks to him," Shizumi muttered, no doubt meaning that to have been under her breath, and flushed slightly as she realized it had been audible, but Hibikitsu just laughed. Was this what it was like, he wondered, having people around him who were not so terrified of him they couldn't make fun of him, complain about him, yell at him when he was wrong?

He was enjoying it immensely.

"Your Majesty," Noniki said, catching his eye. He had one arm around Seikoku's waist, Hibikitsu noticed. "Dear friend" indeed! "We arrived in Awaihinshi with several others, and Seikoku tells me they are all still below and most likely terrified."

"More like you?" he asked, and the young lady burst out laughing.

"Not like him, no," she said fondly. "But good people, your Majesty. Hard-working and honest, just seeking a place where they can be recognized for their talents."

He smiled at her. "We are always happy to have talented people here," he promised. "We will find a place for them. I give you my word."

Shizumi turned at the sound of running feet and was starting to reach for a sword that wasn't there until she recognized the band of warriors who had just burst into the throne room. "Where the bones have you been?" she demanded as they raced over, saluting her and then hastily including the emperor once they'd noticed him.

"Sorry," Geniji answered, gasping for breath. "There were these…winged things…everywhere. We…fought them…off…best we…could." The big woman was red in the face and wheezing, but she held out her hand and the item clasped in it.

Shizumi's sword.

With a happy little cry, she accepted the blade. Then, remembering where she was, she turned to Hibikitsu, shame-faced.

He just smiled. "Far be it for me to keep my own Taikoro from arming herself," he told her. "Especially since I'd rather she not have to resort to her knife to come to my aid."

"Thank you, sire." She felt much more herself once she'd slid the sword into her sash. "Are the skeletons still out there?" she asked her bantao.

Akino shook his head. "They collapsed," he said softly. "Just fell to pieces, all at once."

So Noniki had been correct, Shizumi reasoned. That cloud had been controlling the creatures somehow. There would no doubt be repairs to make—including fixing the palace wall where those strange men had crashed through—and wounded to tend to, but it did sound as if the danger were well and truly past.

"This may sound strange," Hibikitsu declared. "But I find

myself suddenly starved." He glanced around at everyone. "Perhaps my Taikoro and my Rojiri and their friends and warriors would consent to dine with me?"

It was Noniki who cleared his throat. "With all due respect, Your Majesty," he replied, bowing, "though I would be honored, I suspect my table manners are inadequate for such exalted company."

The Echo of Victory laughed, a twinkle in his eye. "Well, then, I hope no one will be offended or scandalized if we dispensed with formalities, just this once?"

Which was how, a short while later, Shizumi found herself and her squad in the Rojiri council chamber with the emperor, Taikoro Maniko, the brothers Kagiri and Noniki, and the young woman named Seikoku as they all sat around the massive council table and dug noisily into large communal bowls of rice and fish and pickled radishes, piling food into smaller bowls and then eating with chopsticks or fingers or both, slurping tea from large earthenware mugs. It was a strange, strange scene, but everyone was laughing and talking and smiling and it felt good. It felt right.

Glancing around him, enjoying the simple food and the simpler camaraderie, Hibikitsu smiled. He could not help but feel that perhaps they had turned a corner. They still had a long road ahead, of course. It would not be easy to wean the nation off its aishone, and there would many who resisted. But with people like these at his side, he hoped that they could make that change. Certainly it felt like they were on the right path at last. With a little luck and a lot of work, he hoped they could actually accomplish his goal, breaking the kingdom's dependence upon old bones, its obsessive reliance upon those relics of the past, and force it into new life instead.

CHAPTER THIRTY-SIX

C hiyu Akaii glanced up at the sentry's shout, reaching for her yanoi. Sure enough, a small boat was pulling up to the dock, a single man standing in the center while two more rowed. As soon as the boat brushed up against the heavy wood pylons he leaped across, landing lightly despite the dark armor that caught the lantern light where his kisoni had slipped loose.

At the sight of that warlike gear, Akaii settled into her stance, her spear angling so its butt was pressed down against the dock's thick planks, its tip aimed at the stranger. "Hold!" she shouted, her voice echoing against the water ahead and the stone walls rising up behind, taking comfort in the flurry of motion to either side as her cohorts took up position around her. "State your name and purpose!" she demanded.

The man did not answer but instead stepped forward, moving at an unhurried pace. A nihono hung at his side, Akaii saw, but his hands were not upon it—rather, they were cupped against his belly, cradling something there. She did not think it was dangerous, given its size, but after the events of earlier that evening she was taking no chances. "Stop where you are!" she insisted again. "If you come any closer, we will have no choice but to cut you down!"

He smiled, that much she could see even though he was still beyond the bulk of the lantern light, his face still in shadow. "I would hope not to suffer such a fate," he said at last, his tone light and amused, "but if it should be so, at least I will know that it was indeed through no one's fault but my own."

And he took one more step, moving into the light.

Akaii gaped as the illumination caught on his round face, his carefully coiffed and oiled chonmage, his impeccably groomed mustache. It was a face she knew, as they all did, but to see it here was beyond puzzling. "Taikoro?" she said, lowering her spear's tip but only slightly. "I had assumed you were inside, up in Aihiri with the others."

Fujibuki Haro smiled. "I was," he acknowledged, "but the emperor sent me on an urgent task, one too delicate to entrust to anyone else." He glanced around at the shattered remnants of bone still being swept up. "I take it there was some sort of trouble?"

"You could say that," Akaii agreed, straightening at last and returning her weapon to its upright, ready position. "We were attacked. By skeletons. Winged ones." She gestured toward the pieces littering the dock behind her. "That is all that remains."

"Ah. Interesting." Haro's eyes lingered on the mess before returning to her and the other aiashe. "It seems you have indeed acquitted yourself well, then." She shrugged. In truth, though they had managed to drag down and bludgeon several of the creatures once they'd received direction on how to go about that, the majority of the destruction had come when the attackers had simply collapsed on their own. Still, she saw no reason to tell the Taikoro that.

"I would hear more of this," he commented now, "but I am afraid I cannot linger. The emperor will be expecting my report as soon as possible." He nodded past them. "Please open the door."

Akaii saluted. "Of course, sir! At once!" She hurried past her fellows, down the dock, extracting a heavy iron key from her sash as she went. As the senior guard on duty, the key was her responsibility. The lock was stiff when she slid the key inside, for it was not used often. Indeed, the fact that it had been opened twice already this past week was highly unusual. After all, very few had the authority to take this route into the city. But the commander of the Honjofu was certainly one of them.

Unlocking the door, she stepped aside. The Taikoro had followed behind her, still moving at a steady pace but without rushing, and now he was nearly abreast. This close, she could see that the item he held was in fact an utume, cleverly constructed to resemble a tiny chest. Perhaps it contained a message too sensitive to trust to a mere courier?

"Thank you," Haro told her. He paused then, and frowned. "I will require someone to light my way," he stated. "You will suffice."

"Me?" Akaii started to protest—after all, she was in charge on the dock at the moment!—but a sharp glance silenced her before she could utter another word. She was only a chuisu, after all. He was a Taikoro and vastly outranked her. As such, the only thing she could reasonably do was salute. "Hai!"

Turning back to the others, she gestured for Yoshitaro to join her. "You are in charge until I return," she told him, handing over the key. "Lock the door behind us." Then, taking the lantern he offered, she stepped through into the narrow tunnel, the light spilling out ahead of her onto the cobbled path.

"What is your name?" Haro asked as they walked, their boots clomping along the hard stones. Though the way was wide enough for them to walk side-by-side, he had fallen in behind her instead and she could hardly argue, even though having him there made the hairs on the back of her neck stand on end.

"Chiyu Akaii," she replied. They were nearly halfway to the next door, which meant at the moment neither it nor the one behind were visible. It seemed as if they were marching through total darkness, her lantern creating a bubble of golden safety around them to keep the shadows at bay.

"I thank you for your sacrifice, Chiyu Akaii," the Taikoro stated formally, and there was something about his voice, some thickening of the words and lowering of his tone, that made her stop and turn, the lantern swinging in an arc that splashed light against the brick walls.

What it revealed behind her made her gasp and tighten her grip on her yanoi, starting to lower it into position. But before she could bring it down to head level the shadowy figure before her was lunging in, closing the distance between them, its one hand still cupped around the utume, the other lashing out with some sort of long, jagged blade that hissed as it cut the air. It bit deeply into her throat, tearing as much as slicing, and Akaii gurgled in surprise and pain, dropping weapon and lantern both as she clutched at the wound, feeling the blood spurting from between her fingers. There was the sound of shattered glass as the lantern broke upon the stones, its flame spilling forth and just as quickly guttering out, but she barely noticed. Already she was starting to shiver, the cold spreading from her neck and quickly turning her limbs numb, her vision beginning to darken far more than the extinguishing of the light could cause.

The last thing she saw was the creature standing over her as she slumped, its eyes and teeth the only bright spots in its dark and blurry form, its long, clawed fingers reaching for her eyes.

"I will not forget you," it assured her, its voice deep and raspy.

She felt a deep, piercing agony, and then darkness took the pain away for all eternity.

END OF BOOK THREE

GLOSSARY

Adai: a kind of soup broth, made from seaweed, dried fish flakes, mushrooms, and water

Ahaiinko: a formal stamp of office used to sign official documents

Aiashe: "foot bone," a foot soldier in Rimbaku's army, typically garbed in maikiro, hanketo, suneoto, and jingaso and armed with yanoi and chokoto

Aikaye: "sea bone," a sailor-warrior in Rimbaku's navy

Aio-akeo: a riverboat that runs the channel between Tabichi and Iwikaru

Aishone: relic bones

Aisho Hasume: Bone Collectors, a group of Buddhist-like traveling priests who wear the skulls and bones of their revered teachers dangling from their belts.

Aitachi: The Relicant Touch, the ability to absorb ancestral memories, skills, and knowledge by touching or consuming objects or people from the past

Akatai: family or household demons; malevolent ancestral spirits

Aragei: chicken that has been chopped into chunks and fried

Atorido: a traditional hanging lantern with four or six sides

Atuma-yio: sweet potato

Awaihinshi: The City of Polished Light, the marble capital of Rimbaku. Divided into six tiers (one for each level of the soul), with a shanty town/slum (Suranmui) at the bottom outside the walls and the emperor's palace at the top. Each tier has an outer wall of a different shade of marble, growing lighter in shade witch each height, from black to white. The tiers are:
One: Aihiri, the Imperial compound at the very top. Walls of purest white marble.

Two: Atsani, where the Daijin and other important nobles live—and home to Sorainasei, the first "town" in Awaihinshi. Walls of palest yellow.

Three: Motohiri, where the most influential merchants and the minor nobles live. Walls of peach.

Four: Sakiriti, mid- to lesser merchants and the most important artisans. Walls of the hue of cherry blossoms (a pale rose).

Five: Bejinuri. Other artisans and craftsmen. Walls of pale violet (red wisteria).

Six: Mazihini, laborers and other menials. The walls surrounding this level are pale blue like water, and the outer walls of the city as a whole.

Bakiro: a bag, typically a large bag used for carrying one's personal items and equipment

Banezhan: a cylindrical ring worn on the thumb when using a bow, most often made of bone, ivory, horn, or jade.

Bannin: guards, watchmen

Baraken: a wooden practice sword, typically made of either teak or bamboo

Bezenkai: a southern province

Birabiro: a town in Korito, closest to the Fyushan-Rimbakan border

Botetsu: a little village in Yunigiri

Buhiyo: a mayor, responsible for a town or small city

Burahone: the Bone Blind. These women's aitachi is so strong they are constantly overwhelmed by memories and knowledge, drawing it from the very elements around them.

Chahito: the pommel or endcap of a sword

Chasai: symbolic baton, typically of lacquered wood with metal caps at both ends and a tassel at one.

Chayaburi: a small, fast sailboat

Chinbiro: a town in Korito, near Birabiro

Chituju: a house steward

Chohu: a prosperous merchant house specializing in gemstones

Chokoto: a straight-edged sword with a ring pommel

Chonmage: a hair bun, particularly favored by warriors

Chosinichi: A "reservoir," someone who can hold absorbed skills for a long time

Chunsin-inori: a full feast, served in three courses, each on its own tray

Cuioburi: the smallest class of military boat, most often used for patrols and search missions

Darakada: "body thief," a sorcerer whose magic allows him to steal another's face and form

Dayabei: the seventh and final day of a sihu, often a rest day

Deo: a breastplate or cuirass, part of a suit of armor

Dobuichi: "animal-touched," those who use their aitachi on animal bones instead of human ones

Dojo Kuge: artistocratic bureaucrats

Doh Bridge: a wide bridge spanning the Zinyang River and connecting Obanari to Hochiro

Edishu River: a small river running from the Tonawa west to the ocean. Awaihinshi sits beside it.

Essa: a doctor.

Esuge: the Rimbakan cedar, the most commonly used wood in the land

Eioha: a form of dumpling

Eikono: a formal outer robe with a round collar, wide sleeves, a long tail, and sewn sides

Enwara: a small town in Bezenkai, south of Ginzai

Eto-riantzu: a large wheeled cart with sliding front doors

Ferume: an inkbrush, used for writing

Fumisoni: a style of kisoni, the most elaborate and formal, with long, wide sleeves

Furotingawa: "floating tower", a legendary tower, long since in ruins, at the southern edge of Rimbaku, near the mouth of a river

Furukotai: the largest town in Korito, home to the regional governor

Fyushu: a rival nation to Rimbaku's north, constantly testing the borders. Symbol: a black gauntlet clenched in a fist.

Ganabo: a massive two-handed war club, usually spiked or studded

Gensaiba: "Living blades," legendary warriors of mythic ability

Ginzai: the nearest large town to the brothers' home

Goji: a folding stool most often used by men in full armor

Gotaiburi: a large, multi-masted boat designed to carry troops

Guisuke bitte: a chest for holding one's armor

Guisuke kai: a stylized stand for displaying armor, usually set atop a guisuke bitte

Haidoto: thigh guards, part of a suit of armor

Hakami: close-fitting pants, often worn under armor

Hakara Ikibanichi: the Brothers of Many Spirits, a monastic order

Hanketo: armored gauntlets

Hantien: a short, padded winter coat

Happoa Kappua: "The Foamy Cup." A tavern in Ginzai

Hakichuekai: a small, brightly colored bird, known for its trilling and its sociability

Heioki: fried octopus balls

Higeibara: the red spider lily, the official crest of Rimbaku

Higinasi: a nation bordering Rimbaku to the southwest. Symbol: a stylized blue wave

Himsu: a town in Hochiro

Hiromura: a small village in Bezenkai

Honjofu: "Bone warrior," Rimbaku's elite military unit. Clad all in black armor.

Honteno: "Emperor's bones," the Rimbaku Imperial Guard. Clad all in red armor.

Horohaba: a lost city of Ritakhou, known as the "City of Beasts" for its renowned menagerie

Hosode: an undershirt, usually plain and unbleached and typically of silk.

Hozaiburi: a large, heavy warship.

Iematsu: the red pine tree, often used for beams and posts

Ikibanichari: Castle of Many Spirits, the mountain monastery of the Hakara Ikibanichi

Iniro: a small, segmented box worn at the belt to hold small items, often beautifully carved and detailed

Irogaso: a circular bamboo hat

Irohito: a small town strategically located at the intersection of the Tonawa and Edishu rivers, guarding the way to Awaihinshi

Ishtaya: a tailor or seamstress

Itoyako: the lily of the valley, known for its soft, drooping petals that shade from white to pink

Ittei: a blunt iron rod with a wrapped handle and a hooked tine just above that, used by guards when they were not allowed to carry swords

Jagimato: a town in Saruto, between the Wagata and Edishu rivers

Jigekugi: lesser bureaucrats, the lowest rank of nobility

Jingaso: a conical iron helm, worn by the aiashe

Jogoturi: "Lords of the Street," a gang in Ginzai

Jubanichi: The "perfect touch"—someone who absorbs quickly and holds for a long time

Kaemusei: "the Silent Change" or "The Silent," a magical being of limitless hunger

Kanashi: a hair stick

Kaoni: a hip- or mid-thigh-length open coat with long, wide sleeves, worn over a kitoro

Karo: a regional governor, who reports to the Emperor

Karute: a helmet, usually with a menatu attached in front and one or more modato above

Kazure: iron plates hanging from the front and back of the deo to protect the pelvis and upper leg

Kenroichi: A solid touch, someone who can absorb decently and hold it decently

Kibango: small sweet dumplings made from rice flour

Kindichi: bosses or kings

Kisoni: A loose robe, wider and looser than a kitoro, that can be worn as either an undergarment or an outer layer.

Kitoro: a silk outer garment, like a wide-sleeved robe, usually decorated.

Koshitsu: a graverobber

Kosshiki: "the Bone Spirit," sword of the Relicant Emperor

Kogotano: a small utility knife, often found in a small channel carved out of a sword scabbard, or in a writing set

Kotone: baby bird

Kune mato: a merchant's safe, usually made of metal or thick wood and with several locks.

Magojifu: a small town in Bezenkai, between Ginzai and the Rumiri river.

Maikiro: a war vest of lacquered plates on a cotton backing, secured by cotton straps, worn by aiashe. Smaller plates hang from the front and sides to protect the groin and thighs.

Mamusha: a large, deadly snake, very aggressive

Matoyan: a small hunting village up in the mountains between Rimbaku and Yatamoro

Matekai: a wizard or wizards.

Megaita: a green tea made with roasted brown rice

Menatu: a warrior's face mask, made of metal and hooked onto or tied to a karute

Modato: a crest affixed to the top of a karute

Mosi: an inkstick, made of soot and animal glue, ground down and mixed with water to create ink

Mukanichi: An "untouched," someone who can't really absorb at all, the lowest of all people

Muraito: A larger town or small city not far above Ginzai, on the southern edge of a mid-sized lake

Nahiya: a townhouse, usually two or three stories tall, with separate apartments on each floor

Naritaba: a pole weapon, a wooden or metal shaft with a curved single-edge blade at the end. The blades were forged in the same way as nihono. Often used by mounted warriors, and by women warriors.

Nafti: a fruit, round and juicy, with mottled green and gold skin and crisp white flesh.

Nigasi: a dry, pressed sweet made of sugar and rice flour.

Nihono: a long sword with a curved, single-edged blade, carried by nobles and elite warriors in Rimbaku

Nizukai: a mythic water dragon, daughter of the sea god Satumasu, "king of all waters"

Nodaki: a "field sword," a longer, heavier nihono typically used against cavalry

Okube: a traditional sash-style belt worn around the waist, particularly with a kitoro

Onokura: a small village in Miniri, near the south end of the river that separates Nariyari and Bezenkai

Otainui: housekeeper or household manager

Otomi: a small fishing village on the shores of the Wagata

Pokanu: a type of bird, tall and ostentatious, with bright and luxurious tail feathers

Ponmei: loose cotton pants with a drawstring tie and tapered ankles.

Quisuin: a poisonous snake

Raeteru: the common tree frog

Rajo: purple yams

Rakawa: a small village in Bezenkai

Riantzu: a traditional portable storage chest, usually made with no nails, screws, or adhesive

Rimbaku: "land made barren from cursed magic," the land after the Schism

Ritakhou: "land rich with blessed magic," the land before the Schism

Rojiri: counselors to the emperor

Rumiri River: the wide river that runs north-south through Miniri, connecting the Tonawa to Rimbaku's southern coastline. It is the dividing line between Bezenkai and Nariyari.

Saisaihyu: a ten-day period of purification and contemplation. During this time, everyone is expected to not allow any outside influence—including the use of aishone.

Sashiko: a style of patching clothing, often in a pattern

Sehiro: a steaming basket, usually woven out of bamboo

Senkuniki: ancestral spirits—typically akatai are considered the darker, more malevolent ancestral spirits, while senkuniki are those more inclined toward benevolence

Senkousa: a Bone Reader. These women have strong aitachi and can actually "read" aishone, telling what memories and knowledge and skills each bones possesses.

Senoha-a: a plant, whose name means "Mother of Thousands." Often seen in gardens and homes but highly poisonous, particularly the flowers.

Shakomi: a town in Bezenkai, a little north of Ginzai

Shatage: a shirt, generally thicker than a hosode and dyed or lightly embroidered or both.

Shugiri daimyo: grand nobles, closest to the emperor in status and power

Shugodiri: lesser nobles

Sihu: week

Sokuichi: A "crude touch" or "rough touch," someone who doesn't absorb easily and needs a lot of material to absorb anything

Sorhu: a wide scarf or shawl, either silk (for milder weather) or wool (for cooler weather)

Subayaki: a species of flower, also called the common camellia, related to the tea plant and to the tsodami but less vibrant in color. Its seeds are pressed to produce Subayaki oil, which can be used for skin care and hair care.

Suneoto: armored shin guards

Suponichi: A "sponge," someone who absorbs quickly

Suzeri: an inkstone, used like a small mortar to grind mosi so that it could be mixed with water to create ink

Suzeri kabo: "inkstone box" or writing box, which held the implements and utensils needed for writing.

Taikamage: a vertical hair bun, clean and elegant, with the hair piled up on top of the head and secured by a front comb and, if necessary, several kanashi

Takaneburi: a long, narrow, flat-bottomed boat mostly used on rivers to ferry freight.

Takotsu Hakara: Home of Brotherhood, the mountain monastery of the Hakara Ikibanichi

Tanakia: a wild animal, essentially a racoon dog, rumored to be able to shape-change to human form

Tanu: a modular set of trunks and cabinets, usually arranged in a stepped pattern.

Tawasiri: the Tower of Ghosts, an ancient tower at the southeast tip of Rimbaku, long since abandoned and believed to be haunted. Originally the meeting place of the matekai of Ritakhou.

Tayomi: a traditional flooring made from compressed rice straws tightly bound together and covered with woven straw

Tehuya: the guard on a nihono, roughly disc-shaped

Tienbao: a rice paddy, typically one tien in size (approximately 3200 square feet)

Tokimichi: A "flutter touch," someone who can't hold the absorbed skills for long

Tonawa River: a major river that branches off from the Zinyang and runs south along the eastern edge of Saruto before turning southeast and then east and separating Hochiro above from Bezenkai and Nariyari below.

Torito: rough hemp work trousers with a drawstring tie and tapered ankles, often paired with a hantien

Tsao: a boat hook

Tsekuri: rice wine

Tsodami: the red camellia, the royal flower

Tsukifuko: the Moon of Lawlessness, a month during which no rules or laws apply

Tsurogo: a double-edged nihono

Tukaiono: pickled vegetables and tubers, such as radish

Ujiro: A favorite dessert in Awaihinshi, a steamed cake made from rice, water, and sugar, done in a variety of flavors.

Umi: a long bow, made of laminated wood, bamboo, and leather and typically taller than a grown man, with the upper half twice as long as the lower.

Uridon: a thick rice noodle, often used in soup

Urigani: the art of folding paper into shapes, particularly animals

Utume: the art of packaging, particularly by wrapping an object in carefully chosen layers of paper

Uzumoya: A covered pavilion.

Wagata River: a tributary of the Tonawa that splits off to the west as the Tonawa continues north past Awaihinshi. The Wagata forms the southern border of Saruto.

Wara: a sturdy straw bag traditionally used to hold rice. A full wara provides enough rice to feed two people for one year.

Watamato: a small town in northern Bezenkai, not far below the Wagata River.

Yanoi: straight-bladed spear.

Yanokai: Rimbakan cypress, very durable and water-resistant

Yatamoro: the kingdom neighboring Rimbaku to the east, across the mountains. Symbol: a winged serpent reared back, ready to strike. Ruled by a High Council.

Yori-toki: a dagger with a thick blade made for armor-piercing. Often worn in conjunction with a nihono.

Yoto: the small river that runs through Ginzai

Yudishu: a small town in Nariyari, headquarters of the Kindichi

Yue Judei: "Good Times," a zaihaya in Bejinuri, in Awaihinshi

Zaihaya: a tavern or pub, a casual place where people can go to drink together

Zinyang River: the "Central River," the large river that runs east-west across Rimbaku right through the center of Chibiri, separating Hochiro and Saruto to the south from Obanari and Yunigiri to the north.

Rimbaku is divided into four regions: Kitini (north), (Chibiri) central, Miniri (south), and (Shitimi) island. Within each region are two or more provinces. They are:

Kitini:

- Tabichi (northwest region, bordering Fyushu above and the ocean to the west)
- Korito (northeast region, bordering Fyushu above and Yatamaro to the east)

Chibiri:

- Yunigiri (northwest, bordering the ocean)
- Obanari (northeast, bordering Yatamaro to the east)
- Hochiro (southern band, bordering Yatamaro to the east)
- Saruto (the capital region, with the ocean on one side and the southern band on the other)

Miniri:

- Bezenkai (southwest, bordering the ocean)
- Nariyari (southeast, bordering Higinasi to the west)

Shitimi:

- Iwikaru (the northern island)
- Tatsuma (the southern island)

Rimbaku is roughly 1200 miles wide by 2000 miles long, or 2,400,000 square miles total area.

Military groupings, smallest to largest:

Bantao -> Squad (4-10)
Shotao -> Platoon or troop (2-4 squads, 16-40)
Chotao -> Company (2-4 platoons, 60-160)
Dantao -> Battalion (4-6 companies, 300-900)
Reitao -> Regiment (2-4 battalions, 600-2000)
Tyodao -> Brigade (3-6 battalions, 1000-3000)
Sudao -> Division (3 or more brigades or regiments, 3k-6k)
Gaodao -> Corps (2 or more divisions, 25-50k)
Gyunao -> Army (2 or more corps, 100k-150k)
Gyunshadao -> Army Group (2 or more armies)
Chukogao -> Regional Theater (the entire military force
    in a region)
Sanseidao -> Front (the entire military force in a war)

Military ranks:

Sotaisho: commander-in-chief, usually the Emperor himself
[Karo: military governor]
Dogenriku: Lord General, the field marshal (in charge of
    tactics, fills in for the Emperor on the battlefield if he
    is not present)
Taisho: general
Issa: colonel
Chusa: lieutenant colonel
Shosa: major
Taisu: captain
Chuisu: lieutenant
Shosu: junior lieutenant
Gunso: Sergeant
Gocho: Corporal

Naval ranks:

Dogenkaishu: Lord Admiral
Kagono: admiral
Kagusho: vice-admiral
Daiso: captain
Kumigashi: commander
Kogashiri: lieutenant commander
Chudai: lieutenant

Special units:

Taikoro: Lord Commander, in charge of an entire elite
force (like the Honjofu or the Honteno)
Chuisu: lieutenant, can command a chotao
Gunso: sergeant, can command a shotao
Gocho: corporal, can command a bantao

ABOUT THE AUTHOR

AARON ROSENBERG is the best-selling, award-winning author of over 50 novels, including the Twin Cities Cryptids urban fantasy/cozy series, the DuckBob SF comedy series, the Relicant Chronicles epic fantasy series, the Areyat Islands fantasy pirate mystery series, the upcoming BEO Reports urban fantasy series, and, with David Niall Wilson, the O.C.L.T. occult thriller series. His tie-in work contains novels for *Star Trek, Warhammer, World of WarCraft, Stargate: Atlantis, Shadowrun, Mutants & Masterminds,* and *Eureka* and short stories for *The X-Files,* World of Darkness, *Crusader Kings II, Deadlands, Master of Orion,* and *Europa Universalis IV.* He has written children's books (including the original series STEM Squad and Pete and Penny's Pizza Puzzles, the award-winning *Bandslam: The Junior Novel* and the #1 best-selling *42: The Jackie Robinson Story*), educational books, and role-playing games (including the original games *Asylum, Spookshow,* and *Chosen;* work for White Wolf, Wizards of the Coast, Fantasy Flight, Pinnacle, and many others; the Origins Award-winning *Gamemastering Secrets;* and the Gold ENnie-winning *Lure of the Lich Lord*). He is a founding member of Crazy 8 Press. Aaron lives in New York with his family. You can follow him online at gryphonrose.com, on Facebook at facebook.com/gryphonrose, on BSky at @gryphonrose.bsky.social, on Instagram at the_gryphonrose, and on X (formerly known as Twitter) @gryphonrose.

If Jane Austen wrote about pirates, this would be that book!

Isabella Parsons is the well-mannered daughter of a baron in Regency England.

Cannon Belle Pearcy is a feared pirate captain raiding the German Sea.

They are one and the same.

But when a handsome Navy commander arrives on the scene, intent upon quelling the recent pirate threat—and wooing the loveliest lady in the region—Bella's two worlds start to collide!

Other problems quickly ensue, including a second Navy ship, an intriguing other suitor, and a deadly threat from her combined past.

Now Bella faces dangers both on land and at sea, in each of her identities. She finds herself battling to keep either from destroying the other, or the people she holds dear. All while struggling with a threat she never expected: true love.

The Adventures of
CANNON BELLE
Aaron Rosenberg

A thrilling new historic romance, full of adventure and intrigue, from the author of the Areyat Isles pirate-fantasy-mystery series and the Twin Cities Cryptids urban fantasy series!